Berkley Prime Crime titles by Victoria Thompson

Gaslight Mysteries

Counterfeit Lady Novels

MURDER ON BEDFORD STREET

A Gaslight Mystery

Victoria Thompson

BERKLEY PRIME CRIME
New York

BERKLEY PRIME CRIME
Published by Berkley
An imprint of Penguin Random House LLC
penguinrandomhouse.com

Copyright © 2023 by Victoria Thompson
Excerpt from *Murder in Rose Hill* copyright © 2024 by Victoria Thompson
Penguin Random House supports copyright. Copyright fuels creativity, encourages
diverse voices, promotes free speech, and creates a vibrant culture. Thank you for buying
an authorized edition of this book and for complying with copyright laws by not
reproducing, scanning, or distributing any part of it in any form without permission.
You are supporting writers and allowing Penguin Random House to continue to
publish books for every reader.

BERKLEY and the BERKLEY & B colophon are registered trademarks and BERKLEY
PRIME CRIME is a trademark of Penguin Random House LLC.

The Edgar® name is a registered service mark of the Mystery Writers of America, Inc.

ISBN: 9780593337127

The Library of Congress has cataloged the Berkley Prime Crime
hardcover edition of this book as follows:

Names: Thompson, Victoria (Victoria E.), author.
Title: Murder on Bedford Street : a Gaslight mystery / Victoria Thompson.
Description: New York : Berkley Prime Crime, [2023] | Series: A Gaslight mystery
Identifiers: LCCN 2022040507 (print) | LCCN 2022040508 (ebook) |
ISBN 9780593337103 (hardcover) | ISBN 9780593337110 (ebook)
Subjects: LCGFT: Novels.
Classification: LCC PS3570.H6442 M86615 2023 (print) |
LCC PS3570.H6442 (ebook) | DDC 813/.54—dc23/eng/20220829
LC record available at https://lccn.loc.gov/2022040507
LC ebook record available at https://lccn.loc.gov/2022040508

Berkley Prime Crime hardcover edition / April 2023
Berkley Prime Crime trade paperback edition / March 2024

Printed in the United States of America
1st Printing

To Dr. Michelle Skeen,
who shared her expertise with me so I could get this one right

MURDER ON
BEDFORD STREET

I

Nobody could accuse Frank Malloy of being a snob. As an Irish Catholic and a former policeman, he was, in fact, the kind of person snobs usually looked down on. He might be a millionaire now, but lots of people still looked down on him because he'd always be Irish no matter how much money he had. This was why he felt a little guilty about feeling snobbish about the prospective client who had just been escorted into his office.

Hugh Breedlove, according to his calling card, was not Irish or poor and would have been shocked to learn Frank had already developed a bad opinion of him. His tailor-made suit spoke of wealth, as did his bright gold watch chain and the large ruby ring on his hand. He was an imposing man with silver hair pomaded into place and a neatly trimmed beard. His expression ruined the effect, though. His frown spoke of contempt as he glanced around and saw nothing that apparently pleased him, including Frank himself.

Breedlove stopped his critical perusal of Frank's modest office only when Frank's secretary, Maeve, announced him. From the twinkle in her eye, she knew Frank's opinion of Mr. Breedlove, who might well be the biggest snob Frank had met in his life so far, and he had met a few.

"Nice to meet you, Mr. Breedlove," Frank said with a professional smile. He'd risen from his desk chair and reached across his desk to shake Breedlove's hand.

Breedlove seemed to hesitate before accepting the handshake, but luckily for him—if he really needed the services of Frank's private detective agency—he finally did. Then he gave Maeve one of his disapproving looks, as if to ask why she was still in the room.

He obviously didn't know he couldn't possibly intimidate Maeve Smith. "Do you want me to take notes, Mr. Malloy?" she asked, her eyes still twinkling.

"I have a matter of the utmost delicacy to discuss," Breedlove informed them both haughtily.

Frank could have told him that all of his clients did, but he said, "I'll call you if I need you, Maeve."

She gave him a mischievous grin before closing the door behind her, and Frank somehow managed not to roll his eyes. "Please sit down, Mr. Breedlove, and tell me how I can help you." Frank motioned to the wooden client chairs that sat in front of his desk.

Breedlove didn't actually take out his handkerchief and wipe off the seat before he sat on it, but he looked as if he would have liked to. Frank's opinion of him did not improve.

"You come highly recommended, Mr. Malloy," Breedlove said doubtfully, glancing around the utilitarian office again.

"May I ask who recommended me?" Frank thought he might want to take some revenge.

Breedlove mentioned the names of two wealthy gentlemen whom Frank had assisted in the past. "They said you could be very discreet."

"They were right, and anything you tell me will be confidential, even if you don't hire me, Mr. Breedlove."

Breedlove seemed to relax a little at that, but only a little. "If I have your word, then . . ."

"Of course. Now why don't you tell me why you need my help?"

Breedlove sighed and folded his well-tended hands in his lap. "My family and I have spent the past five years in London, and we just returned to New York a few weeks ago."

"What took you to London?"

"My work. I'm a partner in an investment bank, and I went over to manage our office there."

"I see. And what brought you back to New York?"

He seemed to brighten at this. "My daughter. You see, she's eighteen now, and we wanted to bring her out in society here in America. I know it's all the fashion to marry a British aristocrat, but we didn't want that for our girl."

Or maybe they didn't have a big enough fortune to attract a British aristocrat, but Frank didn't mention this. He just nodded his understanding.

"As you can imagine, things have changed a lot in the five years we've been gone. Old friends have . . . Well, we were depending on my sister-in-law to help ease us back into society. My brother died while we were away, you see, but I assumed she would still be available. And her daughter had married well, or so we were led to believe. Between the two of them, we expected . . ."

To Frank's surprise, Breedlove's gaze dropped to his folded hands, and he looked almost embarrassed.

"You expected they would sponsor your daughter?" Frank guessed.

Breedlove looked up in obvious surprise. "You know how a young lady is introduced to society?"

Frank tried not to feel offended. That would be petty. "My wife was a debutante."

Plainly, Breedlove was shocked, but he managed to say, "Oh well, I suppose you'd know then."

"Yes. Now you were saying about your niece and your sister-in-law . . . ?"

"Uh, yes, I was. Ellie, my brother's widow, has left the city, it seems. She moved to the country somewhere and no one seems to know where."

That did seem strange, but perhaps Ellie had her reasons. "And your niece?"

"Julia. As I said, we heard she'd married well. Chet Longly, you know."

Frank didn't know, but he nodded to encourage Breedlove to keep talking.

"When we went to call on her, Longly told us . . ." Once again, he dropped his gaze to his folded hands, and for the first time Frank understood that he really did have something painful to tell Frank.

Frank instantly regretted his hasty judgment of Breedlove and leaned forward to indicate his concern. "Has something happened to Julia?"

"Yes, she . . . Longly has put her in an insane asylum."

This was, of course, terrible news. Few people admitted to insane asylums ever returned since there was really no treatment for such maladies. "I'm sorry to hear that." And he really was.

"As you might well be," Breedlove said, warming to his topic. "My wife and I felt obligated to visit Julia. It was the only decent thing to do since her mother was no longer in the city and might not even know what had happened to her."

"That was kind," Frank said sincerely. "It couldn't have been pleasant for you."

"But much more unpleasant for poor Julia." Breedlove was angry now, his cheeks flushed and his eyes blazing with outrage. "You see, there's nothing wrong with her at all. She's just as sane as you and I."

Frank needed a moment to absorb this information. He didn't know much about these things, but he felt sure *poor Julia* would have seen her aunt and uncle as possible saviors and would certainly have tried to convince them she had been wrongly committed. "How did you determine that she's sane?"

"By talking with her, of course. She told us the whole story. Her parents had married her off to Longly against her wishes. She was barely seventeen at the time and couldn't defy them. I do remember the marriage was rather sudden. We had only been in London a few months when we received the announcement, and we joked that there must be a baby on the way, although that didn't turn out to be the case. Julia's son wasn't born for more than a year. But she soon discovered she had made a terrible mistake in marrying Longly."

When Breedlove looked down at his hands yet again, Frank prodded him. "What did Longly do?"

"He is a . . . a libertine, Mr. Malloy. He gambles and drinks and indulges in vices too sordid for Julia to name. He even keeps a mistress whom he takes no pains to hide."

"That's unfortunate," Frank said, keeping his tone completely neutral, "but many wealthy men behave exactly this way."

"Yes, and their wives choose to ignore such behavior, but Julia could not. She apparently demanded that Longly reform his ways and put his mistress aside. She was so adamant that he eventually tired of her nagging and found a doctor to declare her insane."

Such things did happen. Everyone in New York knew the stories of how Commodore Vanderbilt had put both his wife and his namesake son in the Bloomingdale Insane Asylum for no reason other than he was annoyed with them. Mercifully, they had been released after a few months, both being perfectly sane. But all that happened over fifty years ago. Surely, they didn't still lock up sane people on the word of a vindictive spouse. "That seems very cruel," Frank finally said.

"Cruel and inhuman. That poor girl is terrified, and who wouldn't be, locked away with people who really are insane? She begged us to help her, and what could we do but agree?"

At last, this was what he wanted from Frank. "Do I understand that you would like my help getting your niece released?"

"Yes, that's it exactly."

Frank sat back in his chair, considering.

When he didn't respond immediately, Breedlove turned haughty again. "I'll pay you whatever you ask, within reason, of course."

Frank excused the man this time. He was obviously under

a lot of stress. "I'll just charge you my regular rates, Mr. Breedlove, if I do decide to accept you as a client. The problem is, I'm not sure how I can help you."

Breedlove frowned. "What do you mean?"

"I mean, it's my understanding that the decision on whether a person remains in an asylum or not is made either by the doctor treating them or by a judge after a sanity hearing. I don't see how I can help with either one."

"But that's it, don't you see? If the doctors won't release her, and Julia assures us that they simply ignore her when she tells them she is sane, then we will need to present evidence proving that what she says about her husband is true and that he had her locked away to get rid of her."

"So, you want me to investigate this Chet Longly."

"And Julia, too, to prove she isn't what he's claiming she is."

"I see. I could probably help with that."

"And you must be discreet, Mr. Malloy. Above all, we must avoid a scandal."

Rich people were always worried about a scandal. "If there's a trial, it will be impossible to keep things quiet."

"I know that, but Longly must be the villain and Julia the innocent victim and not insane. It is imperative. We can't have our daughter's coming out tainted, Mr. Malloy. It's impossible to keep people from knowing Julia was sent to that place, but they must also know it was through no fault of hers."

It seemed Frank's initial impression of Breedlove had been correct after all. He didn't really care about rescuing Julia. He just wanted to protect his good name. And his daughter's, too. If insanity ran in their family, no one would want the Breedlove girl no matter how large her dowry.

But if Breedlove didn't really care about Julia, Frank did. He couldn't bear the thought of someone being unjustly locked away in an insane asylum. What a horrible fate, one he wouldn't wish on anyone. But he'd need to do one thing first.

"Before I decide to take this case, I'll have to determine for myself whether your niece is sane."

Breedlove did not look pleased. "How will you do that?"

"I'll talk with her. In fact, I'll take my wife along with me. Julia might be reluctant to speak to a strange man under the circumstances."

"But you're not a doctor. How will you know for sure?"

"The same way you did, I suppose. You and your wife were convinced, weren't you?"

To Frank's surprise, Breedlove hesitated. "Yes," he finally said with no enthusiasm. "Yes, we were."

"Then we probably will be, too."

How horrible," Sarah Malloy said when her husband told her about Julia Longly's plight. As a woman, Sarah felt the injustice even more strongly than he did. In truth, she could hardly imagine a worse fate than being locked away in a place like that for the rest of her life. "I know these things happen, but I've never personally known anyone involved."

They were in the private parlor they had created adjacent to their bedroom when they had remodeled this house. They could speak freely here without worrying about their children overhearing something untoward.

"This Mr. Breedlove must be a very kind man to go to

all this trouble. Few people would even care about someone who has been judged insane," Sarah added.

"He's not as kind as you might think," Malloy said.

"What do you mean?"

"I mean, he made it clear to me that he wants us to get Julia out of the asylum and declared sane so that they can bring their daughter out without people wondering if she's somehow tainted, too."

"Bring her out? You mean as a debutante?" Sarah asked in surprise.

"I gather that's the main reason they returned to New York after five years in London."

"Oh dear, I hope they understand that the process isn't as formal as it is in England."

"How is it different?"

Sarah sighed. "In England, the young ladies are presented to the queen in some elaborate ceremony, and they spend the whole season attending a round of parties and dances where they are introduced to eligible young men. It's all very pre-scribed. It used to be like that in America, too, at least in the large cities, but now in New York it's just a dance. The girls do meet some young men, but they're really on their own after that."

"Poor things, having to find a husband all by them-selves," Malloy said with a grin.

"Don't make fun. It really is harder than it used to be, and if your first cousin is in an insane asylum, I imagine it would truly be impossible."

Malloy looked chastened. "But how could it happen in the first place? If Julia Longly is perfectly sane, how could some doctor say she isn't?"

She gave him a pitying look. "All right, let me illustrate. Imagine for a moment that some strange men came to the door. When I asked what they wanted, they took me prisoner and threw me into the back of some sort of ambulance and drove away without explaining anything. How do you think I'd react?"

"You'd be terrified, in fear for your life or at least your virtue."

"Exactly. I'd be calling for help and banging on the doors and trying to escape. And when they finally let me out, I'd be at some strange place that was obviously an institution of some kind. By then I'd be nearly hysterical with fear. Someone claiming to be a doctor might examine me, and I'd tell him what happened, but he wouldn't care because he already knew what had happened. He'd ask me a few questions and I'd be so upset I probably couldn't answer coherently. I'd beg him to help me, and he'd assure me that he would, and then they'd turn me over to the matrons who'd strip me and bathe me and give me some sort of uniform to wear. And I'd tell them how I'd been kidnapped and beg them to help me, but they'd just ignore me because they've heard it all before and everyone in the asylum claims they are sane. Then they'd lock me alone in a room which would make me even more terrified and hysterical. That's how it happens."

"Good Lord," Malloy said, rubbing a hand over his face. "But you'd calm down in a day or two. You'd start behaving rationally again. You could talk to the doctor then."

"And assure him I'm sane," Sarah said with a knowing smile. "He hears that from every patient."

"So how do we prove Julia is sane, assuming she is?"

Sarah took a moment to consider the question. "I guess we

should visit her, as you promised your client we would. We'll probably be able to tell if there's something wrong with her, at least. Insane people do tend to give themselves away."

"And if she doesn't and we think she's all right?"

"Then you find out if what she said about her husband is true and if he did have a good reason for wanting to get rid of her that had nothing to do with her mental state."

"You make it sound easy."

Sarah sighed again. "I only wish it was."

JULIA LONGLY HAD BEEN SENT TO THE MANHATTAN State Hospital on Ward's Island because the facilities on Blackwell's Island had recently been closed and all the remaining inmates sent to Ward's. The spring air was nippy on the ferry ride across the river to the island, but the island itself was an oasis of calm, with large expanses of newly green grass stretching out in every direction. Whoever had chosen it as a location for disturbed people had chosen well. It was difficult to believe it was so close to the endless noise and bustle of New York City, which couldn't be good for someone whose mind was already troubled.

The hospital building itself was enormous, sprawling east and west from the central entrance in a batwing design. Sarah and Frank learned upon entering that the female inmates were located in the west wing. The woman at the reception desk sent a girl to inquire about Mrs. Longly and find out if she could receive visitors. This took a while, but fortunately, the girl returned to inform them that they could see Julia. She then escorted them to a visitation room. The long walk provided an opportunity to question the girl a bit.

"I didn't expect the building to be so large," Sarah remarked.

The girl, who looked to be in her late teens and wore a uniform made of striped material that appeared to be sturdy enough to withstand a myriad of washings, smiled. "That's because it's a Kirkbride building."

"What does that mean?" Sarah asked, genuinely interested now.

"Dr. Kirkbride believed that insane people would get better if they got lots of sunlight and fresh air, and he designed the building so every room has windows. That's why it's so long."

Sarah would have to think about this theory. "But it seems to have an awful lot of rooms."

"Oh, but we need them. We've got about two thousand inmates here now. We had to add on when they moved the inmates from Blackwell's over here."

Good heavens, she'd had no idea the need was so great.

Even though the building was four stories tall, the visitation room was on the first floor. It was a sparsely furnished space with some worn easy chairs, a rag rug that Sarah suspected might have been made by the inmates, and a couple of tables, scarred and bare of any ornamentation. The room did have a window, in accordance with Dr. Kirkbride's vision, and the view was nice since it overlooked the front lawn. It was even open to catch the breeze, although Sarah thought it was still a bit early in the year to be opening windows. She decided not to remove her coat.

"One of the matrons will bring Mrs. Longly down," the girl told them, and left them there.

"They don't spend a lot of money on the furnishings," Malloy observed, glancing meaningfully around.

"They probably don't have much to spend," Sarah said.

"What really disturbs me is that this is a public room. They probably make it look as nice as possible for outsiders to see, and if that's true, what does the rest of the place look like, the part outsiders don't see?"

"I hope it's not as bad as you're imagining, but it's probably worse."

"Yes, and the patients here have no recourse. They might complain to their families, assuming they have a family and that family actually comes to visit them, but would anyone believe them?"

"And even if they did believe them, what could they do about it? Most of the people here are poor. Their families probably wouldn't know how to make a complaint and they certainly don't have the power or influence to force changes."

Sarah sighed. "I wonder why Mr. Longly put Julia here. There are private hospitals that are much nicer."

"Ah, but they cost money. If what Breedlove told me is true, Longly might need his funds to support his vices and his mistress."

"Or he might just be angry enough at Julia to put her here out of revenge. Being confined anywhere would be unpleasant but being here with people she'd consider far beneath her socially would be a special kind of punishment."

"Yes, Longly could be as evil as Julia led Breedlove to believe, and if that's the case, getting Julia released will give us great satisfaction."

Before Sarah could agree, the door opened, and a woman came stumbling into the room. Sarah realized that she had been shoved by the woman escorting her, a stern-faced female in a uniform similar to the one the receptionist and the escort girl had worn. She was obviously the matron. "Here she is," the matron said with disgust.

Julia Longly gave her a look that could have drawn blood on rawhide, but she quickly turned her attention to her visitors. "Who are you?"

"I'm Frank Malloy and this is my wife, Sarah," Malloy said. "Your uncle asked us to visit you."

She seemed surprised at this. "He kept his word. I wasn't sure he would."

"He's very concerned about you," Malloy said.

She smiled at that. "He should be." She turned to the matron. "Could we have some privacy?"

The matron sniffed derisively. "I'll be right outside," she told the Malloys. "If she gets violent, just give a shout."

Julia gave the woman another glare, which she ignored. When the door had closed behind her, Julia's expression smoothed out and she even managed a smile. "I'm so grateful that you've come. Shall we sit down?" She might have been in her own home, welcoming friends. So far, she seemed perfectly normal.

Julia Longly was a young woman in her midtwenties. In spite of the dark circles under her eyes and the fact that her long, dark hair hadn't been combed and hung in a tangle down her back, she was beautiful.

"You needn't be afraid," she said with a slight smirk when they were seated. "I won't become violent."

"We didn't really think you would," Sarah said.

"And please excuse my appearance. They won't let me pin up my hair because I might stab someone with the pins and they seem to have an aversion to combs here as well, so I haven't even been able to straighten it up."

"At least they gave you a nice dress to wear," Sarah said, indicating the tasteful black gown she wore. It didn't fit well, but it was good quality.

"This?" Julia said with a bitter laugh. "This is the visitation dress. We put it on when we have visitors, and we all share it. They don't want anyone to know the rags we must wear when no one sees us."

Sarah didn't know what to reply to that, so Malloy took advantage of the silence to say, "I'm a private investigator, Mrs. Longly, and your uncle hired me to find evidence he could use to get you released from this place."

Julia closed her eyes for a moment as if trying to get control of her emotions. She did have a lot to be emotional about, but she must have realized at some point that displaying her feelings would not help her cause. When she opened her eyes again, she said, "I must admit, I didn't have much faith in him. He was quite upset when I told him what Chet had done, but he just kept saying how bad this would look for poor Ruth. That's his daughter."

Malloy exchanged a meaningful look with Sarah and said, "It doesn't matter why he wants to help you, Mrs. Longly. The important thing is that he does. Now I know it's probably painful for you to talk about, but we need to know everything you can tell us about your husband and why he might have lied to have you committed here."

Julia was, Sarah noted, sitting perfectly erect, just as a lady always should, with her hands folded in her lap. Her expression was thoughtful, but her eyes were something else entirely. She seemed to be studying them intently, as if looking for signs of deceit or perhaps simply to judge their sincerity. Sarah supposed she had a right to be suspicious after what had happened to her.

She must have decided to trust them, however, because she said, "I hardly know where to start. My father died when I was still at school. It was an awful thing and I mourned him deeply. My mother didn't seem to care about my grief, though. She took me out of school and insisted that I marry as soon as possible. I had just turned seventeen when I made my debut, but I was very popular. My mother let it be known that I would have a large dowry, which attracted all the wastrels in the city. One of them was Chet Longly."

"When you call him a wastrel, what do you mean?" Sarah asked.

Julia looked impatient for a moment, but only for a moment, and then Sarah wasn't even sure she had read the emotion correctly because Julia's expression crumbled into despair. "He gambles, you see. And frequents houses of ill repute, engaging in unspeakable debauchery. He'd tell me about all of it and force me to do the things he described. It was horrible."

Her voice broke and she pressed a fist to her lips and squeezed her eyes shut, obviously holding back the flood of emotion her memories caused. Sarah had been right, she had learned not to show those emotions, but Sarah could feel them just the same. How horrible it must have been for an innocent young woman.

"I'm sorry to make you remember these things," Sarah said, "but it's important for us to know what kind of man your husband is."

Julia drew a calming breath, lowered her fist, and opened her eyes. "Yes, I understand. It's just . . . difficult."

"Take your time," Malloy said gently, "and don't think you need to protect your husband. The more we know about him, the more we can help you."

She smiled a little at that. "I have no intention of protecting him, not after he sent me here."

"You were saying Mr. Longly was interested in your dowry," Sarah prodded her.

Julia sighed again. "He had gambling debts. Oh, he courted me very properly. He pretended he fell in love with me at first sight. I was a child, so naturally, I believed him. He was handsome and charming, so I thought I was in love with him as well."

"Then you were willing to marry him?" Malloy asked. Something in his tone made Sarah look at him, but his face was expressionless.

Julia obviously heard it, too, and reacted to it. "At first, but I didn't want to get married right away. As I said, I was still a child, fresh out of the schoolroom. I'd hardly had a taste of society, and I wanted to enjoy it a bit longer. But my mother insisted, and Chet was in a hurry to get his hands on my money. His creditors were pressuring him, apparently. Mother organized a small ceremony and the next thing I knew I was a wife."

"I'm sorry you had to go through that," Sarah said sincerely.

Julia shrugged. "I had no idea how cruel a man could be. He took my innocence and corrupted it, and when he grew bored with that, he took a mistress. He kept her just a few blocks away, and he made no effort to hide it. He'd spend the night with her, leaving me and our son home alone, night after night, and if I complained he'd . . ." She gave a little shudder at the memory. "If I complained, he'd slap me. In front of our son. In front of the servants. He didn't care who saw it."

Sarah instinctively reached out to offer her comfort, but to Sarah's surprise, Julia flinched away. "I'm sorry," Sarah said.

Julia raised a hand to her temple and shook her head. "It's not you. It's . . . You have no idea what they do . . . how they have treated me here."

"I did notice the matron pushed you into the room," Sarah said.

Julia made a sound that might have been a derisive laugh. "That was nothing. They hit me at the slightest provocation, and I don't dare object or complain to the doctor. He doesn't believe me, and they beat me for telling on them. They take great delight in putting me in ice-cold baths and leaving me there for hours. And the food, it's hardly edible. You can't imagine."

"But surely when you see the doctor, he must notice that you're completely rational."

Julia smiled at that, but it was a bitter thing to see. "Except that he thinks I imagine all the things I tell him. The nurses are kind, and no one would dare strike a patient. The food is perfectly acceptable. The clothes we wear are fine. If I say otherwise, I'm delusional."

"I don't suppose he believes the things you say about your husband either," Malloy said.

"Of course not. He's spoken to Chet, who tells him all kinds of lies about me. Why do men always believe other men and think women are lying?"

Malloy had no answer for that, but Sarah said, "For the same reason women believe each other, I'm sure."

"Then you believe me?" Julia asked with just a touch of desperation.

"Yes, but that isn't enough. We need proof that we can take to a judge."

"A judge," Julia echoed in alarm. "Why a judge?"

"Because if we can't convince the doctors here to release

you, your uncle will have to take the case to court and have a judge rule on your sanity."

"A judge," Julia echoed in disgust. "Another man."

"But if we have proof, he will have to believe you," Sarah said.

"But we'll try the doctors here first," Malloy said. "If they release you, we won't have to consult a judge."

Julia didn't look convinced, and Sarah couldn't blame her. She must be feeling rather helpless.

After a few moments, Julia said, "I've been afraid to ask, but do you . . . ? Have you by any chance seen my son?"

"I'm afraid not," Sarah said.

Julia shook her head. "My uncle and aunt haven't seen him either. I do worry about him so much. He must be terrified, and I have no idea what Chet told him about me. Does he think I'm dead?"

"Surely he wouldn't tell the boy a lie like that," Sarah said.

"I doubt he told him I was in an asylum either," Julia said, bitter again.

"How old is he? Your boy, I mean."

"Just turned four, or at least he was when they put me in this place. I don't even know how long I've been here. The days are all alike."

"Do you remember what day you came in?" Sarah asked.

Julia frowned with the effort of remembering. "I think it was February twelfth."

"Then a little more than a month."

"Is that all?" Julia cried. "However will I stand it if I'm here forever?"

"You won't be here forever," Sarah promised rashly, earning a look from Malloy.

"We'll do everything we can to help you, Mrs. Longly," he said to temper Sarah's promise.

"I can't stay here for the rest of my life," she told them, tears finally forming in her lovely eyes. "I'll go mad just like the rest of them. I'll have to kill myself."

Sarah's heart seemed to sink inside her chest. "Don't talk like that. You aren't alone. People care about you."

"If you care about me, then get me out of here."

JULIA WAS EXPLAINING THAT THE SERVANTS WHO COULD verify the things she had accused her husband of were probably too loyal to him to help her, when the matron came in. "Time's up. She's got to go get her lunch."

Julia made a disgusted face, but she rose obediently. "Thank you for coming to see me. I'm so grateful," she told the Malloys.

"Come on." The matron seemed angry, although Sarah could see no reason for it. She could also see no reason for the rough way the matron took Julia's arm and propelled her toward the door.

"Could we speak with you for a few minutes?" Malloy asked before they reached the door.

The matron turned back in surprise. "Me?"

"Yes," Sarah said with a smile. "We have some questions about Mrs. Longly."

The matron gave Julia a glare, which Julia returned. "I suppose, but I'll have to get somebody to take this one back. Give me a few minutes."

They waited, not daring to speak for fear of being overheard, and the matron returned quickly. Before they could ask her anything, she said, "I suppose she told you we beat her and starve her. That's what they all say."

Sarah knew better than to antagonize the woman. "I'm sure you do the best you can with the patients. I'm sure it's a thankless job."

"Thankless is right. Nobody knows what it's like."

"I'm sure they don't. I can't even imagine and I'm sure I don't want to. We appreciate your willingness to speak to us. We won't keep you long. You see, we have just met Mrs. Longly and she seems perfectly rational, at least during our conversation. We'd just like to know exactly what it is about Mrs. Longly that makes the doctors here think she is insane."

The matron smiled in a way that made Sarah's blood run cold. "That one isn't insane. She's just pure evil."

II

FRANK FROWNED. THAT SEEMED A HARSH WAY TO DE-scribe a young woman. "What do you mean?"

"I've seen her kind before. Thinks she's better than everybody else. Smarter, too. Won't follow the rules. Thinks she can trick people into doing what she wants, and she'll do anything to get her way."

"That doesn't sound evil," Sarah said. Frank marveled at how she managed to make it sound like she was confused instead of outraged.

"I said she'd do *anything*," the matron said with a trace of impatience. "If she can't get it by charm or trickery, she'll get violent."

"Have you seen her get violent?" Sarah asked, again still sounding confused.

"Have I *seen* it? Oh no, she's too clever for that, but I see how the other inmates avoid her. They're afraid to get too close."

"Perhaps she's just defending herself," Sarah said. "Are the other patients violent?"

"Not in this section. Oh, we've got some who would slit your throat for you if they got the chance, but they're locked up tight in another ward. This lot is meek and mild unless you stir them up."

"You said you don't think Mrs. Longly is insane," Frank said.

"Not if you think being insane is talking to people who ain't there or thinking you're Queen Victoria. We got a lot of 'em like that, but then we got some who act all right most of the time until you cross them. Then you see their true colors, and she's one of them. You mark my words. Ain't nobody safe from her, but don't worry, we keep an eye on her. She won't get away with anything while she's in here. Now I gotta go. I got work to do."

Before they could object, she was gone.

"My goodness," Sarah said, her eyes wide with astonishment.

"Your goodness indeed. Let's get out of here," Frank said.

They had just gathered their things when the girl who had escorted them in appeared. "Are you ready to leave?"

"Yes, we are," Sarah said.

"I'm to take you out. Can't have people wandering around, can we?"

"Why not?" Frank asked mildly.

The girl seemed surprised. "Ain't safe, and seeing strangers upsets the inmates."

"Why wouldn't it be safe?" Sarah asked as they followed

her down the hallway, back the way they'd come in. "I thought the violent patients were in another wing."

The girl glanced back and shrugged, then turned away again, never missing a step. "You never know what might make an inmate go wild."

Frank exchanged a glance with Sarah, who seemed as disturbed as he felt. The girl left them at the reception desk and the receptionist sent for the wagon that had carried them here from the boat dock. They had a long ferry ride back before they could speak freely about what they'd learned.

By the time the ferry docked on the Manhattan side of the river, and they found their auto, which they'd parked nearby, Frank had had ample time to consider everything they'd learned today. He knew Sarah would have been unable to think about anything else, too, so he was glad when they finally climbed into the electric auto that he had purchased for Sarah several months ago. They hardly ever used their gasoline-powered motorcar anymore since it was loud and difficult to start and drive. The electric was so quiet, they could even discuss the case while they moved through the city.

"Do you think Julia Longly is evil?" he asked Sarah as he turned onto First Avenue.

"I knew you'd ask me that," she replied with a grin. "And I know there are evil people in the world, but surely, a person doesn't become evil by growing up in a wealthy family and having every advantage."

"Why not? We've certainly seen our share of evil rich people. Maybe you just think Julia Longly can't be evil because she's so pretty."

"She is pretty, and maybe that influences my opinion

somewhat. We do expect evil to show on a person's face, don't we?"

"And if what she said about the way her husband treated her is true, she could be excused for being angry and wanting some revenge."

Sarah shuddered. "I wanted revenge myself after hearing her story. Even if only half of what she said is true—and do you imagine they really beat the patients and put them in ice water baths?"

"I have no idea, but Julia said herself the doctors don't believe her, so if no one acknowledges the patient complaints, the staff could get away with anything."

"That's frightening to think about. All those defenseless women at the mercy of the nurses."

"And of each other," Frank reminded her. "Do you believe what the matron said about the other women being afraid of Julia?"

"That was a surprise, I must admit, but after I thought about it, I realized that the staff can't watch the patients every minute and Julia would probably be seen as an easy target, so they may have tried to intimidate her."

"I didn't think of that, but you're probably right, and no one could fault her for defending herself."

"She must have been effective, too, if the other patients are avoiding her. I hate the thought of it, but I suppose it's better than her being injured by an inmate."

"I'm sure she would agree," Frank said with a smirk.

"And that business about Julia being evil because she's led a privileged life, well, I detected a note of jealousy there."

"It's natural for somebody like the matron to resent somebody like Julia," Frank said.

"Yes, it is, but not to punish her for it or to label her evil because she was born into money. I think we have to take what that woman said with a grain of salt."

"I think you're right. Now how do we find out if what Julia said about Chet Longly is true?"

"I've been giving that some thought as well, and I'm afraid the best way would be to consult my mother."

Frank took their lives in his hands for a moment by taking his eyes from the road to give her a wide-eyed look that made her laugh. "Do we need to get your father's permission? You know how much he hates it when she gets involved in one of our cases."

"He doesn't really hate it. He just likes Mother to think he does. But don't worry, she's not going to be *involved*. We just need to find out what she's heard in the way of gossip. A story like the one Julia told us would be a choice topic among the society matrons. If Mother doesn't know all about it, I think we can assume Julia is lying."

"Will you go to see her?"

"I think I'll invite them to lunch tomorrow. It's Saturday and the children will be home. They can have a nice visit before we consult my parents for gossip."

"Your father, too?" Frank asked skeptically.

"I know Father claims he doesn't gossip just because he calls it gathering information, but we all know it's gossip just the same. If Chet Longly has gambling debts and a mistress, Father will have heard about it, too."

"And if Longly is as debauched as Julia indicated, your mother might *not* have heard about it."

"Because the information would be too salacious?" she scoffed. "I think you overestimate the delicacy of society matrons."

*   *   *

As Sarah had guessed, her parents were happy to come for a visit. They had plans for the evening, but they could spend the afternoon with their grandchildren, which was always a treat for both generations. It also gave Sarah's father an opportunity to practice his American Sign Language, which he was learning so he could communicate with his deaf grandson, Brian. Even Sarah's mother was learning to sign.

"Your father and I have found it quite convenient when we want to say something without the servants overhearing," Elizabeth Decker explained to her daughter when the children had finally tired of them and they had retreated to the parlor to visit with Sarah and Malloy.

"Then Sarah and I should always use sign language," Malloy said with a grin. "I'm sure our servants don't want to hear us discussing our cases."

"You might be surprised," Sarah's mother said. "They are probably quite popular among the other servants in the neighborhood since they have such interesting stories to tell."

Malloy looked horrified, but Sarah just shook her head. "We don't really talk about cases in front of them."

"Still, servants know everything, just like I know you didn't invite us here on the spur of the moment because you thought the children might be craving our company."

"Although I'm sure they were," her father added.

Sarah took a moment to study them. They were both still quite attractive in middle age. Her mother's blond hair was only lightly threaded with silver, and her face was remarkably unlined. Her father was even more handsome than in his youth, demonstrating the annoying trait some men had of getting better-looking with age. Their wealth had shielded them from the hard work and hardship that wore poor people down, she knew, but it hadn't protected them from the pain of being alienated from both their daughters. They had lost Sarah's sister forever when she died in childbirth, but Sarah was glad she had chosen to heal the breach and be reconciled with them again. So much good had come of it.

"What makes you think we had another reason for inviting you?" Sarah asked with feigned surprise.

Her mother just gave her a pitying look.

"I told you we wouldn't fool them," Malloy said.

"All right, we just wanted to ask if you knew anything about Chet and Julia Longly," Sarah said, surrendering.

"Oh my," her mother said, glancing at her husband.

Her father's eyebrows rose. "Has Longly hired you for something?"

"No," Malloy said. He had a policy of not revealing the names of his clients, but he had no compunction at all about revealing when someone was not his client.

"That's a relief," her father said.

"Why is it a relief?" Sarah asked.

Her parents exchanged another glance. "Chet Longly is somewhat of a . . . What's the word I'm looking for, dear?" her mother said.

"Degenerate?" her husband guessed.

"Good heavens, he's not that bad, is he? He was quite wild in his youth, but I heard he had settled down at least for a while when he married Julia."

"Wild in what way?" Malloy asked with an interest that made her father blink.

"Gambling and women," he said. "The usual things a young man does before he marries."

Her mother perked up at that. "Did you gamble and chase loose women before we married, Felix?"

"I'm sure you already know the answer to that question, Elizabeth," he replied, not even looking at her.

"But *I* don't," Sarah said with a grin.

"And you never will," her father said. "Now about Chet Longly, what else did you want to know?"

"You said he was a degenerate," Malloy said. "What did you mean by that?"

"That was unfair of me. I'm afraid I was joking to annoy Elizabeth. He may not be the ideal husband, but he's no worse than many other men of equal wealth and position in the city."

"Does he keep a mistress?" Sarah asked.

"Really, Sarah, a society matron never uses that word," her mother scolded her.

"I'm not a society matron, and I know you know if he does."

Her mother sighed. "Rumor has it that he keeps a woman in a house only a few blocks from the one where Julia lives."

"That's very indiscreet of him," her father said.

Her mother looked at him in surprise. "Then you would approve if he kept her farther away?"

"It's just good manners," her father replied, unrepentant.

Sarah rolled her eyes and Malloy had to cover a grin.

"Have you heard anything darker about him?" Sarah asked. "That he might have some shocking habits or interests?"

Both her parents frowned. "Who told you such a thing?" her father finally asked.

"Then you don't know anything more about him?" Malloy asked, dodging the question.

"He spends too much time at his clubs, and he flaunts his mistress, but that's the worst I've heard about him," her father said.

"But perhaps he's more discreet about his other bad habits," her mother suggested archly.

Sarah didn't need to look at Malloy to know he was disappointed. "Have you heard anything about Julia?" she tried.

Her mother took a moment to consider. "I think she must be in delicate health."

"Why do you say that?"

"When they first married, they went everywhere. Julia is quite vivacious, and Chet could be charming when he wanted to. But after their son was born, they were seen less and less. Chet would give the excuse that Julia wasn't feeling well. We all thought it might have been a difficult birth and she hadn't recovered."

Sarah took a moment to think through her next question since she didn't want to reveal Julia's current situation, but she also wanted to find out if it was common knowledge already. "Have you heard anything about her lately?"

She had tried to sound merely curious, but she couldn't fool her mother, whose gaze grew shrewd as she studied her daughter. "I haven't heard anything, but would you like me to find out if anyone else has?"

Malloy jumped in. "I don't think—"

"But now that I think of it," her mother continued, undaunted, "there was something about Julia's mother, Ellie Breedlove. It's been a long time now, but . . . yes, that's it. She disappeared."

"Disappeared?" Sarah echoed in surprise.

"People don't disappear, Elizabeth," her husband said. "That only happens in stage shows."

"I don't mean she vanished in a puff of smoke," she replied, still undaunted. "I mean right after Julia married, she sold her house and packed up and left the city."

"Where did she go?" Sarah asked.

"That's just it, everyone thought they knew where she'd gone because she'd told them, but it turns out she told everyone something different."

"What?" Malloy asked in amazement. "Why would she do that?"

"We thought she was teasing us, and we expected to hear from her once she was settled. She'd send us her address so we could stay in touch. We were sure that's what would happen, but she never did. We never heard from Ellie again."

"But surely Julia knew where she was," Sarah said. "Didn't anyone ask her?"

"She claimed she didn't, and she was obviously heartbroken that her mother would desert her like that. I would be the last to judge her, though. Perhaps she and Julia had quarreled, and some mothers and daughters don't ever get along."

"And Julia was married," her father added. "She probably thought Julia didn't need her anymore."

"Could she have married Julia off to Mr. Longly to get rid of her?" Sarah asked. "Do you remember any talk about them when they married?"

Sarah's mother considered the question for a moment. "Everyone thought it was a good match, and they certainly appeared to be madly in love. It was a bit embarrassing, in fact. Do you remember, Felix?"

"Longly did seem quite besotted. He was obviously pleased with his bride, even after all the loose women."

Malloy had to cover his mouth again, but Sarah didn't find her father's remark quite so amusing. Hadn't Julia said she hadn't wanted to marry Chet Longly?

"We'll be seeing some old friends this evening," her mother said. "I can mention Ellie Breedlove and ask if anyone has heard from her. That will probably lead to some discussion of her daughter and son-in-law as well."

Sarah's instinct was to tell her not to, for fear of spreading the word about Julia's being committed to an asylum, if someone happened to know that, but Malloy said, "We'd be glad to hear anything you find out about them."

"And Felix can find out the latest news about Chet Longly," her mother added with a twinkle. "That should be easy since he's so indiscreet."

D**ID WE LEARN ANYTHING NEW?**" FRANK ASKED SARAH when her parents had left.

"I'm not sure," she said, sitting down on the love seat beside him. "I suppose I should be surprised that my parents thought Julia and Chet were a love match."

"Julia definitely said she hadn't wanted to marry him as quickly as she did, but she also said she thought she was in love with him, at least at first."

"It's certainly understandable for a young girl to fall in love with a handsome man who shows her attention. And no one knows what goes on in a marriage behind closed doors except the two people involved."

"She didn't seem to like that either," Frank said.

"No, she didn't, but now I'm wondering if perhaps she

was just very innocent and found what is perfectly normal between a husband and wife appalling. It does happen, and she was very young when she married."

"I hadn't thought of that, but it is certainly possible. And if she was repulsed, she might have decided to leave his bed. There were no more children, after all."

"And it would explain the mistress, although I suppose I need to find another word to use if I can't say that one," Sarah added with a grin.

"I don't know another word for it, at least not a nice one. And I've heard your mother use it before. I think she may have just been teasing you."

"If she teases me again, I'll certainly ask her what word she uses. Now where do we go from here?"

"I think I need to speak to Chet Longly and find out what he has to say for himself," Frank said.

"About why he put Julia in the asylum," she guessed.

"Yes, and anything else I can find out."

"I can't imagine he'll be very forthcoming."

"I don't know. He might feel the need to justify his actions. That's what I'm counting on."

A loud shriek distracted them. "Oh dear, I think the children may have been left alone too long," Sarah said, rising. "We can talk about this more when Maeve and Gino get back."

MAEVE AND GINO RETURNED SHORTLY. OF LATE MAEVE split her time between working in Frank Malloy's private investigator's office and serving as the live-in nanny to the Malloys' two children, so Saturday was usually her day to watch the children. The visit from Sarah's parents had given her a free afternoon, so Gino had taken her out somewhere in the electric motorcar. Maeve refused to admit that Gino was courting her, although it certainly looked that way to everyone else. They were, she insisted, just friends. She was much too young to think about marriage.

Frank greeted them both when they came into the parlor.

"Where's Mrs. Frank?" Maeve asked.

"She's with the children, and my mother is still out doing whatever she was doing with Mrs. Ellsworth." Frank's mother lived with them in her own private suite, and she had become good friends with their neighbor.

"I should go up then," Maeve said. "But first, tell us if Mr. and Mrs. Decker knew anything about the Longlys." Maeve and Gino sat down on the love seat and Frank took a chair opposite them.

Frank had naturally discussed the new case with Gino, who was his partner at the agency, and Maeve, who kept all the records. "Not much more than we knew already, although they were under the impression that Julia was happy to marry Chet Longly, even if he was a bit wild in his youth."

"Maybe she just pretended she was," Maeve said, confirming Sarah's theory. "Women do that to make their lives more pleasant."

"Is that all you learned?" Gino said with feigned surprise. "I was sure Mrs. Decker would know everything about them."

"Since we've alerted her to the fact that she needs more information, I'm sure she will before another day passes," Frank said. "Oh, she did mention that Julia's mother moved out of the city after Julia got married and nobody seems to know where she lives now."

"That's strange," Gino said.

"Or maybe it isn't strange at all," Maeve said. "Maybe she

got tired of all the rules society made her follow, so she went someplace where nobody knew her."

"Sarah also pointed out that some mothers and daughters don't get along, so maybe she wanted to get away from Julia," Frank said.

"Leaving town seems a little extreme," Gino said. "Couldn't she just have stopped visiting her?"

"We'll probably never find out if nobody knows where she lives," Maeve said.

"Are you talking about Julia's mother?" Sarah asked as she came into the parlor. The men stood. "As my father said, people don't disappear. If she's still alive, we can probably find her. Did you have a nice afternoon?"

"It was great," Gino said. "I could drive that auto forever."

"But it only goes twenty-five miles before it needs to be charged, so forever is way too far," Maeve said.

"Did you barely make it home?" Frank asked with a smirk.

"We had miles to spare," Gino said with a grin.

"*Two* miles," Maeve clarified. "Should I go up to the children?"

"They're fine for a few minutes," Sarah said, taking the chair beside Frank's so the men could sit down. "Malloy and I didn't have a chance to discuss what we learned about Julia's mother. Ellie Breedlove is her name."

"Yes, she's the widow of Hugh Breedlove's brother," Frank said. "Mrs. Decker said no one questioned Julia's marriage. They thought it was a good match and the couple seemed very happy, at least at first."

"So, it seems odd that Julia said she was forced to marry him," Sarah said.

"It doesn't seem odd at all to me," Maeve said. "Maybe

she was lying to get your sympathy. She needs you to be outraged so you'll work harder to help her."

Having been raised by a con man, Maeve always expected the worst from others. In this case she might be right, however. "That's true, she does need us to be outraged. Getting her out of that place won't be easy," Frank said.

"And she was surprised her uncle actually made the effort to hire us to assist him," Sarah said. "I gather she doesn't have much confidence in his strength of purpose."

"If he wavers, we can always remind him of how the scandal will affect his daughter's entry into society," Frank said.

"But that might not be enough, so we need to work fast in case Breedlove decides to give up," Gino said. "What do you think we should do next?"

"I'm going to call on Longly and see what I can find out from him. If he has a good reason for locking Julia up, he shouldn't be afraid to tell me what it is," Frank said.

"And what if he doesn't have a good reason?" Gino asked.

"Then we'll figure out another plan."

"And my mother will probably find out something and tell us in the next few days. She is attending a party tonight and felt sure she could get more information for us."

"I can't believe she didn't know more," Maeve said.

"She said Julia and Chet stopped socializing, or at least Julia did," Sarah said. "Mother thought perhaps Julia was in poor health."

"Did she seem sickly when you met her?" Maeve asked.

"She didn't look her best, of course. No one would after a month in an institution like that, but she didn't seem ill. What do you think, Malloy?" Sarah said.

"Not at all, but why would a healthy young society matron stop socializing? Isn't that all they do?"

"Which is why they call it *society*," Maeve said, grinning slyly.

"Sadly, it *is* practically all they do, aside from the occasional good works," Sarah said. "So yes, it is odd that Julia would give up the parties and the visits."

"Maybe she didn't do it voluntarily," Maeve said.

"But could her husband force her to stay home?" Gino asked doubtfully.

"Do you mean could he lock her up or physically restrain her?" Sarah said. "He probably could have, but I'm sure if he'd done that, Julia would have mentioned it. He might have made it difficult for her by denying her the money to buy the right clothes, and we do know he told people she was ill, at least sometimes. But most likely, he just didn't attend the parties himself. It would have looked odd if she continually attended unescorted and would have made her the subject of unpleasant gossip."

"We'll have to ask her about it when we see her again," Frank said. "In the meantime, we'll find out what we can from Longly himself and your mother."

"When are you going to call on him?" Gino asked.

"I don't know if he has a profession, but I thought I'd go early on Monday morning. Men like him don't start work early."

"I hate to think of Julia languishing in that horrible place any longer than necessary, but I suppose it's foolish to think Mr. Longly would be at home for Sunday-afternoon visitors," Sarah said.

"That was my reasoning," Frank said. "Don't worry. I'm as anxious as you are to free her."

"And the easiest way to do that would be to win Mr. Longly's confidence, I know," Sarah said, "but somehow I don't think any part of this will be easy."

"Easy or not, we'll do it," Frank said. "A young woman's life is at stake."

THE CITY DIRECTORY LISTED CHET AND JULIA LONGLY AS living on Bedford Street, which wasn't far from Frank and Sarah's home on Bank Street in Greenwich Village. Still, Frank drove the electric down because he wanted to give the impression of wealth. He also wore one of his bespoke suits. He found the house easily. It was a three-storied, Federal-style house, but much larger than the others on the street. The stoop led straight up from the sidewalk with no front yard of any kind. The street was quiet with only the occasional businessman on his way to work or servant out on an errand.

Frank gave the brass knocker several resounding whacks and waited, mentally rehearsing the speech he had prepared for this occasion. Chet Longly wouldn't want to talk about his wife's condition, so Frank thought he had figured out the approach that had the best chance of winning his cooperation.

A frowning maid answered the door. Plainly, she wasn't used to visitors at this unusual hour. "I'd like to speak to Mr. Longly. It's a matter of some urgency."

"Is he expecting you?" the girl asked.

"No, but the matter involves Mrs. Longly. Would you give him my card and tell him I won't keep him long?" Without waiting for an invitation, he went in, forcing the maid to step aside or be trampled.

She stepped aside although she looked quite alarmed. "Mr. Longly might not be home," she said, accepting Frank's offered calling card reluctantly.

"Then I'll wait."

Plainly, the girl wasn't used to dealing with such rude visitors, but she said, "Wait here, please," and left him standing in the hallway while she scurried away into the depths of the house.

She kept him waiting almost fifteen minutes, but when she returned, she said, "Mr. Longly said for you to wait for him in the parlor." She escorted him into one of the rooms that opened off the hallway, a stiffly formal place obviously reserved for visitors. Frank had learned from Sarah how to judge the occupants of a house by its decor. This room, at least, had been furnished relatively recently with items bought new. The Longlys had probably purchased the house when they married instead of moving in with Longly's family. A family home would have been cluttered with heavy Victorian furniture passed down through generations.

The room was clean, without a speck of dust anywhere, and the lace-curtained windows looked out onto the quiet street. This spoke of efficient servants who did their jobs even without a wife in residence to oversee them.

Frank was studying the painting of an English countryside when Chet Longly came in. He was a handsome man, tall and slender with abundant chestnut hair and intense brown eyes that looked quite angry at the moment, even though he had the good breeding not to start out by shouting at Frank. "What do you want, Mr. . . ." He glanced down at the calling card he held. "Malloy?"

"As you can see from my card, I'm a private investigator. I've been hired to determine if there is any reason your wife should not have been confined at Ward's Island and to obtain her release if possible."

"Breedlove must have hired you, then. He's the only one who would care."

"Mr. Longly, I know you must be quite angry that someone is meddling in your affairs, but I'm sure you must understand what a shock it was to the Breedloves to discover Mrs. Longly's current situation."

"Are they shocked or simply embarrassed, I wonder?"

Frank refused to be distracted. "They are deeply concerned about Mrs. Longly. They have spoken with her, you see, and they believe her to be completely rational. They can't understand why you've sent her to Ward's Island. Now I'm sure you would not have taken such a drastic step without justification, which means Mrs. Longly's behavior must have alarmed you in some way. I've come to you today to ask you to tell me what it was that drove you to take this drastic step, because if I can give the Breedloves a good explanation, I am sure they will drop their objections and leave you in peace."

Longly studied Frank for a long moment, his dark eyes still intense and obviously angry. "Peace. For your information, Mr. Malloy, I have enjoyed nothing but peace since I sent my wife away. The Breedloves do not trouble me at all."

This was not the reaction Frank had hoped for, but he didn't dwell on that. "Mr. Breedlove has asked me to help him get Mrs. Longly released from her confinement."

"Are you trying to intimidate me, Malloy? You're wasting your time. The only way to get my wife out of that place is through a sanity hearing. Since Breedlove is only concerned with avoiding a scandal that will affect his daughter's coming out, I don't believe for a moment he wants a sanity hearing that will be public and will end up in the newspapers and become the talk of the town."

"In fact, he told me that he would welcome such a hearing because he believes Mrs. Longly will be found perfectly sane and released, an outcome he would like to see publicized."

"I'm sure, since it would reflect badly on me, but I assure you, my wife will never be judged sane and will never be released, no matter what Breedlove's opinion of her sanity might be."

Frank managed not to sigh. "If that is the case, then just tell me why you chose to confine her, and I will explain it to Mr. Breedlove so he can stop his efforts to get her released."

Some emotion flickered across Chet Longly's handsome face, and for a moment, Frank thought he would actually reveal what grievous sin Julia Longly had committed to get herself sent away. But when he finally spoke, Longly said, "My wife's behavior is no one's business, Mr. Malloy, and it is especially not the business of a shady private investigator who is no doubt planning to sell the details to the newspaper that bids the highest. Now I'll ask you once politely to leave my house, and if you do not, you will force me to throw you bodily into the street."

III

Sarah knew her mother wouldn't be occupied before lunch, since morning social calls didn't begin until the afternoon. She had no idea why they were still called morning calls, but neither did anyone else, so she supposed it didn't matter. But with the children in school, she was free to call on her mother and fully expected to be invited to stay for lunch. It had been too long since they had enjoyed a chat, just the two of them.

"Sarah, how lovely to see you," her mother said when the maid showed her in. Her mother had been at her desk in the family parlor, writing letters and probably responding to the most recent invitations she'd received. "I rather expected you to call soon."

"Since you're doing all the work, I thought I should make the effort to hear your report."

Her mother rang for tea, since it was still rather cool

outside, and they settled into two comfortable chairs by the gas fire.

"I'm afraid you're going to be disappointed since I didn't learn very much that is new about the Longlys," her mother said with a frown.

"If you learned anything at all, I'm sure it will help," Sarah said.

"As I told you I would, I started out by asking if anyone had heard from Ellie Breedlove, which started a discussion of her mysterious disappearance. There were five of us, and we all shared a story of our final conversation with Ellie in which she told us she was tired of living in the city and had bought a house in the country where the air was clean and the neighbors didn't know her."

"And she told them all a different location," Sarah remembered.

"Yes, although none of the locations were particularly far away except Newport. I don't know why she chose Newport except that the neighbors who would know her there would only be in town two months of the year at most."

"What were the other locations?"

"Two towns on Long Island, Connecticut, and White Plains. She had promised to send all of us a note with her new address when she got settled, but of course she never did."

"We might conclude that something happened to prevent her, except that she was plainly trying to keep her destination a secret and to create confusion about where it might be for anyone who might try to guess."

"Yes, and her old friends are still mystified by her behavior. Of course, she did lose her husband. We thought she had coped well with her loss, but perhaps we were wrong, and she had decided to move away to escape the bad memories."

"How long ago did her husband die?" Sarah asked.

"About a year before Julia married. Oh, I just realized, Ellie brought Julia out as soon as the year of mourning was over. In fact, the year wasn't quite up but she brought Julia out anyway. We all thought it strange since the girl was still in school and by rights she should have waited another year, until she was eighteen."

"So, her mother took her out of school and married her off as soon as she possibly could after her father died," Sarah mused.

"I'd forgotten the details until just now. Does it mean anything, do you think?"

"I don't know, but it does seem strange. Julia is a beautiful woman, and she would have found suitors no matter when she came out."

"That's probably true. I can't imagine why Ellie was in such a hurry."

Sarah couldn't either. When a woman lost her husband, she usually wanted to pull her other family closer, and Julia was all she had left. And what about Julia? She had lost her father and then her mother had married her off to a virtual stranger and left her alone to manage her new life on her own.

Sarah's mother was watching her closely. "What are you thinking?"

"That Ellie Breedlove was a selfish woman."

"What makes you say that?"

"Because she doesn't seem to have taken Julia's feelings into account at all. Shouldn't she have let Julia finish school and come out later? And then she left her daughter alone with a husband she barely knew. I wonder if Julia knows where her mother is."

"I'm sure she does," her mother said with more assurance than was warranted. "And I can't imagine Ellie not wanting to see her grandson."

No, her mother would not understand that at all. She had claimed both Frank's son by his first wife and an abandoned little girl Sarah had taken in as her own grandchildren, even before adoption had made them a real family.

"Did you learn anything about Julia and Chet Longly?" Sarah asked to change the subject, which had become much too serious.

Her mother seemed grateful for the slight change in topic. "I told you that Chet and Julia no longer socialize, but my friends still had news, although it was very vague. It seems the Longlys had some difficulties with their servants."

"What kind of difficulties?"

"No one really knew, but Mr. Longly let all of them go a month or two ago."

How odd. "All of them? At once?"

"According to one of my friends, yes. Her sister lives nearby, and the sister's servants were buzzing with the news."

"I can imagine. What on earth would you do without any of your servants?"

"It would be a disaster, I'm sure."

"Malloy was going to call on Mr. Longly today. I'll be sure to ask him who answered the door," Sarah said, but her mind was racing. A month ago was when Chet Longly put his wife in the asylum. Were the two events connected in any way? She wished she could tell her mother what had happened to Julia and get her opinion, but she didn't dare. They had to at least try to protect Julia's good name, and the fewer people who knew, the better. "Did you learn anything else?"

"Just a little more about Chet Longly's, uh, lady friend," her mother said.

Lady friend. Sarah would have to remember that. "What about her?"

"I don't have her exact address, but I know approximately where she lives and that Chet Longly frequently spends the night there, leaving his poor wife and child alone. The man is an absolute cad."

Poor Julia, how humiliating. Many wealthy men kept mistresses, but they hardly ever sent their wives to asylums.

"Sarah, what are you thinking?" her mother asked with a worried frown.

"Nothing at all," Sarah claimed.

"I know that's not true. You can't visit a woman like that. It simply isn't done."

"You're absolutely right, it isn't done," Sarah said with an agreeable smile.

So how could she do it?

LONGLY THREW YOU OUT?" GINO MARVELED. FRANK had gone from the Longly house to his office, knowing Sarah would be at her mother's. Maeve and Gino had been eagerly waiting to hear about his visit with Chet Longly.

"Not bodily, although he threatened that if I didn't go willingly."

Maeve and Gino apparently didn't know whether to be appalled or amused, and their expressions were frozen somewhere in between.

"Did you learn anything at all?" Maeve asked finally.

"Just that Longly doesn't believe for a moment that his wife will be judged sane and released from Ward's Island. He guessed that Breedlove had hired us, which was pretty easy to do, but he wasn't the least bit alarmed at the prospect of the situation becoming public knowledge."

"And why should he be?" Maeve said with a frown. "Men can do anything to their wives, and no one bats an eye."

"We're batting an eye," Gino reminded her.

"But we wouldn't have to if the law didn't allow a man to make up fantastic stories and have his wife locked away for the rest of her life."

Neither man had a reply to that. After a moment Gino managed to say, "What do we do next? If Longly won't tell us why he sent Julia away, how can we hope to prove she's not insane?"

"We need more information about what goes on in that house," Maeve said.

"Did you forget Mr. Malloy just got thrown out of that house?" Gino asked.

"Not thrown out," Frank insisted. "Just asked to leave."

"*Told* to leave, I'm sure," Maeve said. "And obviously you can't go back, so someone else will have to do it."

"And who would that someone be?" Frank asked, sure he already knew the answer.

He was right. Maeve grinned. "Me."

MAEVE MAY BE RIGHT," SARAH TOLD MALLOY THAT AFternoon. He had come home early to find out what she had learned from her mother. Since the children weren't home from school yet, they were in the downstairs parlor. "Mother said her friend's sister reported that Chet Longly fired all of his servants right around the time he had Julia sent away."

"I've known people to fire a servant or two, but not all of them at the same time," Malloy said. "I didn't know much about keeping up a big house until we got this place, but now I do. How could you manage without some help?"

"You couldn't. I assume he has some help now."

"A maid answered the door, and the place was clean. I didn't see any dust in the parlor, in any case."

"Oh, Malloy, I'm so proud of you for noticing," she exclaimed with far more enthusiasm than the deed warranted. Malloy knew it, too, and gave her a mock glare. "But you see, you found proof that Mr. Longly has some household staff now, so he didn't waste any time replacing the ones he sent away."

"But why would he send them all away in the first place?"

"I've been trying to figure that out myself. It does seem very strange, but if he was planning to put Julia in the asylum, this could have been part of his plan."

"What do you mean?"

"I mean that servants can develop a loyalty to their employers. Most do, even if the employers don't deserve it."

"And you think they may have had some loyalty to Julia," Malloy guessed.

"It stands to reason. Mr. Longly is somewhat of a cad. Servants know everything that goes on, so they would have known about his mistress and probably more about the way he was treating Julia than either of them realized."

"That's alarming," Malloy said, obviously thinking of their own servants.

"Don't worry, our servants know you treat me well. But since Mr. Longly was going to put Julia away, he wouldn't want the loyal servants to know. They might interfere in some way or even try to prevent it from happening."

"I never thought of that."

"It could be very awkward, so the easiest thing to do was send them away and hire new servants who are loyal only to him."

Malloy was nodding. "And he wouldn't even have to worry about what they thought of him afterward. It would be hard to have them lurking around thinking he's a devil for what he did to his poor wife."

"I'm sure it would. The problem is that since he replaced all the servants, questioning the current ones won't do us any good."

"Because they probably don't know what happened before they were hired."

"Exactly."

"Then how do we find out? If we could locate the servants he fired . . ."

"Which would be extremely difficult, especially since we don't even know their names and Mr. Longly isn't likely to tell us, but I have an idea."

"Does it involve Maeve helping?" Malloy asked, a hopeful look on his face.

"It does," she was happy to tell him. "I know she gets jealous because you and Gino do most of the investigation, so this should make her very happy."

THAT EVENING, AFTER THE CHILDREN WERE IN BED, Sarah explained her plan to Maeve. "My mother and I are going to visit one of Julia's neighbors who happens to be the sister of one of my mother's good friends, and you're going with us. You'll pretend to be my maid so you can talk to the other servants."

"Wouldn't it be better if I talked to the Longlys' servants?"

"We don't think so. If Chet Longly fired all of his servants just before he sent Julia away, the new ones probably don't know anything about her or what happened, but Mrs. Kindred—that's the sister of Mother's friend—heard about it from her own servants."

Maeve nodded. "That's not what I had in mind, but I see what you mean about the new servants not knowing what happened with Julia before they got there."

"Since they'll have heard Mr. Longly's story about why his wife no longer lives there—whatever that may be—and also the gossip in the neighborhood from other servants, they may actually have a completely wrong idea of what went on, so talking to them could even be misleading. I think this is a better idea."

"Even though it only requires one afternoon," Maeve said sadly.

"I know you were hoping to get a job in the Longly household, but maids work very hard," Sarah reminded her. "You should be glad I'm sparing you that."

Maeve grinned. "Real maids work very hard. I usually figure out a way to avoid working very much."

"Then this should be even easier for you. All you have to do is talk."

Sarah let her mother pick them up in her carriage the next day since the electric wasn't large enough to seat three comfortably and her mother wasn't enthusiastic about traveling in their gasoline-powered motorcar, especially with Maeve driving it. The carriage was slower, but it served the purpose.

"I've thought of the perfect excuse for visiting Opal Kindred," her mother told Sarah and Maeve when they were seated in the carriage.

"I knew you would," Sarah said. "What did you come up with?"

"I will ask her to serve on the Ladies Committee for the hospital. We're always looking for people because it's such a tiresome job."

"What do you do?" Maeve asked.

"We distribute clothes to the poorer patients, so they have something to wear when they leave. We knit socks and write notes to our friends asking them to donate to help us buy the clothes."

"Those are important things," Sarah pointed out.

"But not very glamorous, which is why we're always looking for people to help. Most women in my social circle would rather organize a tea or a ball to raise money."

"I don't suppose you can blame them," Maeve said.

"I don't suppose you can. Now what will you be doing, Maeve, while Sarah and I are recruiting Opal?"

"Gossiping with the servants," Maeve said. "They were the ones who knew what happened to the Longlys' servants, so I'll see if I can convince them to tell me what they know."

"I have every confidence in you," Sarah said.

Sarah's mother sighed. "Now I wish we were joining you, Maeve. Your task sounds so much more interesting than ours."

"And I would welcome you," Maeve said with complete sincerity, "except the servants aren't likely to say a word in front of you."

Her mother smiled at that. "Am I so very intimidating?"
Maeve smiled back. "Yes."

The trip to Bedford Street didn't take long. The women
paused on the sidewalk, looking around when the coachman
had helped them down.

"That's the Longly house," Sarah said with a nod. "The
one on the corner."

"Julia seems to have done well for herself," her mother
said, "although this is no longer a fashionable part of the
city."

"Which is why Malloy and I settled here," Sarah said.

"Maybe the Longlys didn't want to live in a fashionable
part of the city either," Maeve said.

"I'm sure it was Chet Longly's decision," her mother said.
"And living here would provide him with some measure of
privacy."

"With no high society matrons as neighbors to spy on his
comings and goings," Sarah said with a grin.

"He's still being watched by his neighbors, though,"
Maeve reminded them.

"And the high society matrons, as you call them, still
hear about his comings and goings," her mother said.
"Shall we?"

She led the way up the front steps and rapped the
knocker. The maid who answered seemed surprised to see
three females on the doorstep, but when Sarah's mother presented her card and asked to see Mrs. Kindred, she graciously asked them to step inside while she went to see if her
mistress was at home.

Which, Sarah supposed, was the proper use of the word
mistress.

She returned in just a few minutes to inform them Mrs.

Kindred would be delighted to receive them, but she did give Maeve, who was dressed as a maid and looking appropriately obsequious, a questioning look.

"I'm afraid we had my maid with us while we shopped this morning," Sarah said, "and I didn't want to leave her waiting in the carriage. Could she just sit here in the hall while we visit with Mrs. Kindred?"

"I suppose that would be all right," the girl said, giving Maeve another uncertain glance.

"You'll be fine," Sarah assured Maeve with just the right amount of unconcern. Rich people didn't often concern themselves with the comfort of their servants.

The maid led them to what was obviously the formal parlor, reserved for guests and special occasions, where Opal Kindred awaited them with obvious pleasure. She was a plump woman around thirty with a face that could conceal no emotion. Her brown hair was carefully styled, and her gown was the latest fashion, although it did not flatter her. Sarah remembered her vaguely from growing up as the daughter of one of the oldest families in New York.

"Mrs. Decker, what a nice surprise," Opal said. "I've ordered some tea and . . . Is this Sarah?"

"Yes, I hope you don't mind that she came along. I thought for sure you'd remember her."

"Oh, I do. It's lovely to see you again."

"She's Mrs. Malloy now," her mother said.

If Opal Kindred found it odd that Elizabeth Decker's daughter had married an Irishman, she was too well-bred to show it. "I can't remember the last time I saw you, Sarah," she said as she saw her guests seated on the sofa and took a chair opposite them. The room was furnished in the Louis XVI style, with elaborately carved pieces featuring laurel leaves, swags, oak leaves, and acanthus scrolls, and upholstered in vivid satins.

"Sarah retired from society when she married," her mother said. She could have explained that Sarah's first husband had been a lowly physician and Sarah herself had rebelled from her upbringing to become a nurse and a midwife, but she didn't want to distract Opal from the matter at hand.

"And you're reintroducing her?" Opal guessed, obviously hoping she had been selected to help Sarah reenter society.

Her mother also chose not to answer that question, since Sarah might well have contradicted her if she had tried to confirm Opal's guess. "The two of you are practically neighbors. Sarah and Mr. Malloy live on Bank Street."

Plainly, Opal was determined to accept whatever Elizabeth Decker said with delight. "Really? Then we *are* practically neighbors. It's such a nice part of the city, don't you think?"

"We've been very happy here," Sarah said quite truthfully.

"You must be wondering why we've come," her mother said, and launched into her plea to Opal to join the hospital committee.

Sarah sat back and waited, knowing Opal would be only too glad for a change of subject when her mother was finished.

MAEVE WAS SITTING ON ONE OF THE CHAIRS IN THE hallway when the maid returned from escorting Sarah and her mother upstairs. The chairs had obviously been chosen for style rather than comfort. The carved bunches of grapes on the back made relaxation impossible. Maeve jumped to her feet when the girl reappeared.

"I hate to leave you here," the girl said.

"She always does this to me, taking me along to carry her packages when she shops and then leaving me to wait while she visits somebody. I'm parched. Could I get a glass of water?"

The girl glanced back at the closed parlor door. "Will she be mad if you aren't waiting when she comes out?"

"Your mistress will ring when they're ready to leave, won't she? I can come back then."

The girl smiled. "Come on to the kitchen then. I have to fetch the tea tray."

"Maybe we can sneak some cakes," Maeve said, following her down the back stairs to the kitchen.

"Mrs. Kindred wants tea for her and two guests," she informed the cook, who had been resting with her feet up when the girls entered.

The cook made a disgusted noise and looked Maeve up and down. "And who might you be?"

"I'm Mrs. Malloy's maid, Maeve Smith."

"Mrs. *Malloy* has a maid?" the cook scoffed. "Lace-curtain Irish, is she?"

"She's society," the maid informed her importantly.

"And he's a millionaire," Maeve added, unwilling to have the Malloys maligned.

"La-di-da," the cook said, unimpressed. She rose and started preparing the tea tray.

The maid got Maeve a glass of water and introduced herself as Winny.

"I never knew Mrs. Decker to visit Mrs. Kindred before," Winny remarked as Maeve refreshed herself.

"I couldn't say, but I do know why she's come," Maeve confided. "I heard them talking in the carriage."

Even the cook perked up at that, although she didn't even glance at the girls as she continued preparing the tea tray while the water boiled.

"Why?" Winny asked.

"Well, she's pretending to recruit her for some committee or other, but really she wants to hear the gossip about the Longlys."

Winny's eyes widened. "Does she now? How on earth did she know about the Longlys?"

"She's friends with Mrs. Kindred's sister, who heard it from Mrs. Kindred, who, I gather, heard it from you."

"Not from me, but from her lady's maid," Winny said, "although we all knew about it."

"Did Mr. Longly really fire all his servants?" Maeve asked with wide-eyed wonder.

Winny glanced at the cook as if for permission to tell the tale, but the cook pretended not to notice. "All kinds of strange things happened at that house."

"What kinds of things?" Maeve asked eagerly.

Winny looked around again, as if checking for eavesdroppers but of course no one was near except the cook. "First of all, one of the maids went missing."

"What do you mean *missing*?"

"She just wasn't there one day, and nobody knew what happened to her."

"Not even the other servants?"

"If they did, they didn't say, although everybody had a good guess."

"What did they guess?"

"Well," Winny said, glancing around again. Plainly, she

enjoyed the drama of the situation. "They said she was Mr. Longly's *favorite maid*, if you know what I mean."

Maeve didn't have to pretend to be shocked. She hadn't expected this, although she knew perfectly well that maids were often considered fair game to their employers. "Do they think there was a baby?"

"No one knows but why else would she just leave like that, without a word?"

"And no one knows where she went?"

Winny shook her head.

"And that happened before he fired all the other servants?"

"Yes, a month or two before."

Maeve was trying to make sense of this. "Did something else happen? I mean, to make Mr. Longly angry with the servants?"

Winny nodded solemnly. "Another servant vanished."

"Another favorite maid?" Maeve guessed.

"Oh no, this was the boy's nursemaid. The Longly boy. He's about four years old."

"Did Mr. Longly get her with child as well?" Maeve asked, feigning shock at such a thought.

Winny actually laughed at that, earning a scowl from the cook, who finally deigned to look up, and Winny sobered instantly. "She was old and plain, so he wouldn't have been interested in her, but she vanished just the same."

"And the other servants didn't know what happened to her either?"

"There were stories, of course. Someone saw a wagon taking something away in the night, and somebody else claimed they heard screams, but nobody is sure about anything except the nursemaid wasn't there the next day."

"And then Mr. Longly fired the rest of his servants?"

"Not too much longer after that. They didn't even say good-bye," Winny said. "They just left one morning with their valises and a month's wages."

"How do you know the part about a month's wages?" the cook challenged.

Winny stiffened but she turned to the cook with the confidence of one who knows she is correct. "They told me, didn't they? I saw them leaving that morning."

"That's the first I heard of it," the cook said. "Maybe we don't keep you busy enough if you have time to be watching who walks down the street."

"I was washing the window, wasn't I? I couldn't help but see."

"I guess you couldn't help but go outside to find out why they were leaving either."

"No, I couldn't, and you're just as glad that I did. Otherwise, we'd be wondering to this day."

"Not to this day," the cook told her with a smirk, "since they all came back a week later."

THE OTHER LADIES ON THE COMMITTEE WILL BE VERY glad to welcome you, Opal. Thank you so much for being willing to help," Sarah's mother said with creditable enthusiasm. "I'll send you an invitation to our next meeting."

Poor Opal didn't look very excited about her new commitment, but she managed a polite smile. "I'll look forward to it."

"I'm so glad your sister mentioned you when I saw her the other night," her mother said. "She made me think of you."

Now Opal looked a bit alarmed. "Why did she mention my name?"

"Oh, we weren't talking about you, if that's your concern. I happened to ask if anyone had heard from Ellie Breedlove. That's Julia Longly's mother, you know."

"Is it?" Opal asked, apparently a little confused.

"Yes, and no one had. She left the city for country life when Julia married, and her friends have lost touch with her. In any case, we were discussing Ellie, and your sister mentioned that you and Julia were neighbors."

"Yes, we are," Opal confirmed, obviously feeling herself on firmer ground now. "They moved here when they married."

"Chet Longly was such a rogue as a young man," her mother said. "I was surprised he chose Julia."

"I think everyone was," Opal said obligingly.

"I suppose you've gotten to know Julia quite well, being neighbors," Sarah said, recognizing that it was time for her to step in.

Opal frowned. "Not really. Julia is . . . She's difficult to get to know."

"Is she?" Sarah's mother said. "I found her quite charming when she was first married and we used to see her."

"She can be charming when she wants to be, I suppose, but she didn't waste any of it on her neighbors. I get the feeling she didn't think we were worth the effort. She spends her time elsewhere."

Sarah's mother gave her an apparently shocked glance, and Sarah said, "I thought she had withdrawn from society because her health was bad."

"Withdrawn?" Opal scoffed. "Hardly. She is always going somewhere. She has this smart little carriage, and her driver is always taking her someplace, day and night."

But not to society functions, or Sarah's mother and her friends would have seen her, or so her mother believed.

"Oh, I just happened to think," Opal was saying. "Being out day and night might have ruined her health, as you say. That would explain why she hasn't been home for a few weeks."

"Are you sure about that?" Sarah asked, thinking word must be getting out that Julia wasn't at home anymore.

"Yes, I called on her the other day. I was concerned, you see, because I hadn't seen her lately." Did Opal sound a little defensive? More likely she was just nosy and wanted to know where Julia had been.

"That was very good of you," Sarah said to encourage Opal's continued confidence. "We should all look after our neighbors."

"Yes, one never knows, does one?" Opal looked at Sarah's mother, who solemnly agreed.

"What did they tell you when you called on her?" Sarah asked.

"They said she was taking a rest in the country. Oh, I wonder if she went to stay with her mother. That would make perfect sense."

Sarah nodded. "Indeed it would." If it were true.

Opal frowned. "I suppose that explains about her driver, too."

"Her driver?" Sarah asked.

"The coachman who took her everywhere. You see, Mr. Longly sent all their servants away. We thought at first he had fired them, but then they all returned, all but the coachman. But if Julia had gone to the country, I suppose they didn't need him anymore."

IV

Yes, the maid did say the Longlys' servants came back after a week or two," Maeve confirmed when she joined Sarah and her mother in the carriage, and they'd shared what they had learned. "All except Vogler, the coachman. The Kindred servants were quite sad about that, too."

"Why is that?" her mother asked.

Maeve smiled mysteriously. "Apparently, he is very handsome."

Sarah found that interesting. "Isn't it the footmen who are supposed to be handsome?" she asked her mother, remembering this tidbit from her youth.

"Absolutely, but handsome or not, finding footmen nowadays is difficult."

Sarah was sure this was true. "Didn't Opal say that Julia often went out in her carriage?"

"I believe she said Julia went out day and night."

"With her handsome coachman," Maeve said, no longer smiling. "That sounds strange."

"But we don't know where she was going," Sarah said, remembering the distraught woman she'd met at the asylum. "And maybe the coachman being handsome didn't have anything to do with it. She could have just been trying to avoid her husband."

"And she might have been doing good works, for all we know," her mother said.

"I will be sure to ask her when I see her next," Sarah said, thinking she should probably make another trip out to Ward's Island very soon. She was accumulating a lot of questions for Julia.

"I don't suppose we can fault her for wanting to avoid her husband, though," Maeve said, "especially if he got a maid with child."

"What a horrible man," her mother said with a small shiver.

"And don't forget whatever happened with the nursemaid," Sarah said. "Julia will probably know that, too."

"Will it help her, though?" Maeve asked. "Even if her husband is Satan himself, she could still be judged insane."

"Insane?" her mother echoed in surprise. "Did someone accuse her of being insane?"

Sarah winced. They hadn't intended to tell her mother or anyone else about Julia's stay in the asylum, but Maeve had accidentally let the cat out of the bag.

"Oh dear," Maeve said with genuine regret.

"It's all right," Sarah told her, thinking that it was time to confess to her mother anyway. "Mother, I didn't tell you before because we were trying to protect Julia, but her husband has had her committed to an insane asylum on Ward's Island."

"Dear heaven, no wonder you're so anxious to help her," her mother said. "The poor thing!"

"Yes, and the more we find out about Chet Longly, the more I think she deserves our help."

"If he's as bad as we suspect, he might have *driven* her insane," her mother said.

"I don't know how they decide on someone's sanity, but the more we know about him, the more we can help Julia. Maybe he will be so eager to keep his misdeeds quiet that he'll have Julia released."

"Isn't that blackmail?" Maeve said, feigning dismay.

"We won't be asking him for any money," Sarah said. "We'll just be asking him to behave in a civilized manner."

"Some men find that impossible," her mother warned.

As Sarah knew only too well from working on cases with Malloy.

The coachman let Sarah and Maeve down at Sarah's house and took her mother home. When Sarah and Maeve were alone in the parlor, Maeve sat down beside Sarah on the sofa and said, "We still need to find out what happened at the Longly house."

"And I suppose you're volunteering your services," Sarah said with a sigh.

"Who else could go?"

"They obviously need a coachman," Sarah pointed out reasonably. "We could send Gino."

"Gino could be a chauffeur, but I doubt he'd pass for a coachman."

"Besides, all the female servants in the neighborhood

would be chasing him," Sarah pointed out with a small smile.

Maeve scowled, but she apparently had no intention of being drawn into a conversation about Gino's attractiveness to women. "And he's not likely to hear much gossip out in the mews. We need someone in the house if we want to find out what happened to those two women."

"Maeve, they said the maid who disappeared was Mr. Longly's *favorite maid*, and they suspect she was with child. You know what that means."

"It means you think I might not be safe. But I'll be careful. I'm not some naive country girl who will swoon if the master notices me. I'll even take a knife with me in case he tries anything."

Sarah stared at her in horror. "A *knife*?"

"Just a small one. I don't intend to murder him, just discourage him."

Sarah laid a hand on her heart. "That makes me feel so much better," she said sarcastically.

"You never give me enough credit. I know how to take care of myself."

"I know you do, but you're a young girl, and he's a man who may have already defiled at least one servant."

"We don't know that for sure," Maeve pointed out.

"But we do know servants disappear from that house. I can't take a chance with your life, Maeve."

To Sarah's relief, Maeve seemed to be convinced or at least she chose to stop pressing her case. After they had lunch, Maeve went to the office for a few hours until she had to walk Catherine home from school. Sarah drove the electric down to the Lower East Side to the maternity clinic she operated there. She had made her living as a midwife before she married Malloy, and she never wanted to stop delivering babies. Since the pregnant women in that part of the city often had no help at all and might even be homeless, she had opened the clinic to aid them and to give herself the occasional opportunity to bring a baby into the world.

She didn't expect to deliver a baby today unless someone had a surprise for her, and the two midwives she employed made most of the deliveries now, but there was almost always a new baby to snuggle, and she could help if someone in labor came in unexpectedly. Besides, the drive down and back would give her time to think about what she had learned today and what it could all mean.

FRANK WAS GLAD WHEN MAEVE LEFT THE OFFICE THAT afternoon to fetch Catherine from school. He hated it when she pouted because she couldn't get her way, but he had to agree with Sarah. After the things Maeve told him they had learned at the Kindred house, he couldn't allow Maeve to put herself in danger. She'd gotten a job as a maid before in other cases, but never because a servant had gone missing.

"One thing has been bothering me about what Maeve told us," Gino said, having appeared in Frank's office doorway.

"Everything about what Maeve told us has been bothering me," Frank said, "but tell me the one thing you're worried about."

"You always say the servants know everything, and I suppose it's true. We never had any servants, but my mother knows everything, so I guess it's the same thing. Anyway, if Chet Longly did do something to the maid who disappeared, even if he just sent her away, and if he did something to the nursemaid who vanished, the servants would know all about it, wouldn't they?"

"The Longly servants would know at least something about it, yes. I imagine you can't keep any secrets when people live so closely together."

Gino came into the office and sat down in one of the client chairs. "And we know that Longly sent his servants away for a week or two."

"That's right. We assumed that he'd fired them, but he brought them back again."

Gino nodded, as if still putting his thoughts together. "So, if he did something bad to those two women and the other servants knew it and he sent them away, why would they come back again?"

Frank leaned back in his chair. "I see what you mean. If they knew he'd done something untoward . . ."

"Or more than one thing untoward," Gino said.

"Why would they still want to work for him?"

"That's what I'm wondering."

Frank considered the possibilities for a moment. "They might have been afraid to leave him," he said, trying out the theory to see how it sounded.

"More afraid to leave him than afraid he would rape or kill one of them?"

"You're right, that doesn't make sense. But why send them away at all if he's just going to bring them back again? That doesn't make sense either."

"Not much of this case does, so far, but let's figure this out," Gino said, leaning forward so he could rest his forearms on Frank's desk. "What happened while they were gone?"

"Longly sent Julia to the asylum."

Gino nodded. "I don't know how these things work, but

I imagine either Longly took her there or they sent some staff to get her."

"If all this suspicious stuff was going on, she wouldn't be likely to go anyplace with Longly voluntarily, so he would have had to restrain her somehow."

"I don't know him, but I can't imagine any man doing something like that without attracting a lot of attention. Even if he put her in a carriage, she'd be screaming and fighting, wouldn't she?"

Frank nodded. "Knowing what we do of Julia, I'm sure she would. Even in New York, people might try to stop you if they heard someone screaming and carrying on. You're right, a man used to behaving well in public would have a difficult time dealing with a scene like that."

"Which means the asylum probably sends some staff out to collect new patients. They'd know how to handle them, and they'd have restraints and an ambulance to put them in."

"And no one would think it odd if a person inside the asylum's ambulance was screaming and carrying on."

Gino shook his head. "It gives me chills, thinking of an innocent woman being treated like that."

"Me, too, but it does explain why Longly wouldn't want his servants around to see it happen. Sarah and I already decided that was the reason Longly sent them away, but we didn't know then that they'd come back. They may have been with the family a long time and he didn't want to lose them."

"If the servants had been with them a long time, they'd know there wasn't anything wrong with Julia. Would they have tried to save her, though?"

"That's hard to say, but I can see where Longly might not want to take a chance. If they didn't see her being taken

away, he could tell them any story at all about where she went. He could tell them she went to visit family or shopping in Europe or to a rest cure in the mountains. They might be suspicious, but what could they do?"

Gino had no answer for that. After a long moment he said, "We need to question the Longly servants."

Frank ran a hand over his face. "I know. Any idea how to do that without involving Maeve?"

Gino sighed. "Not a single one."

WE NEED TO VISIT JULIA AGAIN BEFORE WE DO ANYTHING else," Sarah informed Malloy when he told her about his conversation with Gino. "She probably knows everything we'd find out from the servants, and if she does, we don't have to put Maeve in danger."

They were in their private parlor, where Maeve wouldn't overhear them and get ideas.

"You're right. I'd like to speak to a doctor at the asylum, too."

"What are you going to ask him?"

"The same thing I asked that nurse: What makes them think Julia Longly is insane when she acts so rational?"

"I'd like to know that, too, and also if anyone oversees the nurses and the way they treat the patients. I'm still disturbed by the things Julia told us."

"Unless she was exaggerating to get our sympathy," Malloy said.

"I know she might have been, but you have to admit, it would be easy for the nurses to abuse the patients if no one is watching them."

"And as Julia pointed out, if the patients complain, no one would believe them," Malloy added.

"Exactly. Can we go out to Ward's Island tomorrow?"

"Yes. I should give Mr. Breedlove a report on our progress so far, too, but I'll wait until we visit Julia in case she has more information for us."

"Julia is fortunate her uncle was willing to help her," Sarah said. "Think of how awful it would be to have no one to advocate for you if your husband locked you away."

"And no one to hire us to find out the truth," Malloy said with a small smile.

"Yes, we're wonderful, aren't we," Sarah said with an answering smile.

"For Julia's sake, let's hope so."

THE WEATHER WAS WARMER ON WEDNESDAY MORNING than it had been a few days earlier when they had made their first visit to Ward's Island. The receptionist didn't look very pleased to see them, especially when Frank said they would like to speak to the doctor in charge of Mrs. Longly's care after they visited her, but they were escorted back to the same visiting room and instructed to wait.

This time Julia walked into the room under her own power, and Sarah noticed a different matron had accompanied her, one who evidently did not feel the need to shove her to get her to move.

Sarah had expected Julia to look worse than she had before, more worn and more frightened, but oddly, she met their gaze with confidence and even a glimmer of pleasure. Her hair was combed and tied back with a ribbon, and her face had color in it. "Mr. and Mrs. Malloy, how nice to see you again so soon." She turned to her escort. "Thank you, Matron," she added as if they were in a drawing room and the matron were a servant who had performed her duty well.

The woman looked at her sharply, but she only said, "Call me if you need me," to the Malloys and slipped out of the room, closing the door behind her.

"Have you come to get me out?" Julia asked as she had before.

"Not yet, unfortunately, but we're working very hard on your case," Sarah said.

"We want to have as much information as possible before we approach a judge," Malloy added.

Julia smiled a bit sadly. "That is difficult to hear, but I suppose these things are complicated. Let's sit down and you can tell me why you've come."

They sat in the worn chairs they had occupied the last time. Today the open window let in a mild breeze. "We've heard some rumors about things that happened at your home shortly before your husband had you committed," Malloy said.

Her expression darkened. "I suppose my husband accused me of all sorts of terrible things."

"Your husband refused to tell me anything at all."

This obviously surprised her. "Who did you speak to then?"

"As my husband said, we heard some rumors," Sarah said, not wanting to name Opal and create a rift between the neighbors. "We heard that one of your maids disappeared. Can you tell us what happened to her?"

Julia closed her eyes and shook her head as if in silent

denial, but when she opened her eyes she said, "The girl didn't disappear. Chet sent her away."

"Where did he send her?"

"How would I know? Where do men send a girl they've debauched and gotten with child? It wasn't the first time, either. He has a penchant for pretty young girls, regardless of their social standing, and he has no difficulty seducing them. He's quite charming when he puts his mind to it, which is how he fooled me into marrying him."

"Does he force them? The girls, I mean," Sarah asked, thinking about her concerns for Maeve's safety.

Julia laughed mirthlessly at the suggestion. "He doesn't have to force them. They practically fall at his feet."

"You said your husband sent her away. Do you know what happened to her?" Malloy asked.

She was still amused. "He doesn't discuss these matters with me, as you can imagine. For all I know, he turned her out into the street."

Sarah winced, although many girls had suffered that fate after falling pregnant to the master or his sons, either willingly or unwillingly. This was only one of the many reasons places like her maternity clinic were so necessary.

Before Sarah could think of another question, Malloy said, "We also heard your husband keeps a woman in a house near your own."

Julia was no longer amused. Anger flashed in her lovely eyes, but she must have realized how futile it would be to indulge herself in it because she merely said with obvious disgust, "Yes, the infamous Mrs. Nailor."

"You knew about her then?" Sarah asked. She really didn't know much about how these situations were handled by the people involved. She did know that while women often knew all the details of other men's indiscretions, they rarely acknowledged their own husbands' paramours.

"Chet flaunted her, so how could I not? But in the end, I was grateful for her because he no longer tortured me with his demands." Julia met Sarah's gaze unflinchingly and Sarah saw a woman who had endured humiliation and survived. How much longer could she endure this current ordeal?

Sarah couldn't let sympathy stop her, though. They needed to know exactly what Chet Longly had done, no matter how painful it was for Julia to recount it. "Do you know why your husband decided to have you committed to the asylum at this particular time?"

Sarah saw another flash of anger, as she might have expected, but Julia Longly must have been determined not to surrender to even the slightest degree of hysteria, knowing how it would be viewed in this place. "I have asked myself that question a hundred times. I admit, I have not been a happy wife, but who could blame me under the circumstances? I don't believe I behaved differently than any other woman in my situation would. I begged and pleaded and I screamed and cried, whatever seemed appropriate for what I was enduring, but a man should expect such a response when he does the things Chet did to me. I must admit, I think he actually enjoyed my suffering. Eventually, he became bored with me, however, and turned his attentions elsewhere."

"How long ago was this?" Sarah asked.

Julia seemed quite offended by the question, so Sarah quickly amended it.

"I just meant that if it was recently, perhaps that was why he sent you away."

But Julia shook her head. "No, it was not recently. I have enjoyed my husband's neglect for over a year now. Since I was no hindrance to him, I can't imagine why he decided to send me away at all. He cannot divorce a woman who is insane, and I don't imagine he wants another wife in any case. I'm very much afraid he has just done it to be cruel to a woman whose only crime was loving him so much, I overlooked his faults until it was too late." Her eyes filled with tears, but she set her jaw and refused to allow them to fall.

Sarah blinked in surprise. She hadn't realized Julia loved her husband quite so much. But then she probably didn't want to admit it after all the things he'd done to her.

"Don't lose hope, Mrs. Longly," Malloy said. "Your uncle is determined to free you, and we are doing all we can to assist him."

"I'm very grateful, Mr. Malloy, but you can't imagine how difficult it is to wait. And I miss my son. Have you seen little Victor, by chance? Can you tell me how he is?"

"We haven't seen him, I'm sorry to say," Sarah said. "Your husband refused to give Malloy any information at all and ordered him to leave before he could even ask about Victor."

"I can't imagine what lies Chet is telling him about me. The child will probably be terrified of me," Julia said, angrily swiping at the tears in her eyes.

"And he doesn't have his nursemaid to take care of him either," Sarah said, remembering the other missing servant.

"What do you mean?" Julia asked.

"I thought you knew, but perhaps we misunderstood. We heard that your son's nursemaid has gone as well."

Julia frowned. "Gone?"

"Yes, the story we heard involved screams and the nursemaid disappearing in the night."

Julia stared at Sarah for a long moment, and for the life of her, Sarah could not read her expression. "I wonder who told you all this. What a storyteller they must be. Miss Winterbourne left of her own accord. There may have been some screaming, since it was my husband's behavior that drove her to leave even though she adored little Victor, but I assure you she didn't *disappear* at any hour of the day or night. What a lot of nonsense."

"And then your husband dismissed the rest of your servants," Sarah said, not making it a question.

"My, my, you really are well-informed. Yes, Chet did dismiss the rest of our servants. That should have terrified me, and it would have if I'd known what he was planning, but I was merely confused and naturally upset because can you imagine having to replace all of your household help at once? Or living without them while you do it?"

"Did he explain why he had let them go?" Malloy asked.

"Chet never explains himself to anyone, but when the brutes from this place arrived in their filthy ambulance and bound me hand and foot and threw me inside of it, I realized why he had emptied our house of everyone except little Victor and me."

"Would your servants have helped you, do you think?" Sarah asked, which was what she and her cohorts believed.

She smiled at that, a sad and ironic twisting of her lips. "*Helped* me?" she scoffed. "They would never have helped me. Chet paid them, and he had their loyalty. No, he sent them away to still their tongues."

"Still their tongues?" Sarah echoed in confusion.

"They couldn't tell people he had sent his wife to an asylum if they didn't know, could they?"

"No, I don't suppose they could," Sarah said, glancing at

Malloy to see if he remembered they had suspected this. He did.

Julia didn't notice. "Chet might want to rid himself of me, but he wouldn't want people to know how he had accomplished it. He'll make up some story about a trip or something and then tell people I died of a fever. He couldn't do that if a houseful of servants had seen those beasts carrying me away."

Sarah and Frank had thought badly of Chet Longly, but apparently, they had still given him too much credit.

"Your husband seems to care a lot for his good name," Malloy said.

"He does, but it is more than that. He cares for little Victor's good name. His son's future is important to him, and he will do anything to protect it. That is why he has gone to such lengths to make sure I am alone and defenseless."

Defenseless. It was such a terrifying word, and women were almost by nature defenseless when faced with the physical and social powers of men.

"You aren't quite defenseless, Mrs. Longly," Malloy said. "You do have some friends."

She bestowed on him a gracious smile, giving Sarah another glimpse of the woman she had been when she was a society matron instead of an inmate of an asylum. "I am fortunate indeed. But only if you succeed, Mr. Malloy. I am powerless on my own."

"I assure you, we will not give up," he promised, which Sarah thought was a little rash, considering how difficult the task would be, but she didn't say so. No use discouraging Julia. Her life was difficult enough without crushing the little hope she had.

"I'm just wondering if you've given any thought to what you will do when you are released," Sarah said.

"What do you mean?" Julia asked.

Could she really not have thought about this? "I mean where you will live and how. Mr. Longly isn't likely to welcome you back and I can't imagine you'd want to live with him again."

"Certainly not!"

"But perhaps you have friends who will take you in," Sarah said. "We understand that you were quite active socially."

"I don't know who could have told you such a lie," Julia said coldly, as if Sarah had insulted her.

"We were given to understand that you went out frequently, and we assumed it was to pay social calls," Sarah said quickly in an attempt to clarify.

Julia nodded solemnly. "Now I understand who must have given you so much false information about me. Which of my neighbors did you chat with, Mrs. Malloy?"

Sarah smiled apologetically. "I told you, we heard rumors."

"I'm sure my neighbors were only too happy to enthrall you with tales of my misdeeds. I can only wish I was able to make social calls, but Chet had cut off all contact with the people we once knew. I was no longer welcome in their homes."

"Your neighbors saw you frequently going out in your carriage, though," Malloy said.

"When did that become cause for censure, Mr. Malloy? Yes, I confess to asking my coachman to take me for long drives when I could no longer bear being a virtual prisoner in my own home. Sometimes I would go to a library or a museum. If that is worth gossiping about, my neighbors must live hopelessly dull lives indeed."

"Many of them probably do," Sarah said, remembering her own thoughts about the main duties of a society matron. "I'm sorry we distressed you, but we had to ask about these things. Your husband will certainly oppose us when we try to free you, so we needed to know the truth."

"You will be astonished by the truth, Mrs. Malloy. Chet will never allow it to come out if he can possibly prevent it."

"Fortunately, he doesn't have any control over us, Mrs. Longly," Malloy said.

The matron came in then and informed Julia her time was up.

"I am very grateful to you both for your help," Julia said as they all rose. "Please don't forget me."

Sarah thought her heart would break at those simple words. How easy it would be to do just that. They had no ties to Julia Longly, and her uncle could simply decide he had done enough and give up his efforts to see her released. What would become of her then? And how many other perfectly sane women had shared her fate?

"We aren't going to forget her," Malloy said into her ear as they watched Julia leave.

She smiled at him, grateful that she had chosen such a good man as her husband.

A few moments later, a nurse came to the door and escorted them to the doctor's office. The room was plain, with nothing hanging on the walls and no personal touches to soften it, but like all the rooms in this Kirkbride building, it had a large window that provided lots of daylight and fresh air. Dr. Ziegler rose from behind his battered desk to welcome them. He was a stocky, middle-aged man whose fair hair had almost completely deserted him. Wire-framed glasses perched on his large nose and magnified his eyes in a disturbing way.

Frank shook his hand across the desk and introduced himself and Sarah.

"And you are family of Mrs. Longly?" he asked when Frank and Sarah had been seated in the two mismatched chairs facing his desk.

"I'm a private investigator," Frank said. "I've been hired by her family to help them prove her sane so she can be released."

The doctor frowned. "Her uncle hired you, I assume?"

"Yes, Mr. Breedlove. Have you spoken with him?"

"He asked to see me when he first visited Mrs. Longly."

"Then you know he does not believe Mrs. Longly should be a patient here," Frank said.

Dr. Ziegler leaned back in his chair and studied both Frank and Sarah for a long moment. "Many people who did not live with the patient will often be outraged when she is committed here. This is because they did not see the behavior that led to it. They remember the person from an earlier time perhaps, when she was not afflicted."

"But, Doctor," Sarah said in that reasonable voice she used to convince people she was right, "we didn't even meet Mrs. Longly until she had already become a patient here, and we also have found her to be completely rational."

"The patients are often capable of seeming that way for periods of time," Ziegler said, "especially with people who they believe might help them win a release, but I assure you, we do not keep people here if they do not belong here."

"Then maybe you can tell us what it is about Mrs. Longly

that makes you think she belongs here," Frank said, trying to match Sarah's reasonable tone.

Ziegler spoke slowly, as if choosing his words carefully. "Most of our patients are here because they have lost touch with reality. They see things or hear things that only they can see and hear. They behave in ways the rest of us consider strange. Some of them are violent and dangerous, but most of them are harmless and only need to be here for their own protection. We have the facilities to make sure they don't harm themselves or put themselves in danger and that others do not take advantage of them."

"Do you make any effort to cure them, Doctor?" Sarah asked.

He took the question with remarkable grace. "Some people do recover, the ones who simply needed time to rest and restore themselves, but they are few, Mrs. Malloy. Sadly, we do not perfectly understand the human mind, and we have not found a way to cure most of these people, so we merely keep them safe and provide for them."

"But Mrs. Longly doesn't fit into any of those disturbing categories," Sarah said. "Why is she here?"

Dr. Ziegler frowned. "Mrs. Longly is a special case."

Frank didn't dare meet Sarah's eye since he knew that statement would have made her furious. "What do you mean by that?"

"I mean that she is not insane in the usual way, and she does not behave the way most people believe an insane person behaves."

"Doesn't that mean she isn't insane, then?" Sarah asked, not bothering to hide her outrage.

"Just because a person does not rant and rave does not

mean they are sane, Mrs. Malloy. Their mind may still be disturbed in other ways."

"What ways, Doctor?" Frank asked.

Dr. Ziegler shifted in his chair, a sure sign that he was not comfortable with the discussion. "I explained all this to Mr. Breedlove when he came to see me."

"Then explain it to us, too," Frank said.

The doctor sighed. "When Mr. Longly asked us to admit his wife, he was adamant that we keep her presence here confidential, and if someone asked about her, we were not to reveal anything about her."

"But you spoke to Breedlove," Frank reminded him.

"Because he was her uncle and determined to see her released. I felt it was my duty to explain to him why that should never happen, but you are no relation to Mrs. Longly at all. I have only your word that you work for Mr. Breedlove, and even if you do, I cannot assist you in trying to win her release."

"What if I told you that Longly's reason for forbidding you to tell anyone about his wife's condition is just because he wants to protect his good name?" Frank said.

"You needn't bother. Mr. Longly told me that himself. In point of fact, he wishes to protect *his son's* good name, and who can blame him?"

"Dr. Ziegler," Sarah said, far more reasonably than Frank would have done, "if you cannot tell us why Mrs. Longly has been placed here, perhaps you will be good enough to tell us how a patient here is deemed to be cured, since you did say this sometimes happens."

He gave her a small smile, not fooled by her question. "It is a difficult process, as it must be, since we must be certain the patient can take care of herself and will not harm herself or others if released. Often, the family—if there is one—will refuse to take the patient back, so we must find a place for her to live as well."

"But who makes the decision to let someone go?" Frank prodded.

"The doctors here must agree, of course. We must see the patient's improvement over a long period of time. The patient must also answer many questions to test their judgment. Then a judge must declare the person cured after hearing our testimony and speaking with the patient."

"And that's the only way?" Frank asked.

Dr. Ziegler shrugged. "It is the only way I know of, and let me assure you, under our system of safeguards, Julia Longly will never be released from this institution."

V

Sᴀʀᴀʜ ᴀɴᴅ Mᴀʟʟᴏʏ ᴡᴇɴᴛ ᴅɪʀᴇᴄᴛʟʏ ꜰʀᴏᴍ Wᴀʀᴅ'ꜱ Iꜱ-land to their office to inform Maeve and Gino of what they had learned.

"I guess I'd go for carriage rides, too, if I had a handsome coachman," Maeve said when Sarah and Malloy had filled them in. Gino had carried in an extra chair, and they were gathered around Malloy's desk in his office.

"Really?" Gino asked with mock surprise. "I'd expect you'd want to drive yourself."

"I would, too," Malloy said, earning a glare from Maeve.

"The important thing," Sarah said to get them back on track, "is that she had a reasonable explanation for everything her husband and her neighbors accuse or suspected her of doing."

"And you're going to believe her over them?" Gino asked.

"It's not a question of whom we believe," Sarah said, hoping this was true. "We just need to weigh all the information and decide if it proves Julia is sane or insane."

"But doesn't that mean we have to decide what is true and what isn't?" Maeve argued.

"I don't think so," Sarah said. "Perfectly sane people lie when it suits them. The question is, Does lying prove Julia is insane? And so far we don't even know if she was lying about anything."

"Besides," Malloy said, "if Longly won't talk to us, we have no way of knowing if his version of events is any different from hers."

Sarah nodded her enthusiastic agreement. "We know the neighbors think some strange things happened at the Longly house."

"Yes," Maeve said. "Disappearing servants and unexplained carriage rides."

"But they only know what they saw and not what went on in the house, and what we haven't considered is that the *strangest* thing to happen at the Longly house was Julia being carried away and locked in an asylum."

They all stared at Sarah for a long moment in surprise. Plainly, none of them had realized they should have been considering this.

Malloy leaned forward across his desk, bracing himself on his elbows. "And we know that Chet Longly is responsible for sending Julia to Ward's Island. He admitted that much himself."

"If he's responsible for that," Sarah continued, "as we know he is, then he could well be responsible for everything else, too, just as Julia claims."

"Even the carriage rides?" Gino asked with raised eyebrows.

"If it's true he kept Julia a virtual prisoner and she used them to escape, then yes."

"Unless Julia is lying about all of it," Maeve pointed out.

"That hardly seems possible," Sarah said, sure that was true.

"I think it hardly seems possible Chet Longly kept a woman like Julia a virtual prisoner," Maeve argued.

"Normally, I would, too," Sarah argued right back, "but Julia had been stripped of everyone who might have helped her. Her father died. Her mother left the city, and no one knows where she is. Her aunt and uncle had moved to London. Mr. Longly told her friends she was ill so they wouldn't call on her, and she wasn't allowed to call on them. Like most women, she probably had no money of her own, so how could she leave? Where could she go? How would she support herself? She has her son to think of as well. If she couldn't take care of herself, how could she take care of him? And if she left him behind, what would become of him?"

"I just realized," Gino said uneasily, "we don't really know what happened to Julia's mother, do we? Not for sure, anyway."

"You're right," Malloy said, leaning back in his chair again. "Breedlove and Sarah's mother told us she'd moved out of the city, and that might have been her intention, but why would she cut off all contact with her friends and family? No one has given us a satisfactory explanation for that."

"Do you think she might be dead?" Maeve asked.

"That's certainly one explanation for why someone is never heard from again."

"And if she isn't dead, why did she take such pains to vanish like that?" Sarah asked.

"Because she was frightened of something," Gino guessed.

"Or someone," Maeve added.

"I guess we have to count that as another strange thing associated with the Longlys," Sarah said.

"And if the person Julia's mother was frightened of was Chet Longly, then he could be responsible for all of it," Maeve said.

They considered that for a long moment.

"I suppose he could be," Malloy said at last, "and the fact that he wouldn't talk to me makes him look very suspicious."

"As does his decision to put Julia on Ward's Island," Sarah said. "She would have seen most of this as it happened, since it happened right in her house."

"And she might even know what became of her mother," Gino said.

"Or at least suspect," Maeve said. "If she accused her husband or somehow revealed that she knew . . ."

"That would give him an excellent reason to send her to a place where no one would ever believe anything she said again," Sarah said grimly.

"I wonder why she didn't mention it to us when we visited her," Malloy said.

"If that's the real reason Mr. Longly sent her away, she might be afraid to," Sarah said.

Maeve gave a theatrical sigh. "Oh my, if only we could find out what happened in the Longly house, then we could know for certain if Julia is telling the truth or not."

The other three glared at her, but she simply smiled innocently and waited.

After a long moment of silence, Sarah felt compelled to say, "I did ask Julia if her husband forced himself on the servant girls."

Gino's face turned beet red, but Maeve simply looked mildly interested. "And what did she say?"

"She said he didn't have to force them. He simply used his charm."

Maeve smiled at that. "Then I am perfectly safe from him."

Gino wasn't amused. "We don't really know what happened to those women."

"Julia said her husband sent them away," Maeve said. "If he sends me away, I'll just go home."

"They might not even hire you," Malloy pointed out.

"I've been thinking about this. No one has said they hired a new nursemaid for the boy. I could bring sterling references, and I have the added advantage of actually knowing how to take care of children."

"Maeve may be immune to charm, but she can certainly *use* it when she wants to," Sarah reminded them. "There's a good chance she could get hired."

Maeve smiled smugly at the endorsement. "If they don't want a nursemaid, I'll tell them I'm willing to be a maid. I'll even work without a salary until I prove myself."

"Let's hope you don't have to humble yourself that much," Gino said, making her smile more broadly.

"Then I can do it?" Maeve said. "Mrs. Frank, you'll have to take Catherine to school and pick her up while I'm gone."

"And put the children to bed myself," Sarah said. "I know, but I can't see another way to find out what really happened inside that house."

Gino pinched the bridge of his nose, as if he were getting a headache. "I wonder if they need to hire a new coachman."

"If they do," Maeve said generously, "I'll put in a good word for you."

* * *

THE NEXT MORNING, MAEVE SET OUT FOR THE LONGLY house. She walked the few blocks from Bank Street to Bedford Street, enjoying the mild spring weather and the pleasant Greenwich Village streets. The Longly house was the largest one on that block, and it looked well kept. After satisfying herself that she had gleaned all the information about the neighborhood that she could from simply observing it, she made her way to the back of the house, which was the proper place for someone seeking employment to approach.

A maid answered her knock and the girl looked her up and down, taking in her simple suit and shirtwaist and her modest hat. "Can I help you?"

"I was told that you might be in need of a nursemaid, so I'd like to apply for the job. I have references." Indeed, she did. Mrs. Frank had written them for her last night, and every word in them was true except for Mrs. Frank's name. She had signed it using her first husband's name in case Mr. Longly happened to see it and recognize the name Malloy.

"Nobody told me nothing about that," the maid said with a frown.

"Maybe you could let me talk to the housekeeper," Maeve suggested with a friendly smile. "She probably knows."

The maid, still uncertain, obviously decided to err on the side of caution and let Maeve in. "Wait here while I get Mrs. Pauly."

Maeve stood patiently in the small area inside the back door. Interior doors led to what appeared to be the kitchen and the butler's pantry and a third to the back staircase, which the servants would use. After a long few minutes, a plump, middle-aged woman wearing a serviceable dress and a quizzical expression approached her through the butler's pantry.

"Kate said you're looking for a job as a nursemaid," Mrs. Pauly said, looking Maeve over as Kate had done. She seemed to approve.

"Yes, I am. I heard you might be looking for someone, and I'm going to lose my position soon because the children are too old for a nursemaid now, so I thought I'd come by and find out."

"You're awfully young," Mrs. Pauly said.

"I'm older than I look. I'm twenty-three," Maeve lied. "And I have four years of experience taking care of two children, a boy and a girl. I have a letter of reference from my employer, Mrs. Brandt, if you'd like to see it."

Maeve rummaged in her purse and pulled out the slightly wrinkled envelope, but Mrs. Pauly made no move to take it. She was still studying Maeve. "Who told you we needed a nursemaid?"

Maeve never even blinked. "Winny. She works for Mrs. Kindred, your neighbor."

Mrs. Pauly wasn't pleased by this information, if her frown was any indication.

"Was she wrong?" Maeve asked uncertainly. "I hate to think she got my hopes up and made me bother you if it was just a joke."

"Those females are the biggest gossips," Mrs. Pauly said in disgust. "What else did she tell you?"

Maeve hardly had to act at all to appear distressed. "Only that you might need a nursemaid for a little boy who was four years old. I asked her if you'd advertised, and she wasn't

sure, but she knew the one you had was gone off somewhere."

"We didn't advertise. The maids have been looking after
the young master, but we can't keep that up forever. I told
Mr. Longly just this morning that Victor needs someone."

Maeve smiled hopefully. "If you have maids looking after
him, they aren't doing their work, are they? And the child
needs someone who knows how to keep a child amused."

Mrs. Pauly looked her over again, this time with a bit
more approval. "Come inside and let me see what you have
to say for yourself." This time, she took the envelope from
Maeve's hand and led the way back into the butler's pantry,
where she asked Maeve a lot of questions.

Plainly, the woman was used to hiring staff and she knew
how to sniff out someone lying about their qualifications.
Fortunately, Maeve didn't have to lie very much at all since
she had really been a nursemaid for Brian and Catherine, in
addition to her occasional forays into detective work. When
she did have to lie, she did it very well, and after only half
an hour, Mrs. Pauly said, "Would you like to meet Master
Victor?"

"I would love to," Maeve said with complete sincerity.

Mrs. Pauly led the way up the back stairs to the third floor.
Nurseries were often relegated to this distant part of the house
so the children wouldn't disturb the adults with their noise.
"He's a quiet child. Too quiet, if you ask me, but then . . .
Well, never mind. He's no trouble at all or at least that's what
the girls say."

Mrs. Pauly tapped on the door but didn't wait to be invited in. She opened the door to a bright room filled with
sunshine, but to Maeve's surprise, the little boy, who had
been sitting on the floor playing with some tin soldiers,

jumped up and ran to the maid who was sitting nearby, hiding behind her and peering out at them with obvious alarm.

"It's just me, Master Victor," Mrs. Pauly said cheerfully. "I've brought someone for you to meet."

The little boy didn't seem pleased to hear it. He remained huddled behind the maid, who had risen when Mrs. Pauly entered and who seemed at a loss as to how to handle the situation. "See the nice lady who has come to meet you, Master Victor," the girl said, trying to get him to release her skirts, which were clutched tightly in his little fists.

He was a handsome boy with dark curls and cheeks still chubby with baby fat. His large brown eyes seemed haunted, though, and Maeve couldn't miss the fear in them. Why would he be afraid of her?

Maeve dug in her purse and pulled something out that she kept clutched in her fist. She moved slowly over to the boy and then hunkered down so she would be at eye level with him. "Hello, Master Victor. I'm Miss Smith. How do you do?"

When the boy didn't speak, the maid nudged him. "Manners, Master Victor."

"How do you do?" he replied in a whisper.

Maeve smiled her approval. The boy stared back at her, his eyes still wide with fear, but Maeve was glad to see a hint of curiosity now, too.

"I wonder if you like candy. I have a peppermint here that I've saved for you. Do you like peppermints?"

Victor hesitated, but finally he nodded once, very quickly.

Maeve held out her hand and opened her fist to reveal the peppermint she'd pulled from her purse.

The boy glanced up, looking for approval from the maid

whose skirt he still clutched. At her nod, he snatched the peppermint.

"What do you say?" the maid prompted.

"Thank you," he said, again in a whisper. He seemed afraid to speak aloud. Perhaps he had been chastened for making too much noise.

"You're welcome." She looked pointedly at the toy soldiers that were arranged as if for battle. "Are your soldiers fighting a war?"

He shrugged.

"I can show you how the armies were arranged at the Battle of Gettysburg. The little boy I take care of now knows all about that."

"Master Victor wouldn't know about it," Mrs. Pauly said.

"It's a very famous battle. Would you like for me to show you?" Maeve asked Victor.

For the first time, curiosity overtook the fear in his eyes. He nodded vigorously.

Maeve set her purse aside and sat down on the floor where Victor had been sitting with his soldiers. She began to move the soldiers around. After a few moments, she glanced over at where he still hid behind the maid's skirts. "Come here and I'll show you. Do you have some blocks? I need them to make the town."

He hesitated again but only for a moment. Then he was scrambling to fetch a wooden box that turned out to contain an assortment of blocks. Then he was sitting beside Maeve and handing her blocks so she could build a very makeshift version of the town of Gettysburg, where one of the pivotal battles of the American War between the States took place.

Maeve was vaguely aware that Mrs. Pauly and the maid had a whispered conversation before Mrs. Pauly left, probably to attend to her duties. The maid stayed on, which was only right. Mrs. Pauly would be a fool to leave her master's son alone with a complete stranger.

Victor eventually lost interest in the battle, and they used the rest of the blocks to build a castle where the soldiers could live. By then it was lunchtime, and Kate, the maid who had answered Maeve's knock this morning, delivered a tray with meals for Victor, Maeve, and the maid watching Maeve, whose name was Iris.

Kate was much more friendly this time.

"It's nice to see Master Victor smiling," Kate said, gazing fondly at the child as Iris set out the plates on the nursery table.

"Is he usually an unhappy child?" Maeve asked, not having to feign her concern.

"Just lately he is," Kate said, lowering her voice. "Some things happened that scared him."

Maeve wondered if he'd seen his mother being taken by the men from Ward's Island, but she didn't dare ask. "That's terrible."

Kate shrugged.

"We don't talk about those things," Iris said sharply, silencing Kate on the subject. Kate scurried out, leaving Maeve an opening to ask more questions later.

After lunch, Master Victor was to take a nap, so Maeve read him a story from one of the books on a shelf in the nursery and tucked him into his small bed in the bedroom adjacent to the playroom.

Mrs. Pauly appeared as Maeve was advising him to close his eyes. "Did you like playing with Miss Smith, Master Victor?"

"Yes, I did. Very much." He was no longer whispering, Maeve noticed with delight.

"Perhaps we'll invite her back. Would you like that?"

"Yes, I would. Please do invite her back."

"I enjoyed playing with you, too, Master Victor," Maeve assured him, and Mrs. Pauly ushered her out of the boy's bedroom.

"You're very good with the boy," Mrs. Pauly said.

"He's a sweetheart."

"I've told Mr. Longly about you. He would like to meet you."

"Should I come back this evening then?"

"No, he's here now. Come with me."

Maeve knew a moment of trepidation. She had expected Longly would want to meet the person he was hiring to care for his only child, but she'd thought she would have had more time to prepare. She drew a fortifying breath and followed Mrs. Pauly down to what turned out to be a library that Mr. Longly apparently used as his office. The room contained several bookshelves that gave it a cozy feel, and comfortable chairs created a conversation area where Longly could visit with friends if he so desired. The lingering odor of pipe smoke told Maeve that Longly spent some time here.

He rose from his desk, a large, rolltop affair cluttered with papers, when the women came in, and Mrs. Pauly introduced them. Maeve had to admit he was a handsome man. Mr. Malloy should have warned her, but perhaps he didn't notice things like that. The way Longly looked her up and down, he was pleased by what he saw as well, and even in this situation, Maeve could feel the pull of his charm. He wouldn't have to try very hard to seduce every maid in the house if that was his desire.

"Mrs. Pauly tells me you have won Victor's heart," he

said. His voice was deep and seemed to touch a chord somewhere in her chest.

"I have found that little boys cannot resist a good battle
with toy soldiers."

"I seem to recall that myself. I have read your letter of
reference, Miss Smith. This Mrs. Brandt seems heartbroken
to be losing you."

"And I am heartbroken to leave them, but the children
no longer need a nursemaid. I had forgotten how much fun
it is to have charge of a young child again. I should dearly
love to care for Master Victor."

"How soon can you start?" he asked.

Maeve felt her heart lift. She couldn't wait to tell Gino
how easy this had been. "I can be here tomorrow."

"Will Mrs. Brandt be willing to lose you on such short
notice?"

"She knew I was coming here today, and she expects me
to leave soon. In fact, I think she will be relieved not to have
to find work for me when the children are in school."

"Very well then, we shall be glad to welcome you tomorrow, Miss Smith."

Maeve knew she looked grateful, although not for the
reason Mr. Longly probably thought. "Thank you for your
confidence, Mr. Longly."

He had not asked her to sit, which was proper considering her status as a servant, so she simply nodded politely and
followed Mrs. Pauly out.

"The master is a good man," Mrs. Pauly said. "He's had
his troubles, but that's over now. You should have an easy
time of it here."

Which was a curious thing to say, but Maeve decided not

to mention it. "Doesn't Mrs. Longly want to meet me?" she asked with just the right amount of innocent ignorance.

Mrs. Pauly stopped so suddenly, Maeve almost ran into her. "It's best you know right off. Mrs. Longly is in poor health, and she's gone away for a rest cure, so you won't be seeing her."

"I'm sorry to hear it," Maeve said, thinking that was probably an appropriate thing to say.

"Yes, well, it's very sad, but it's for the best. And we don't speak of her, especially around the boy."

Maeve didn't bother to hide her surprise. Anyone would be shocked by such a statement, but she nodded her understanding. "Of course."

They had reached the back door where Maeve had come in. "We'll see you tomorrow, Miss Smith."

Maeve needed all her willpower to resist the urge to skip down the alley to the street. She couldn't wait to tell everyone about her success.

I WOULD HAVE TOLD THEM I'D BE THERE TONIGHT, BUT I didn't want to seem unreasonably eager," Maeve explained to Sarah after telling her what had happened at the Longly house. Sarah sat on the edge of Maeve's bed while the girl packed for her new "job."

"Yes, tomorrow is awfully soon, but I'm sure Julia Longly will appreciate your sense of urgency. I can't help thinking how awful it must be for her, day after day in that place."

"I know. I haven't even seen it, and I had a nightmare about it last night," Maeve said, shuddering dramatically. "Should I take this, do you think?" She held up a rather nice dress that she wore to church on the rare occasions that she went.

"That's probably too fancy for a nursemaid. You might think no one will see it if you don't wear it, but someone might snoop into your things."

"You're right. No sense in raising any questions." She hung it back in her wardrobe.

"What is the little boy like?" Sarah asked.

"According to the housekeeper, he's been very quiet lately, and he was actually frightened when I came into the nursery. I was able to cheer him up, though. We played soldiers."

"Do you think he knows what happened to his mother?"

"That would certainly explain why he seems frightened, but even just losing his mother so suddenly, even if he didn't see her taken away, would have been a shock to him. Mrs. Pauly told me they don't speak of Julia in front of him."

"I can see why. No one would want to explain what happened to her, but it's also cruel to leave him wondering. Children can imagine all sorts of awful things."

"Although it's hard to imagine anything worse than what really happened to her," Maeve said.

Sarah could only agree. "What did you think of Mr. Longly?"

"A good-looking man and he was very nice to me. I can see the female servants falling under his spell if he tried to woo them."

"Don't tell Gino that," Sarah advised her.

Maeve gave Sarah a mischievous grin that did not bode well. "Mrs. Pauly said something odd, though."

"What did she say?"

"That Longly had his troubles, but they were over now."

"I wonder what troubles she meant," Sarah mused. "Of course, if Julia and her husband were arguing over his bad behavior, the servants might have taken his side. Julia did say he had their support because he paid them."

Maeve stopped folding the shirtwaist she'd been about to put into her suitcase and considered that for a moment. "I can see where a servant would be respectful to the person who pays his salary but earning a servant's support takes more than that."

Having never been a servant, Sarah had no knowledge of this. "How would someone earn a servant's support?"

But Maeve had never been a servant either, at least not a real one. "I'm not sure, but I'd guess it would be the same way you'd win anybody's support. The servant would have to believe you were in the right."

"How could anyone believe Chet Longly was right to lock his wife in that place?"

Maeve shook her head and placed the folded shirtwaist in the suitcase. "Or maybe they're afraid of him. I mean, if he could send his wife to that place so easily, he could surely send one of them there, too."

"I hadn't thought of that," Sarah said, newly horrified. "You must be very careful, Maeve. If he thinks for a moment you're any threat to him . . ."

"How could a nursemaid be any threat to him? I don't even know what he did to Julia until somebody tells me. I'm just going to take very good care of his son and gossip like crazy with the other servants."

"And you'll leave if you get so much as a hint that you're in any danger. Don't worry about bringing your things with you. If you have to, leave them. We'll replace them."

Maeve smiled in delight. "Maybe I'll purposely forget to bring them home, then. But I know how to escape from a difficult situation, Mrs. Frank. My grandfather taught me that when I was a child."

Maeve's grandfather, who had raised her, had been a con artist, so Maeve possessed an interesting assortment of skills, in addition to being an excellent liar.

"And at least you aren't far away from home if things get difficult," Sarah said. "But I'll be thinking about you the whole time."

"I'll be fine," Maeve insisted, "and if trouble comes, I'm ready." She raised her skirt to reveal a knife in a rather fancy leather sheath strapped to her calf.

"Good heavens, I thought you were teasing about taking a knife!"

"If Chet Longly thinks he can force me to do anything, he's in for a surprise."

"Do you know how to use that?" Sarah asked uneasily.

"I wouldn't have it if I didn't, but I don't expect to need it. I'll be finished at the Longly house before they even know I was there."

"Just don't tell Malloy about the knife," Sarah advised.

Gino didn't come home with Malloy that evening, so Maeve was denied the pleasure of telling him herself that she'd gotten the job at the Longly house. Malloy was just as concerned as Sarah about Maeve's assignment, but she distracted him by asking his advice on what she should try to find out. Sarah was pretty sure Maeve already knew what to do, so she enjoyed watching Maeve's rapt expression as Malloy advised her. Sarah decided she could learn a few things from the girl.

THE NEXT MORNING, SARAH DROVE MAEVE TO THE Longlys' house in the electric so she didn't have to carry her heavy suitcase. She dropped her at the end of the street, though, so Maeve could walk up to the door as if she had trudged her way through Greenwich Village like a proper servant.

Mrs. Pauly welcomed her and escorted her back to the nursery, where the nursemaid had a bedroom right next to Master Victor's.

Victor and a maid were eating breakfast when Mrs. Pauly and Maeve came into the nursery, and the boy jumped up, obviously pleased to see her.

"You came back!" he cried.

"Of course I came back," Maeve said, setting down her suitcase so she could catch the boy when he propelled himself into her legs and wrapped his arms around her.

"Miss Smith is going to take care of you from now on, Master Victor," Mrs. Pauly said. "The way Miss Winterbourne used to."

He looked up at Maeve, his brown eyes wide and his arms still wrapped around her as if he'd never let her go. "You won't leave me and go to heaven, will you?"

Maeve blinked in surprise at the question. "I'm not planning to go to heaven for a very long time," she managed.

"Master Victor, that's not a proper question to ask people," Mrs. Pauly said sternly.

His little face crumpled. "But I don't want her to leave me."

Maeve's conscience tweaked her hard at that. She'd probably be leaving him in a matter of days. "It's hard when people leave us, isn't it?" she said to him. "But we're not going to think about sad things today. We're going to have fun just as soon as you finish your breakfast. Show me what you're having this morning."

Properly distracted, Victor hurried to show her his nearly

clean plate, and she praised him for eating so well. A glance in Mrs. Pauly's direction told her she'd impressed the housekeeper, but more important, she now had an excuse to ask some questions about Miss Winterbourne and why Victor thought she'd gone to heaven.

The maid stayed with Maeve all morning, but she must have given Mrs. Pauly a good report of Maeve's abilities, because she left Maeve alone with the boy after lunch. But maybe that was just because Victor was due to take a nap and how much harm could Maeve do when he was asleep?

When she'd tucked him in, Maeve made her way downstairs to the kitchen, hoping to encounter some of the servants who could answer a few of her questions. She found the cook rolling out piecrust.

"Master Victor sleeping, is he?" the cook asked. She was a round woman with powerful arms and very few teeth.

"Yes. I thought I'd take this time to meet any of the staff I haven't encountered yet. I'm Maeve Smith."

"I reckon we all know your name," the cook said. "I'm Mrs. O'Hara. Have a seat. Miss Winterbourne used to come down when the boy slept, and we'd have a chat. I'm glad to see you're not too good for the likes of us. Would you like some cake? It's left over from last night's dinner."

"I had some for lunch, but I wouldn't turn down another slice," Maeve said.

Mrs. O'Hara set some water on to boil for tea and she cut Maeve a generous piece of the cake. When the tea was ready, Mrs. O'Hara sat down at the kitchen table where Maeve had already taken a place at the opposite end from where Mrs. O'Hara had been rolling out the pastry.

"Was Miss Winterbourne the nursemaid before me?" Maeve asked casually.

But Mrs. O'Hara didn't take the question casually. She frowned and turned her troubled gaze to the cake in front of her. "She was that."

"Master Victor must have liked her very much."

"We all liked her. She was a fine lady."

Maeve ate a bite of the cake. It was delicious. If she wasn't careful, she'd soon be as round as Mrs. O'Hara. "Victor seems to think she went to heaven," Maeve tried, smiling a little to take the sting out of the words.

Mrs. O'Hara studied her face for a long moment, as if looking for signs of deceit. Fortunately, Maeve knew how to look completely innocent. "We told him that, so he wouldn't expect her to come back."

"Then she didn't die," Maeve said. "That's a relief."

"She's never coming back. The boy needs to accept that," Mrs. O'Hara said grimly.

Which wasn't exactly a confirmation. "I certainly won't tell him otherwise, but I don't want to say the wrong thing. Did she die?"

Mrs. O'Hara laid down her fork and looked Maeve full in the face. "There's some things we don't talk about in this house. Miss Winterbourne is one of them."

VI

FRANK EASILY FOUND THE ADDRESS HUGH BREEDLOVE had given them as his residence. He had telephoned Breedlove last night and arranged to meet him at his home this morning. Apparently, Breedlove didn't want anyone at his bank to know he was meeting with a private investigator.

The Breedloves had chosen to live in a more fashionable part of the city than the Longlys. They were between Fifth and Sixth Avenues on a quiet, tree-lined street of brownstones. A wrought iron fence enclosed a tiny front yard where not a single dead leaf marred the perfection of the landscaping.

A maid answered the door and showed Frank in without making him wait, since Breedlove was expecting him.

The Breedloves must not have brought any furniture with them from England since everything in the parlor where the maid led him was brand-new. Breedlove had been sitting in a chair by the gas fire, reading the newspaper. He laid the paper aside and rose to greet his visitor.

"Bring us some coffee, please," he instructed the maid. She nodded and left, closing the door behind her.

"I hope you have some good news for us, Malloy," he said when Frank was seated on the sofa opposite him. The fire had obviously been lit to chase away the chill in this seldom-used room, but it hadn't yet done its job.

"What we have is mostly gossip, but it indicates something wasn't right in the Longly household."

"We already know that, and gossip won't help Julia," Breedlove said with a frown.

"Which is why we have placed someone in the house as a servant. She will find out what led up to Julia being sent away and what Longly was up to, both before that and since."

"*She?* You're relying on a female?" Breedlove scoffed, far from pleased.

"I have found that females are the best when it comes to talking with servants. Besides, the Longlys didn't have many male servants so our chances of getting a man in there were small."

Breedlove was still frowning. "How long do you think this will take?"

"A few days at least. I know it's difficult, knowing Mrs. Longly is still at Ward's Island, but we have to discover something that will convince a judge to release her, and that is bound to take some time."

Breedlove scowled. "My daughter is having a whole new wardrobe made for her debut. It's costing me a fortune, so we need for Julia to be released before the ball."

"We're doing everything we can, Mr. Breedlove. My wife

and I are as anxious as you are to see Julia freed." Although for very different reasons, but Frank knew better than to mention it.

"I've hired an attorney," Breedlove said, surprising Frank, although it probably shouldn't have. They'd need one to represent Julia when they went before a judge.

Frank nodded his approval. "Who is it?"

"Karl Klein."

Luckily, Frank had a lot of experience hiding his emotions because the name Karl Klein made him want to wince. Klein did represent a lot of wealthy people and he did frequently win his cases, but it was more often through the greasing of palms than his skills in the courtroom. "And he understands what happened to Julia?" Frank asked, wondering why Klein was willing to take on a case in which the clients were desperate to keep the details a secret when Klein made sure his name appeared in the newspapers when he won.

"Yes, and he assured me he could get Julia released."

Now Frank was confused. "Do you still want us to keep working?"

"Yes, yes," Breedlove said impatiently. "Klein will need everything you can find out, but he assured me that in the end, Julia will be free."

Frank didn't want to think about how Klein could make a promise like that, but it wasn't his concern. "Do you want to know what we've learned so far?"

Breedlove shrugged. "I suppose so."

"Two female servants disappeared from the house. Julia believes at least one of them left because Chet Longly seduced her and got her with child."

"I thought he had a mistress," Breedlove said with more than a little distaste.

"I'm just telling you what we've heard. We don't know what's true and what's not."

"Is that all?" Plainly, Breedlove hoped it was.

"Longly also let all of his servants go shortly before Julia was taken away, and then he hired them back again."

"That doesn't make any sense," Breedlove said.

"No, it doesn't. That's one reason we put Miss Smith in the Longly house. She is going to try to figure out exactly what happened and why. I also spoke with Julia's doctor."

"That idiot," Breedlove said. "I wouldn't trust him to remove a splinter."

What had given Breedlove such a low opinion of Dr. Ziegler? "He told us that for a patient to be released from the hospital there, the doctors must agree that the person has regained her sanity and will no longer be a danger to herself or others."

"Did he now? Well, Klein told me it only takes the word of one judge to free somebody. He said there's really no way for a doctor to tell if a person is sane or not, so if it's a matter of the doctor's opinion, it can just as easily be a matter of the judge's opinion."

"I see," Frank said uneasily. Could that be true? If so, it might be easier to get Julia released than he'd thought. "But we'll still need as much evidence as possible to convince the judge."

"That is my understanding. We can't expect the judge to take my word that Julia was placed there under false pretenses."

"Especially since you weren't even in the country when it happened," Frank reminded him. "We will continue to find out as much as we can about Chet Longly and his reasons for locking Julia away."

"If he's seducing the servants, that could easily explain why he wanted to get rid of Julia," Breedlove said.

"That did occur to me, but we don't know for sure what happened to those women."

"But we do need to show the judge that Chet had his own reasons for wanting Julia out of the way. That's what Klein told me."

"Which is exactly what our operative is trying to find out."

"And Julia herself can show that she's perfectly rational. You've seen her. You agree, don't you?"

"We've seen no indication that she is insane," Frank said, unwilling to be unequivocal.

"Klein said he will question her before the judge to prove her mental state. Let the doctors try to convince the judge otherwise after that."

Before Frank could agree, someone tapped on the parlor door. Breedlove bid them enter, and the maid carried in a tray with the coffee. A well-dressed, middle-aged woman came in behind her, earning a frown from Breedlove.

"Amelia, I told you I would handle this."

"It involves me, too, Hugh." She turned to Frank, who had risen to his feet. "Are you Mr. Malloy?"

"Malloy, this is my wife," Breedlove said with notable reluctance.

"Pleased to meet you, Mrs. Breedlove."

She nodded to acknowledge him and told the maid she would pour. When the girl was gone and the door closed behind her, she turned back to Frank. "Please sit down. I want to know what you have learned about Chet Longly."

Frank gave her a brief description of the few things he had told her husband while she poured the two men some coffee.

"Do you think we can convince a judge Julia is sane enough to be released?" she asked when he had finished.

Frank took a moment to consider his answer. He didn't want to make any promises he couldn't keep. "Mrs. Longly seemed very rational when my wife and I visited with her. I think she could impress a judge, but I'm afraid I don't have any idea if that is enough to convince him to release her."

"It simply must be," Mrs. Breedlove said. "We cannot leave Julia in that horrible place."

At least she didn't mention her daughter's wardrobe expenses. "She is very fortunate to have family members who are concerned for her."

"We know our duty, Mr. Malloy," Mrs. Breedlove said, folding her hands primly in her lap.

But had they realized how far that duty might extend? "Then you are planning to take Mrs. Longly in when she is released?" he said.

"Take her in?" Mrs. Breedlove echoed in amazement.

"She'll need someplace to stay," Frank pointed out reasonably. "Under the circumstances, she can't go back to her husband."

"Heavens no," Mrs. Breedlove agreed.

"I don't know her situation, if she has any money of her own, but some arrangements will have to be made."

"She'll stay here, of course," Breedlove said. "At least until we can determine what is best."

His wife shot him a look that was half-surprised and the other half horrified. She could hardly contradict her husband in front of a stranger, though. Such things were simply not done, but she said, "Are you sure that is the best thing, Hugh?"

"The best thing would be for her to go home to Chet, but

he isn't likely to take her, is he?" Breedlove said with no pretense at courtesy. "Would you have me put her out on the street?"

Mrs. Breedlove glanced at Frank, obviously painfully aware of their audience. "She would probably prefer to have her own place."

"And I would prefer not having to deal with her at all, but I have no choice. Perhaps I can convince Chet to make some kind of settlement on her, but unless that happens, we will have to provide for her."

"She has grounds for divorce," Frank said helpfully. "She could marry again."

He had no trouble at all reading Breedlove's thoughts. If Julia married again, her new husband would have the care of her. "I hadn't thought of that."

"But *divorce*, Hugh," his wife said as if the word left a bad taste in her mouth. "No one we know ever got divorced."

"The Vanderbilts did," he reminded her, probably referring to William and Alva Vanderbilt, who had ended their marriage a few years ago. "If they can do it, Julia can. Chet would probably be glad to be rid of her."

He was undoubtedly right about Chet. "I'll probably be seeing Julia soon," Frank said. "Can I tell her she can stay with you when she is released? I know she's concerned about her future."

Before Breedlove could confirm his offer, Mrs. Breedlove said, "Are you sure she will be released? You didn't tell me anything you've learned that would prove she is sane."

"She will do that herself," Breedlove said impatiently. "You spoke with her, Amelia. You know she's perfectly fine."

"But she was such an odd child," Mrs. Breedlove said. "Don't you remember?"

"She's not a child now, and she is not insane," Breedlove insisted. "She can prove it simply by talking to the judge."

Yes, Julia could probably make a good showing, but would it be enough? The pressure was on Frank and his crew to give her as much help as they could, because if it wasn't enough, she would spend the rest of her life in that place.

THE COOK HADN'T WANTED TO TALK ABOUT THE Longlys anymore after informing Maeve they didn't talk about Julia, so Maeve had answered her questions about her previous life with a series of lies she invented on the spot. She didn't like to lie—it required you to remember what you'd said so you didn't contradict yourself—but she couldn't very well admit that she worked for a private investigator, could she?

"Do you have any men working at the house?" Maeve asked when she had satisfied the cook's curiosity. The cook had gotten up and started rolling out her piecrusts again.

"Just Mr. Longly's valet, but he doesn't spend much time in the kitchen," the cook said with a sniff. Plainly, she thought the valet was too full of himself. "Don't get any ideas about him, though. He's fifty if he's a day and he's French."

"I don't have any ideas about any men, especially if they're French," Maeve assured her. "But if the valet is the only man, then I guess Mr. Longly doesn't keep a carriage."

"What makes you say that?" the cook asked with a frown.

"Who would drive it?"

"Oh well, we had a coachman, but he's gone now."

Maeve feigned surprise. "He quit, I guess. It's hard to keep men in service nowadays or so I've heard."

"It is that. You don't hardly see anybody with a butler anymore," the cook agreed.

"Is Mr. Longly hard to work for?" Maeve asked.

The cook instantly stopped rolling the pastry and looked up warily. "What do you mean?"

"I mean did the coachman quit because he couldn't get along with Mr. Longly, because if he quit for another reason, I might know someone who'd be interested in the job."

The cook nodded, obviously relieved. "You might ask Mr. Longly if he's hiring. He's a good man, Mr. Longly. Your friend won't have any trouble with him at all."

That was quite an endorsement and not what Maeve had expected. "Does that mean I won't have any trouble with him either?" Maeve asked.

The cook didn't even look up. "Not if you take good care of Master Victor, you won't."

"I'm not worried about that, but in some houses, well, a girl has to make sure she doesn't get caught alone because the master might feel free to take some liberties."

"Mr. Longly won't be taking any liberties. I told you, he's a good man. You'll be safe here now."

"Now?" Maeve asked, wondering what was different *now*.

The cook didn't look up. She was concentrating on picking up the piecrust and putting it into a pan without stretching it. Maeve had learned the importance of that from their neighbor Mrs. Ellsworth. "You'll be safe here," she amended. "Now you'd best get back upstairs so you're there when Master Victor wakes up. He gets upset if he wakes up alone."

Maeve knew when she was being dismissed. She'd learned

a little, at least, although she was having a difficult time reconciling what she was hearing about Longly from his servants with what she already knew about him. Did a *good man* keep a mistress right under his wife's nose? Or fire all his servants? Or get them with child? But the two women who had told her Longly was a good man were middle-aged and far from attractive. Maybe they never saw that side of him.

Victor didn't wake up for another half hour, so Maeve had an opportunity to jot down some notes from her conversations this morning. She didn't want to forget anything.

Victor wanted to draw a picture when he woke up, and Maeve was surprised to find an abundance of drawing paper, pencils, and even a package of crayons. The boy was not yet a masterful artist, but he was enthusiastic. He also insisted Maeve draw something, too. She was not a masterful artist either, but she managed a crude version of the Longly house.

Victor drew what appeared to be two human figures. One stood in an archway of some kind and the other stood nearby.

"Who is that in your picture?" Maeve asked when he presented it for her approval.

"That's Miss Winterbourne," he said, pointing to the figure in the archway. "She's flying out to heaven."

Maeve studied the picture, trying to make sense of it. Could the archway be a window? She glanced at the row of windows in the nursery and realized they were roughly the same shape as Victor had drawn. Did he really think Miss Winterbourne had flown out the window and gone to heaven? "And who is this?" she asked, pointing to the other figure.

This figure was hardly human at all. Victor had mostly scribbled it, making it completely black with no discernable face and only the vaguest suggestion of a human figure. "That's the bad lady," he said, then jumped up. "Let's play soldiers."

He had gone over to the shelves that held his toys to fetch the box of soldiers. Maeve studied the picture for another moment while Victor upended the box and spilled the soldiers out onto the floor. "Hurry, Miss Smith," he said.

Maeve laid the picture on the table and quickly gathered up the art supplies to return them to their rightful place. When she sat down on the floor next to Victor, she asked as casually as she could, "Who is the bad lady?"

"I don't know," Victor said, focusing all his attention on setting his soldiers upright.

Maeve knew perfectly well that if pressed, a young child will simply refuse to answer if he doesn't feel like it. How many times had she seen it with Catherine and Brian? Still, she couldn't resist. "Where does the bad lady live?" Because if she lived here . . .

"In her house," Victor said.

Not in *this* house, then. "Does she come to visit?"

Victor's little face screwed up with impatience. "Sometimes. Are you going to build the town again? We need to do that battle."

"Yes," Maeve said with a smile. "I'll get the blocks."

I keep thinking I should go by the Longly house and check on Maeve," Gino said. He'd come home with Malloy and was staying for dinner. They were waiting in the parlor until the meal was served.

"Which is sure to get her fired," Sarah told him. "You know female servants aren't allowed to have gentleman callers."

"Do we have any way to contact her? Or any way for her to contact us if she gets in trouble?" he asked.

"Maeve can take care of herself," Malloy reminded him. "She's done this before, you know."

"And almost got herself killed in the process," Gino said with a frown.

Sarah considered telling them about the knife and decided that would be foolish. "Even Julia herself thought Maeve would be safe from Longly's attentions."

"And Maeve is hardly going to invite them," Malloy added.

"And if he does try something," Sarah added, "Maeve can just leave the house and run home in a matter of minutes."

"I'd still feel better if I knew she could send for help if she needed it."

The sound of someone ringing the doorbell startled them.

"Mrs. Ellsworth doesn't usually call at dinnertime," Malloy remarked.

Their neighbor had often called at strange times, but Malloy was right, not usually at dinner, unless it was a problem with her daughter-in-law, who was expecting a child. Sarah knew a moment of anxiety while they waited for their maid to answer the door. To her relief, she didn't recognize the voice of the person who had come.

Sarah half expected Hattie to escort a visitor into the parlor, but she came in alone.

"There's a message for Mrs. Brandt," she reported with a small smile. That had been Sarah's name before she married Malloy, and it was the name she had signed to Maeve's reference. Hattie handed Sarah an envelope.

"I think Maeve may have found a way to communicate

with us," Sarah said, tearing it open. "Who delivered this, Hattie?"

"Somebody's maid. I never saw her before."

"They live over on Bedford Street," Sarah said. Everyone fell silent as she read the note. "Gino, are you looking for a job?"

He broke into a grin. "What does she say?"

"She says they may be hiring a coachman."

His grin vanished.

"Can you drive a carriage?" Malloy asked.

Gino was frowning now. "I can drive a wagon."

"And take care of the horses?" Sarah asked.

"I don't know anything about taking care of horses."

"Then Longly isn't going to hire you," Malloy said.

"I could lie," Gino said.

"Not a good idea," Sarah said. "He'll be able to tell if you don't know what you're doing."

"Maybe I could hire somebody to help me then," Gino said.

"Like who?" Malloy asked skeptically.

"Somebody must be taking care of the horses now, even if they aren't driving for Longly."

"That's certainly true," Sarah said.

"I could use the money Longly pays me to pay them to look after the horses," Gino said, his grin firmly back in place.

"A brilliant plan," Malloy agreed, "so long as the person is willing."

"I can wander over there tomorrow and find out. Maybe this person knows where the former coachman is, too. We'd like to ask him a few questions, wouldn't we?"

"We certainly would," Malloy said.

"And Maeve won't have many opportunities to go out to the stables and question the groom."

"Probably none at all," Sarah said. "At the very least you can try to discover where the coachman can be found."

Gino leaned back in his chair and sighed contentedly.

"Feeling better now?" Malloy asked.

"I wonder if I can hire somebody to drive the coach for me, too."

M AEVE SHOULDN'T HAVE BEEN SURPRISED TO SEE MR. Longly come into the nursery after she and Victor had finished their dinner. Parents who cared about their children usually did visit them regularly even when they had staff to care for them. Victor was overjoyed to see his father, as Maeve would have expected, and Mr. Longly greeted him warmly, picking him up for a hug.

"How do you like your new nursemaid?" he asked the boy, giving Maeve a conspiratorial wink that rather shocked her.

"She plays soldiers with me. She knows all about battles."

"Does she?" Longly asked with genuine surprise. He gave her a questioning look.

"The little boy I used to take care of was very interested." Longly nodded his understanding.

"Master Victor is quite the artist," she added, hoping for an opportunity to discuss the strange picture he had drawn.

Longly frowned. "I hope you haven't been drawing pictures of the bad lady."

Victor stuck out his bottom lip. "Miss Smith isn't scared of her."

"We don't want any more bad dreams, do we?" Longly said, still kind but stern.

"I'm not scared of her either." But Maeve could tell he was. "Are you going out?"

"For a little while," Longly said, making Maeve remember he had a mistress nearby, "but Miss Smith will be here."

"Will the bad lady come?"

"No, she won't. I've told you before, Victor. The bad lady will never come again. Now show me what battle your soldiers were fighting."

At first Maeve thought the scream was part of her dream, but then she was awake, and someone was still screaming. For a minute she didn't know where she was and the room was pitch-dark, offering no clue. Then she remembered she was at the Longly house, in the nursemaid's bedroom, and she recognized the screams were a child having a bad dream. Longly's words about bad dreams from earlier rang in her ears as she shrugged off the lethargy of sleep and turned on the electric lamp. She found her wrapper and hurried to Victor's room next door.

She found the lamp next to Victor's bed and turned it on, creating a puddle of light in the darkness. Victor seemed to still be asleep, tossing and struggling with some unseen demons.

"Victor, wake up," Maeve cried, sitting on the narrow bed beside him and shaking him.

His eyes flew open and for a moment were filled with terror, until he recognized her. "Miss Smith, the bad lady came!"

"No, she didn't. It was just a dream," Maeve assured him.

"But she was here. I saw her!" he wailed.

"You were dreaming, sweetheart. Dreams can seem very

real, but as soon as we open our eyes, they're over and they can't hurt you."

"The bad lady can hurt me," Victor said, still terrified.

"Don't you remember? Your papa told you the bad lady is gone, and she won't ever be back."

"Not ever?"

"Not ever," Maeve promised rashly, having no idea if the bad lady was even real.

Maeve had wrapped her arms around him, and now she heard the sound of bare feet slapping against the floor nearby. In another moment, the maids burst into the room, stopping dead when they saw Maeve comforting the child.

"Is he all right?" Kate asked.

"We heard him screaming," Iris said.

Both girls had obviously been awakened by the sound. They were both in their nightclothes. "He's fine now," Maeve said, patting Victor on the back.

He raised his head and frowned at them. "Why are you here?"

The girls smiled at the question. "You woke us up, Master Victor," Kate said.

"But I was asleep. Miss Smith said."

"Don't worry about it, Master Victor," Maeve said.

"I want to see Papa. Why didn't he come, too?"

Maeve looked up at the maids, but they were very uncomfortable and refused to meet her gaze. "He probably didn't hear you like we did," Maeve said.

"Go get him, then. I need him," Victor said, pouting.

But when Maeve looked back up at the maids, they were both shaking their heads and giving her a warning look. Plainly, getting Mr. Longly wasn't possible, which probably meant he was spending the night elsewhere.

"We don't need to wake your papa," Maeve said. "I'm here, and I'll stay with you until you fall asleep again."

"I don't want the bad lady to come," Victor said. He looked as if he might cry.

"I won't let her come," Maeve promised. "I'll keep you safe. Kate and Iris will keep watch, too, won't you?"

Both girls solemnly agreed.

"Lie back down and I'll tuck you in again."

"You won't leave me?" Victor said.

"No, I swear." She eased him back down and pulled the covers up to his chin.

When Victor closed his eyes, Maeve motioned to the girls that they could leave. She watched the boy as his breathing slowed and sleep claimed him again, sitting very still so she wouldn't disturb him until she was sure he would no longer notice.

As she waited, she thought back to all the things Victor had said about the bad lady. Plainly, someone had frightened him badly, and everyone in this house knew about it but her. Tomorrow she would insist that someone tell her, too, although she wasn't sure how she could force them to if they refused, and she was very much afraid they might.

GINO GOT AN EARLY START SO HE WOULD ARRIVE AT the Longly house at an hour when a substitute groom would be most likely to be caring for the horses. He easily located the house and the mews behind it, where the horses were kept. As he'd expected, there were rooms above the stables, so the coachman probably lived back here as well. To his relief someone was feeding the horses. Gino was relieved to see there were only two and the Longly coach was a small one. He could probably handle it if he had to.

"Good morning," Gino called, startling the young man who was attaching a feed bag to one of the horse's heads.

When he looked up, Gino saw he was hardly more than a boy. "Did you want something?"

Gino kept his smile firmly in place. "I was looking for the Longlys' coachman."

"He's gone," the boy said. He was dressed in work clothes and had obviously been mucking out the stalls.

"Gone where?" Gino asked, hoping he sounded surprised.

"Who knows? They don't pay me to keep track of him. They just pay me to take care of the horses now that he's gone."

"And drive, I expect," Gino tried.

The boy gave him a pitying look. "I just take care of the horses. I don't even really work for Mr. Longly. I work for Mr. Thompson next door. Longly pays me extra to look after his nags until he hires somebody else."

Gino let his smile grow wider. "Then Longly is going to hire another coachman?"

The boy shrugged. "I hope not. I like the extra money."

Gino didn't want to discuss that. "Any idea why the last fellow left?"

"What do you care?" the boy asked. He probably had to wait for the horses to finish feeding, so Gino would have at least a few more minutes with him.

"Just wondering if Longly is one of those men who are never satisfied no matter how hard you work."

The boy brightened with understanding. "You want to know was Vogler fired."

"And if he was, why?" Gino clarified.

The boy glanced around as if checking for eavesdroppers. Seeing none, he said, "Vogler thought he was too good for this job, but he kept it because of Mrs. Longly."

"Did he feel sorry for her?" Gino asked ingenuously. He knew that nobody felt sorry for beautiful women.

The boy gave a bark of laughter. "Not hardly. He was sweet on her. She's a looker, and she liked him, too. You could tell. They say . . ."

"What do they say?" Gino prodded on cue.

The boy waggled his eyebrows suggestively. "They say he did more than drive her carriage."

Of course they did. Gino also knew that people gossiped about beautiful women even without just cause. "If he did, why did her husband keep Vogler on?"

"Maybe he didn't know."

"If the servants were talking about it, so was everybody else. He must've known."

The boy shrugged. "Maybe he didn't care. Or he just didn't notice. He's got his own woman, you know. She just lives two blocks away. I see him walking over there all the time."

"How do you know he's going to see a woman?"

"Everybody knows. She lives on Morton Street. Has her own house. Not as nice as this one, but she lives there all alone. Says she's a widow, but everybody knows what she is."

"So, you're telling me Mrs. Longly was carrying on with the coachman and her husband didn't care because he has a mistress just a few blocks away?"

"I'm just telling you what I hear." The boy looked Gino over. He was wearing a suit and looking pretty good, if he did say so himself. "Are you thinking you can take up where

Vogler left off with Mrs. Longly? It's been over a month now. She's probably getting lonely with him gone."

Gino wanted to punch the smug grin off the boy's face, but that wouldn't accomplish anything except maybe making a bad impression on the people in the Longly house. The important thing was the boy had revealed an interesting fact: He apparently didn't know that Julia was locked away in an asylum. And wasn't that interesting?

VII

Maeve did not have an opportunity to speak to anyone about Victor's nightmare until the boy went down for his afternoon nap. She had given the matter a lot of thought and had decided to start with Mrs. Pauly. The maids might get in trouble for telling her something they weren't supposed to speak about, but she thought she could appeal to Mrs. Pauly's sense of responsibility as head of the household staff.

As soon as Victor was asleep, Maeve hurried downstairs. She found Mrs. Pauly in the butler's pantry making entries into a ledger. She looked up and smiled when Maeve came in. Her smile was a little tentative, but her voice was sure when she said, "Maeve, is something wrong?"

"I wondered if I might speak to you for a minute about Master Victor."

"I'm sure if you have a question about his care, Mr. Longly would be the one—"

"I'd rather not discuss this with Mr. Longly unless you think it's proper."

Plainly, she was not happy, but she said, "All right. What is it?"

"Victor had a nightmare last night. He said the bad lady had come back."

"Maeve," Mrs. Pauly said with exaggerated patience, "surely you know that children have nightmares all the time."

"Victor had drawn a picture earlier. It showed Miss Winterbourne in a window and the bad lady was nearby. He told me Miss Winterbourne flew out the window and went to heaven."

Was it the light or had the color really gone out of Mrs. Pauly's face? "Children's imaginations——" she began, but Maeve was having none of it.

"And Mr. Longly discussed the bad lady with Victor when he visited the nursery last evening. Plainly, this woman is very real to Victor, and I need to know why if I am to help him."

Mrs. Pauly carefully closed the ledger she had been writing in, and Maeve had the impression she was more interested in giving herself time to think than in the ledger itself. She then straightened it on the table and folded her hands on top of it before looking back up at Maeve. "Miss Winterbourne was Master Victor's nursemaid before you."

"I know. You told me that."

"She . . . There was a terrible accident."

"What kind of accident?"

"The kind that no one ever wants to see. She . . . she fell out of one of the nursery windows."

Maeve couldn't help her gasp. No matter what she had

imagined, it wasn't this. "How could she fall out of the window?"

"No one knows."

"Did . . . did Victor see it?" Maeve asked, horrified anew at the very thought.

"He was in the nursery when it happened. We don't . . . We don't know what he saw."

"He must have seen something. He talks about her flying out the window."

"That's what we told him. We told him she flew out the window and went to heaven. We didn't want him to be frightened."

"Then who is the bad lady?"

"We don't know. Master Victor started talking about her a few days later, but no one else was in the nursery with them that day. We think he might have had a dream and gotten it mixed up with what really happened."

"Then Miss Winterbourne is dead?"

"Obviously. No one could survive a fall like that."

Why hadn't the Kindred servants mentioned this to her? Surely, everyone in the neighborhood would know about such a tragedy, so they couldn't have hoped to keep it a secret. "How can you let Master Victor stay in the nursery after that? Aren't you afraid he'll fall, too?"

"Mr. Longly had someone come in and nail the windows shut. It won't happen again."

Maeve was stunned. No wonder no one wanted to talk about Miss Winterbourne. But was it really an accident? How did a grown woman *accidentally* fall out of a window, especially in the winter?

Or did Chet Longly have something to do with it?

*   *   *

Gino had been turned away from the Longly home when he'd asked to speak to someone about the coachman's job. They'd told him Mr. Longly wasn't at home and it didn't matter anyway because he wasn't planning to hire a new coachman. Gino wondered where Longly could be so early on a Saturday morning and decided he simply hadn't come home at all the night before. The life of a rich man must be very interesting.

He had spent the rest of his morning wandering through the neighborhood and asking the men working in the various stables if they knew where Vogler had gone. They all had something suggestive to say about Vogler's relationship with Julia Longly, but no one seemed to know where Vogler might be found now that he no longer worked for her.

Gino was about to give up when he came to the last house on that side of the street. The stables here were immaculate, which Gino noticed because he'd seen stables in all conditions during his morning rounds. An older man was polishing a very fancy carriage when Gino found him.

His gray hair flopped in his eyes and his clothes were worn and dirty. He looked Gino over with some amusement. "If you're looking for work, you shouldn't dress like some swell. Nobody will take you serious."

Gino instantly regretted his choice of attire. Maybe that's why no one had been helpful to him this morning. "Thanks for the advice, but I'm not looking for work. I'm looking for my old friend. He worked for the Longlys, last I heard, but they told me he's gone and they don't know where."

"Vogler, is it?" the man asked with a frown.

"That's right," Gino said, brightening as if at the prospect of locating his friend. "You know him?"

"We all know each other, but Vogler, he keeps to himself."

"He does," Gino said as if he knew Vogler well. "I guess that's why no one can tell me anything."

"What is it you're wanting with him, then?"

"I shouldn't say. You won't want to help me then," Gino said a little reluctantly.

"I don't know about that. You said Vogler was an old friend. Was he a good friend, too?"

"Not exactly," Gino said, taking a chance. This fellow sounded like he didn't care for Vogler, so maybe he would betray him out of spite.

"So, he was a bad friend?" the man guessed, his amusement back.

"He owes me some money," Gino said. Maeve would be impressed he'd come up with the perfect lie. "He said he'd pay me last week, but he didn't and now I find out he's disappeared."

"Not disappeared. Just moved on."

"And I don't suppose you have any idea where."

The man studied Gino for another long moment. "How much does he owe you?"

"Twenty dollars," Gino said. A significant amount for a working man, almost a month's wages.

"Then it would be worth a dollar to you to find out where he is, I guess."

Gino got the hint and pulled a silver dollar from his pocket. He'd add this to the Breedloves' bill. He held it up but didn't hand it over yet.

The man nodded his satisfaction. "He didn't have any

trouble finding work. He just had to be careful to find a widow who would appreciate his pretty face but who didn't have a husband to get jealous."

"Is that what happened with Longly?"

"Vogler didn't say, but we all knew it was just a matter of time until Longly noticed what was going on."

"Was something really going on? I mean, ladies don't usually carry on with their coachmen, do they?"

"Or any of their other servants," the man agreed, "but it wasn't so much what Vogler did as where he took her."

"Where did he take her?" Gino asked, not having to feign his surprise.

"Places no lady should go," the man said with a curl of his lip. "But that's just what people say. People say a lot of things, I've noticed."

"They sure do, and they say it whenever a woman does anything unusual."

"That they do."

"And what do they say about where I can find Vogler?" Gino asked, growing impatient.

"They say he went to work for a widow." He gave Gino the name and the street. He didn't know the address, but Gino could find it, he was sure.

He handed the man the silver dollar, and he pocketed it with practiced speed.

Gino thanked him and turned to go, but before he took a step, the man said, "Be careful, young fellow. That Vogler is a mean one."

Gino promised that he would.

Now, which was more important, getting the job at Longly's or finding Vogler? Gino set out for the street the old man had given him.

* * *

Maeve still had a lot of questions about what had happened to Miss Winterbourne, but she was sure Mrs. Pauly wouldn't answer any of them. She'd told Maeve what she wanted her to know, and she would simply be annoyed if Maeve kept questioning her. That was the disadvantage of consulting the highest-ranking servant in the house. Fortunately, Maeve knew someone who might be more forthcoming.

"I saw you go into Mrs. Pauly's lair," the cook said with a smirk when Maeve arrived in the kitchen. "I figured you was too good for the likes of me now."

Maeve smiled conspiratorially. "I just had to ask her about something, but she wasn't much help."

"So, you came back to me," the cook said, pouring the tea she had already made. Plainly, she had been certain Maeve would seek her out.

Maeve waited until she had set a piece of cherry pie in front of her, too. "I needed to know what happened to Miss Winterbourne."

The cook froze. She had just been about to sit down in the chair opposite Maeve's and she eventually did, but not until an awful moment of reaction had passed. Maeve knew that expression. If the cook had been Catholic, she would have crossed herself at the mention of one who had died so violently.

"And what did Mrs. Pauly tell you?"

Maeve took a sip of her tea, as if to fortify herself. "She told me Miss Winterbourne fell out of one of the nursery windows, but that can't be true, can it?"

The cook frowned. "Why not?"

"Because how could someone be so careless? Those windows are large, but you'd have to lean pretty far out to lose your balance."

"Nobody knows how it happened," the cook said, as if that settled it.

"Don't they? Or do they just not want to say it out loud?"

"I don't know what you're talking about," the cook said, her face set the same way Mrs. Pauly's had been. She didn't want to tell Maeve anything more either, but Maeve didn't have to be as careful with the cook, who wasn't her boss.

"You know exactly what I'm talking about. You all must have thought it. She had to have jumped."

Plainly, the cook *hadn't* thought it at all. "That's a terrible thing to say!"

"Yes, it is, but what other explanation makes sense?"

"She . . . she fell," the cook insisted. "She never would've jumped, surely not with Master Victor in the room."

Which may well be true. She decided she'd gotten the most out of shocking the cook and she didn't want to alienate her. "I'm sorry. I shouldn't have been so blunt, and you're right, I didn't know her, so I shouldn't judge."

"No, you shouldn't. Miss Winterbourne would never do something like that. Besides, she had no reason."

But maybe she did have a reason and she'd kept it a secret from the rest of the staff, a reason that involved Chet Longly. Maeve wouldn't suggest that, though. "Whatever happened, it must have caused a real scandal in the neighborhood."

"Oh no, not at all," the cook said quite confidently.

"Why not?"

"Because they never heard about it. She fell in the back of the house, you see. No one saw it except the staff here. Mr. Longly didn't want . . . Well, he likes to keep his business

private, so he told the police she fell, and the undertaker
took her away and that was that. No one the wiser."

G INO HAD TO ASK ONLY ONE PERSON, A MAID ON HER
way to market, to find the house where Vogler now worked.
Everyone, apparently, knew the Widow Hart. By then it was
afternoon and Mrs. Hart might well be out in her carriage,
but Gino's luck was holding. The carriage was in the stable
and a good-looking young man sat out front in a patch of
sunlight, his chair tipped back against the stable wall. He
was puffing on a cigar and staring off into space.

"Vogler?" Gino said with a friendly smile. No sense in
alarming the fellow.

Vogler looked up, not a bit alarmed. "Who wants to
know?"

Gino had given this some thought and he'd decided that
honesty might serve him well in this situation. He pulled
out his card and handed it to Vogler. "I'm a private investigator."

Vogler studied the card for a moment before looking up
at Gino. "And what are you investigating?"

Plainly, Vogler's conscience was clear. "Mrs. Longly's
uncle hired me."

Vogler frowned. "Hired you for what?"

"Don't you know what happened to Mrs. Longly?"

Vogler glanced down at the card again and his frown
deepened. "Did something happen to her?"

Could he not know that Longly had sent her to the asylum? "How long have you been gone from the Longlys'?"

"Since he fired me. I don't know, a month or more, I
guess."

"Why did he fire you?" Gino asked.

"He didn't just fire *me*," Vogler said a bit defensively. "He let everybody go. All the staff."

"That seems strange. Was he planning to leave the city or something?"

"He didn't tell me his plans," Vogler said bitterly. "He just gives me this letter of reference and tells me he doesn't need my services anymore."

"And he did this with all the staff?"

"I don't know what he gave them. They're a tight-lipped bunch. Not friendly at all. But they all left, every single one of them . . . Well, except for Winterbourne. That's the nursemaid. She'd already jumped out the window, so I guess you'd say she already left," he added with an ugly smirk.

Gino couldn't hide his surprise. They'd known the nurse-maid left, but this was news. "She killed herself?"

Vogler shrugged. "He hushed it up. Longly, that is. Told everybody it was an accident, but all the women was whispering about it. They didn't whisper to me, mind you, but it was easy to see they knew it wasn't no accident."

Did Maeve know? And did this mean she was in some kind of danger? He'd have to get a message to her somehow, even if he had to knock on the door and ask for her. In the meantime, though, he had to get as much information as he could out of Vogler. "You said Longly let all the remaining staff go, but they're all back now."

"They are?" Vogler was flabbergasted. "How do you know?"

"I know," Gino told him. "I told you, I'm investigating. What I don't know is why Longly hired everyone back but you."

Vogler was still taking this in. "He hired them *all* back?"

"Yes, all but you. Can you think of any reason why?"

"That son of a—"

"Maybe he thought you were too close to Mrs. Longly," Gino suggested.

Vogler looked up at that, his expression wary. "What do you mean?"

"I think you know what I mean. Everybody I asked about you thought you and Mrs. Longly were lovers."

To Gino's surprise, Vogler actually laughed at that. "Lovers? Not in my wildest dreams."

Was Vogler really that good of a liar? "But you did spend a lot of time with her," Gino reminded him.

"Because I drove her carriage, and she went out a lot."

"Where did she go?" Gino asked, remembering this was a question they needed to be answered.

Vogler's expression turned sly. "Wouldn't you like to know?"

In point of fact, he would, but he wasn't going to start by offering a bribe—which was doubtless what Vogler was angling for—when he could get the same information for free. "Does your new employer know what people were saying about you and Mrs. Longly?"

"She doesn't care about gossip," Vogler claimed.

"Doesn't she?" Gino asked in mock surprise. "I expect a widow like Mrs. Hart would be careful about her reputation, and no lady wants people saying she's lifting her skirts for her driver."

Vogler tipped his chair forward with a thump and jumped to his feet. "Nobody's saying that."

"But if I happened to tell Mrs. Hart people are saying that about your previous employer, well . . ."

"All right," Vogler said, furious now but holding his temper because he now understood Gino held the upper hand. "What did you want to know about Mrs. Longly?"

"Like I said, where did you take her?"

Vogler took a long moment to grind his teeth, but he finally managed to say, "Different places."

"Don't be difficult, Vogler," Gino warned. "I had a long morning."

"Gambling joints, mostly," he ground out.

Gino couldn't help it. His jaw actually dropped open. "Gambling?"

Vogler glared at him in contempt. "You didn't think I took her to church, did you?"

This didn't make any sense. Why would a woman like Julia Longly go to a place like that? Even the high-class gambling houses where rich people went were no place for a lady. Men went there to encounter a much different type of woman who could be had for a price and instantly forgotten.

"Did she gamble?" Gino asked stupidly.

Vogler gave him a pitying look. "I don't know because I didn't go in with her, but what do you think?"

Surely, she did, but where did she get the money? Gino also knew that the only true winner at games of chance was the house, and Longly was unlikely to cover her losses. But maybe Julia did have a lover whom she met there and who financed her escapades. Gino had so many questions, but Vogler wouldn't be able to answer any of them.

"Did Longly really hire all the other staff back?" Vogler asked a bit plaintively.

"I'm afraid so," Gino said, but he took pity on the man. "But don't take it too personally. Mrs. Longly isn't going to need the carriage anymore, so he doesn't need a driver."

Vogler smiled mirthlessly. "I guess he found out what she was up to. It was just a matter of time."

Gino wasn't going to confirm or deny, so he thanked

Vogler for his help, but before he turned away, Vogler said, "Did Tamar come back, too?"

Gino had no idea, but he said, "Tamar?"

Vogler shook his head. "I guess not. She'd been gone for months even before Longly let the rest of us go. I was just hoping . . ."

"Hoping what?" Gino prodded in case this was important. Vogler really seemed to care about this girl.

"She got hurt. Fell down the stairs. Longly sent her somewhere, they said. To get better, but I never heard . . ."

"I really don't know, but I can find out."

"Could you? You owe me, you know. For all I told you."

Gino wasn't sure if he owed Vogler or not. He wasn't even sure Vogler had told him the truth, although Gino couldn't think of any reason the coachman would make up such a strange tale. "Yes, I'll let you know what I find out."

Gino's mind was spinning as he walked away. Two servants had met with terrible accidents at the Longly house. He didn't want to think what that meant.

Before Maeve had left for her new job, she and Sarah had agreed that she would try to get away on Sunday morning, using the excuse of attending church. It might not work, because Longly might be one of those employers who insisted their staff attend the same church they did, but Sarah had determined to stay home on Sunday morning just in case, and Malloy never went to church, so they were both waiting for her. Mother Malloy had helpfully taken both children with her to Mass.

Gino had reported to them what he had learned about Vogler yesterday and his claims to have taken Julia to gambling houses and about the two servants who had terrible accidents while working at the Longly home. Both pieces of news were disturbing enough that Sarah and Frank were tremendously relieved when Maeve walked in on Sunday morning, safe and sound.

"I had to tell them I'm Catholic so they didn't make me go to church with them," she announced.

"But you *are* Catholic," Malloy said.

"I don't know what I am, but now they'll probably treat me like I have some dread disease." Many people still viewed Catholics as somewhat suspect. "It couldn't be helped, though. I had to get away because I have something important to tell you."

They sat down around the table in the breakfast room while their cook, Velvet, served Maeve breakfast, since she'd had to fast before the Mass she wasn't really attending to keep up her pretense.

She told them about Victor's drawing and what he'd said about the bad lady and her suspicions that Miss Winterbourne couldn't possibly have fallen out the nursery window.

"What do *you* think happened?" Malloy asked her.

"I thought she might've jumped, but the cook was horrified when I suggested it."

"Nobody wants to believe someone they know committed suicide," Sarah said, "although Gino located the coachman, and he thinks Miss Winterbourne jumped."

"Did he say why?" Maeve asked.

"No, and Gino didn't think to ask. He was probably too shocked at that moment."

"Did the coachman say anything else?"

Sarah and Malloy told her what Gino had learned about Julia's exploits.

"I'm glad to know Julia wasn't carrying on with her driver," Maeve said, "but how could she have been doing the things he claimed?"

"It is hard to believe," Sarah said. "And how could Mr. Longly not have known?"

"Maybe he just wasn't paying attention to Julia," Malloy said. "He's got his mistress to keep him occupied, don't forget."

"And he apparently spends the night at her house at least sometimes," Maeve said. "Maybe he just didn't care what Julia did."

"Or maybe Julia wasn't going to gambling houses at all," Sarah said. "The neighbors thought she was visiting friends and Julia herself said she just had Vogler drive her around so she could get out of the house. Vogler's claim is rather outlandish. He could just be making up slanders about Julia to get even with Mr. Longly for firing him."

"I can't imagine Longly not caring that his wife was visiting gambling houses, but I can easily imagine her wanting to get out of the house and away from him," Maeve said.

"He does seem to be rather heartless," Sarah said. "Gino also found out from Vogler that another maid was injured. Her name was Tamar and she apparently fell down the stairs. We didn't hear any neighborhood gossip about either Tamar or Miss Winterbourne, so Longly successfully covered up both incidents."

"There's no one at the Longly house named Tamar now," Maeve said. "Do we know what happened to her?"

"Vogler said Longly sent her away, but he didn't know where," Malloy said.

Maeve frowned. "But what we do know is that one of Longly's maids was seriously injured and sent away, and the nursemaid died in a horrible manner, and then he sent his wife to an asylum, and he's managed to keep all of this a secret from everyone outside of his house."

"I can see why a man wouldn't want people to know he'd sent his wife to an asylum," Malloy said, "but why keep the injury to the maid and the death of the nursemaid a secret?"

"Unless he had something to hide," Sarah said. "If he was responsible for the injury and the death, and Julia knew it . . ."

"Then he might have sent her away to silence her forever," Maeve concluded. "But none of our theories explains who the bad lady is or how she might be involved, at least in Miss Winterbourne's death."

"Could she have been one of the other servants?" Malloy asked.

"I've been trying to figure it out, but if she was, why didn't Victor recognize her?"

"She might be a figment of his imagination," Sarah said. "Children often have a difficult time understanding what is real and what is imaginary."

"Maybe you're right. His drawing could have been anyone, after all."

"I guess you asked him who she was," Malloy said.

"He said she was the bad lady, that's all. I just remembered, I did ask him where she lives, thinking he would tell me she lived in the house, but he said she lives in *her* house."

"He said that?" Sarah asked in amazement. "Then maybe he did recognize her, if he knew she lived somewhere else."

"Do you suppose . . . ?" Malloy mused.

"Do we suppose what?" Sarah prodded.

"What about Longly's mistress? She lives nearby, doesn't she?"

"Just a few blocks away, if the rumors are true," Sarah said.

"Do you suppose *she* could be the bad lady?" Malloy asked.

Sarah and Maeve gaped at him for a long moment. "But how would she dare come into Julia's house?" Sarah asked.

"Yes," Maeve said, nodding vigorously. "That would require a lot of nerve."

"But if she was jealous enough," Malloy said, obviously still trying to figure it out. "Remember, we thought Chet Longly might be interfering with the servants. If this Tamar was with child, he might have tried pushing her down the stairs to cause a miscarriage."

"Women have been throwing themselves down stairs for centuries and it seldom works," Sarah said, speaking as an expert on the subject of pregnancy. "But Chet Longly probably doesn't know that."

"And if he did injure her but not cause her to lose the baby, sending her away would be the next logical step," Maeve said.

"Sadly, *sending her away* probably means he just turned her out to fend for herself," Sarah said, "but it's a solution men have also used for centuries."

"But what about Miss Winterbourne?" Maeve asked.

"After the fiasco with Tamar, Longly might have decided the simplest way to get rid of a troublesome female was to kill her," Malloy said. "And he may have gotten his mistress to do the dirty work."

"Or she may have done it out of jealousy," Maeve said.

"But to kill a woman in front of his son," Sarah said. "How much of a monster *is* Chet Longly?"

"He may not have intended that part," Malloy argued. "Or maybe the woman acted on her own."

"Someone needs to find out just what kind of a person this mistress is," Maeve said. "Could she really have pushed a woman out a window in front of a little boy?"

Sarah noticed Maeve was looking directly at her. "Are you talking to me?"

"Well, I can't go because I've got to take care of Victor," Maeve reminded her with an innocent smile.

"Yes, you have to take care of Longly's child instead of ours," Malloy said with just a hint of sarcasm.

"And look how much information I've gotten in just a few days," Maeve reminded him.

"Which leaves me to visit a woman everyone in society would consider hardly better than a prostitute who might also be a murderer," Sarah said with a dramatic sigh.

"I'll go with you," Malloy said.

"She's hardly likely to admit to anything with you there," Maeve scoffed.

He glared at her, but she didn't even blink.

"Gino can go with me," Sarah said, shaking her head at both of them.

"She won't admit anything in front of him either," Malloy said.

"He'll be my chauffeur," Sarah said. "We'll take the motorcar so it will look natural. That way he'll be close by if I need to be rescued, although that hardly seems likely."

"You better be right," Malloy warned.

"Don't worry," Maeve said with a grin. "Mrs. Frank might as well wear a priest's collar. She'll have this woman confessing everything to her in five minutes."

"If she even has anything to confess," Sarah said.

"When will you go?" Maeve asked.

"This afternoon if we can find Gino," Sarah said. "What could be more natural than a Sunday-afternoon visit?"

"I told Gino to come by the house this afternoon so we could tell him what Maeve found out," Malloy said.

"Oh dear, what if Mr. Longly decides a Sunday-afternoon visit is natural for him, too?" Maeve said.

"Then I'll embarrass him," Sarah said.

"But won't he recognize you and wonder what you're do- ing there?" Maeve asked.

"He's never seen her," Malloy said.

"It's settled then," Sarah said. "We'll wait for Gino and then I'll go and beard the evil mistress in her den."

VIII

Gino was only too happy to drive Sarah to Mrs. Nailor's house on Morton Street. Sarah had found the exact address helpfully listed in the city directory. It was close enough to walk, but ladies like Sarah always rode. Besides, she wanted to make an impression and she also needed Gino nearby to placate Malloy. Their noisy gasoline-powered motorcar certainly got them noticed.

Sarah waited for Gino to climb down and open her door for her. Then he took her duster and goggles and waited while she unwrapped the length of tulle from her head, where it had protected her hat from being blown halfway across the city. When she was free of all her traveling gear, she made her way up the front steps of the neat brownstone.

The house was small, narrower than most of the others on the street, but nothing else set it apart. Anyone could have lived there.

A maid answered her knock so promptly that Sarah knew their arrival had been observed. Sarah expressed her wish to see Mrs. Nailor and the girl took her card to see if the lady of the house was at home. Sarah had high hopes that curiosity would compel Mrs. Nailor to see her even though she was a complete stranger.

She waited longer than she had expected to, but finally the girl returned and escorted her upstairs to the parlor where Mrs. Nailor awaited her. Sarah couldn't help noticing the girl had a slight limp, which was unusual for a servant. A maid who might tire easily or not be strong would not be able to perform her arduous duties and would never be hired in the first place. But maybe a woman like Mrs. Nailor had to take what she could get.

When she entered the parlor, Sarah understood at once that Mrs. Nailor had taken a few minutes to make herself presentable. Perhaps she hadn't even been appropriately dressed for visitors, since a woman in her position couldn't expect to be visited by anyone except her protector. At any rate, she was appropriately dressed now in a lovely day dress of sprigged cotton. The only thing unusual about her appearance was that it wasn't unusual at all.

Sarah wasn't sure what she had expected, but she had assumed a mistress would possess obvious charms: beauty of face and figure and a sultry sexuality that would attract and hold a man's attentions.

Mrs. Nailor had none of those things.

She was a handsome woman, but only because she took pains with her appearance. Her golden hair was done in a flattering style and her complexion was flawless. Her dress had been made to suit her, although her figure was far from

fashionable. She was plump, with dimpled cheeks and probably dimpled elbows and knees, if Sarah was any judge. She
smiled tentatively, her bright blue eyes wary, when the maid
announced Sarah. She offered her visitor her hand.

"Welcome, Mrs. Malloy. Please sit down. May I offer you
some refreshment? Tea or coffee or perhaps you would prefer
some lemonade."

"Lemonade sounds wonderful," Sarah said, taking a seat
on the plush sofa. She had been so busy making note of
every detail of Mrs. Nailor's appearance that she hadn't really noticed the room itself. It was tastefully furnished, with
a sofa and two easy chairs arranged before the fireplace. Velvet drapes hung at the windows over lace sheers. Various
paintings adorned the walls although, Sarah noticed, no
family portraits.

Mrs. Nailor took one of the chairs after instructing the
maid to bring them some lemonade. "I don't think we've
met before, Mrs. Malloy."

Her statement was loaded with unspoken questions, and
Sarah had no desire to toy with the woman, so she answered
them. "My husband is a private investigator. He has been
hired to help Julia Longly regain her freedom."

Mrs. Nailor didn't seem too surprised at this news. "Mr.
Longly mentioned that he had been visited by a private investigator."

Sarah had nothing to add, so she waited, knowing most
people could not bear silence and would fill it even if they
had to reveal something personal to do it.

After a moment, Mrs. Nailor said, "Why have you come
to see me, Mrs. Malloy? You can't think I would do anything
to help Julia Longly."

"No, but I thought perhaps you could understand why I would. You see, I can only imagine how horrible it would be to be locked away in an insane asylum when I was perfectly sane."

"Is that what you think then? That Julia Longly is perfectly sane?"

"I've spoken with her myself, twice," Sarah said. "It is obvious to me that she does not belong in that place."

"And you think that speaking with her twice qualifies you to judge, I assume." Mrs. Nailor was angry although she was too well-bred to show just how much, which was very interesting. Sarah had not expected a kept woman to be so well mannered.

"How many times have *you* spoken with Mrs. Longly?" Sarah countered.

Mrs. Nailor nodded in acknowledgment of Sarah's point. "You are correct. I have never spoken with her, but I have heard about her behavior firsthand from Mr. Longly for the past four years, so I have a bit more information than you do, I'm sure."

"Information provided by the man who had her committed," Sarah said.

"Do you think that was something he did lightly?" Mrs. Nailor asked in outrage. "I assure you he tolerated her conduct for a long time before she finally forced him to take action."

Before Sarah could reply, the maid tapped on the door and brought in their lemonade. Sarah was glad for the interruption since it gave her a chance to prepare her arguments, but then Mrs. Nailor said, "Thank you, Tamar."

"Tamar?" Sarah echoed in surprise.

"Yes?" the girl replied, stopping on her way out of the room.

"I . . . just . . ." Sarah stammered. "Did you work at the Longly home?"

The girl stiffened in alarm and glanced at Mrs. Nailor, who said, "It's all right, Tamar. You may go."

She scurried out without so much as a backward glance, and this time her limp was pronounced.

"How did you know she worked for Chet?" Mrs. Nailor demanded.

Sarah took a moment to think. "One of the other servants told us. They said she was injured," she tried, not sure what story Mrs. Nailor might have been given.

"She was seriously injured," Mrs. Nailor said with a frown. "You can see she still limps."

"From falling down the stairs," Sarah said.

"You are very well-informed."

"One of the other servants was concerned about her, because she was sent away."

"Sent away?" Mrs. Nailor scoffed. "She was sent here to recover."

Which was much better than simply being turned out to fend for herself. But if Longly wanted to keep Tamar's injury a secret, sending her here was a good decision. "It was good of you to take her in."

Mrs. Nailor's dimpled face hardened into a frown. "I know what you're thinking, that I had no choice, but believe me, I was happy to take Tamar after what she went through."

"What did she go through?" Sarah asked with genuine interest.

"Ask Julia."

Sarah sighed. "I know you aren't going to speak ill of Mr. Longly—"

"And you think that is because he is my protector, but it is simpler than that, Mrs. Malloy. I won't speak ill of Mr. Longly because he has done nothing wrong."

Sarah reminded herself that Mrs. Nailor had heard only Longly's version of things. He surely had shown himself in the best light and justified all of his actions, but if he was willing to put his wife in an asylum, there was no telling what he might do to his mistress. "Women seem to fare badly at the Longly house."

"If you mean Tamar, then yes, she did fare badly."

"And Miss Winterbourne actually died," Sarah said.

Mrs. Nailor winced. "I wonder Julia mentioned her to you."

Sarah chose not to respond to that. "Tell me, Mrs. Nailor, have you ever been inside Mr. Longly's house?"

She stiffened at the question. "Certainly not."

"Not even to meet Mr. Longly's son?"

Now Mrs. Nailor simply looked confused. "I should very much like to meet Victor, but that would be highly inappropriate."

"You've never seen him then?"

"Never."

She met Sarah's gaze unflinchingly, so directly in fact that Sarah believed her. "Do you know that Victor witnessed Miss Winterbourne's, uh, accident?"

"Mr. Longly has never been sure of that, but it is his great fear."

"Victor also talks about a bad lady who frightens him."

Mrs. Nailor considered that for a moment, and then her expression hardened again. "I see now. That's why you asked if I had ever been in Chet's house and met Victor. You think I'm the *bad lady* who pushed Miss Winterbourne out the window."

"Do you believe she was pushed?" Sarah asked, not even feigning her surprise.

"Of course she was pushed, Mrs. Malloy, but you're wasting your time here. If you want to know what really happened, you need to ask your friend Julia. She's the one who knows."

"Are you accusing her of killing Miss Winterbourne?" Sarah asked.

"Who am I to accuse anyone of anything?" Mrs. Nailor asked bitterly. "I know what you think of me, that I'm no better than a common prostitute. You even think me capable of cold-blooded murder. And you believe Julia Longly is a saint just because she happens to be legally married to Chet Longly, but you couldn't be more wrong. You have insulted me enough for one day, Mrs. Malloy. I'm afraid I'm going to have to ask you to leave. I'll send my maid to show you out."

With that she rose and left the room, her head held high. Sarah felt a bit of a fool, although she wasn't sure if that was because she believed this woman or because she knew she shouldn't. Mrs. Nailor had every reason to protect Chet Longly or perhaps just to believe everything he told her, and Sarah was sure she did believe what she had said today. But if Chet Longly was as evil as they had come to suspect, his mistress was wise to stand by him, if only for her own safety.

Sarah was hoping for a word with Tamar, but a different girl came to show her out and when she asked about Tamar, she was told the girl had other duties.

Gino was idly polishing a fender on the motorcar when Sarah came out. "Any luck?" he asked as he held her duster up so she could slip it on.

"Not much, except that I'm now fairly certain that Mrs. Nailor is not the bad lady."

"Who could it be then?"

"I don't know, but Mrs. Nailor suggested I ask Julia Longly." Sarah started wrapping the length of tulle to secure her hat.

Gino frowned. "How would she know?"

"She wouldn't . . . unless she is the bad lady herself."

YOU DO REALIZE THAT MRS. NAILOR HAS EVERY REASON to defend Chet Longly and condemn Julia, don't you?" Frank asked when Sarah and Gino had returned from their visit to the mistress's house. They had settled in the parlor while Sarah recounted her conversation with the woman. Mother Malloy had taken the children to the nursery so they could speak freely.

"Of course she does, and the expression on Tamar's face when I asked if she had worked at the Longly house proves something terrible happened to her there. She's still limping, for heaven's sake."

"Would Longly send her to his mistress's house if he was the one who hurt her, though?" Gino asked.

Frank looked to Sarah for a reply. He hadn't been rich long enough to understand why rich people did the things they did. In point of fact, he probably never would, but Sarah had grown up in that world.

"I've been asking myself that, too," she said. "Most men in his position wouldn't particularly care what happened to a servant girl whom they had injured. No one is likely to even care except the girl herself and perhaps the other servants, but Longly is obviously a very private man. He might take care of the girl in exchange for her silence."

"And Mrs. Nailor is in no position to refuse to accept her," Frank said.

"Don't forget we thought the girl might be with child," Gino said, blushing a little at the sensitive topic. "Do you think Mrs. Nailor would take her if she's carrying Longly's baby?"

"The baby was just a guess on our part," Sarah reminded them. "And Mrs. Nailor seemed protective of the girl, which makes me doubt the theory about a baby. She wouldn't even let me speak to her."

"Maybe she just didn't want you to hear what the girl had to say about Longly," Frank said.

"That's possible, I guess. I wish you'd been able to spend a little more time with Longly," Sarah said. "I don't think we have any idea what kind of man he really is."

"He's a man who doesn't like strangers poking around in his business," Frank said. "That is the one thing I'm sure of."

"Who does?" Gino asked. "I don't think we can condemn him just for that."

"But we can condemn him for it if he's hiding a murder," Frank said.

"If he's determined to hide it, how will we ever find out the truth, though?" Gino asked.

The telephone rang before anyone could reply. Its shrill alert made them all jump.

"I'll answer it," Sarah said, hurrying to get to it before her maid made the trek from the rear of the house.

The telephone sat on a table in the hallway and Sarah got it just after the second ring.

"Sarah, dear, I have news for you," her mother said.

"Is it about our case?"

"Indeed. I may be able to get some information about the person who moved away from the city."

Sarah knew better than to guess at a name. Her mother could mean only Julia's mother, Mrs. Breedlove, but neither of them wanted to say anything on the telephone, where an operator might be listening in hopes of hearing something scandalous she could sell to the newspapers. "When can I get this information?"

"If you come to visit me tomorrow morning, I will tell you all about it."

Sarah smiled. This must be important information indeed.

SARAH DROVE THE ELECTRIC OVER TO HER MOTHER'S house on Monday morning. Her mother welcomed her when the maid escorted her into the family parlor. She had ordered tea and it had already been set out in anticipation of Sarah's arrival.

"This must be serious," Sarah said, eyeing the tea tray.

"I didn't want to be interrupted," her mother said with a mysterious smile. She poured them each some tea and when she was done, she said, "I may have some information about Julia Longly's mother."

"You've found her?" Sarah said in surprise.

"Heavens no, but I kept asking around about Ellie Breedlove, and someone finally suggested I speak to Patricia de Groot. That was when I remembered that she and Ellie had been close friends. I think they met at school or at least rather early in life. If anyone would know where Ellie was, Patricia would."

"Do you know her?"

"I know her the way everyone in society knows everyone else, but we aren't really friends."

"And have you spoken with her?"

"No, I have not," her mother said. "Regardless of what your father may think, I know I'm not really a detective. I thought there would be only one opportunity to approach Patricia on this subject, and I didn't want to spoil your chance of really learning something."

"Oh, Mother, I'm so proud of you," Sarah exclaimed.

"One must know one's limits," her mother said primly. "I do know that I can get us in to see Patricia, though. She would hardly refuse a visit from me, even if we aren't close friends, and I can honestly say I am concerned about Julia and I believe she needs her mother's help."

Sarah frowned. This was a delicate situation. "We can't tell Mrs. de Groot that Julia is in an insane asylum."

"Of course not. I was thinking we could hint very strongly that Julia's husband was abusing her in some way, and she needs a place of refuge. Her mother's home would be the ideal place for her, except we don't know where her mother is."

"Would Mrs. de Groot think Julia would know? Because Julia may well know. I didn't think to ask her."

"She may, but we can simply say Julia has said she does not know."

"You're right, we can. Maeve would be disappointed that I didn't immediately realize we could lie," Sarah said with a smirk.

"She certainly would."

"Finding Mrs. Breedlove would be wonderful," Sarah said. "She can help us prove that Julia doesn't need to be in the asylum, and when Julia is released, she could go to stay with her mother."

"Would Ellie really be able to help prove Julia is sane? She hasn't seen her for a long time, or at least I assume she hasn't."

"I hadn't thought of that, but we can take Mrs. Breedlove to visit Julia. I'm sure she would be as convinced as we are that Julia is in her right mind."

"I would hope so, although I wonder how much weight a mother's word would carry. Mothers are supposed to believe the very best about their children, after all."

"You may be right, but it can't hurt. At the very least, she can offer Julia shelter since her aunt and uncle aren't particularly eager to have her in their home. When would you like to visit Mrs. de Groot?"

Her mother smiled sweetly. "I was hoping you would be free this afternoon. I'm not sure if this is an at-home day for Patricia, but we can at least leave our cards, which would raise her curiosity and make her more likely to be at home the next time we call."

"I happen to be free, and I have the electric motorcar, so I can drive us."

Her mother smiled broadly at that. "I can't wait to tell your father I got to ride with you."

The two of them set out after lunch. The de Groots lived only a few blocks away, but they naturally chose to ride, and her mother would surely have ordered her carriage if Sarah hadn't had her motorcar. The de Groot house was a stately, marble-fronted row house with a neat patch of lawn inside the wrought iron fence.

A maid answered the door and accepted their calling cards. "I'll see if Mrs. de Groot is at home. If you'll wait in here, please." She showed them into the receiving room, a cramped space just off the foyer specifically for accommodating unplanned visitors until the lady of the house decided if she wanted to see them or not. Mrs. de Groot might well be home but decide she didn't want to see those calling on her, in which case the maid would simply say she was *not* at home, thus saving her from insulting her visitors by refusing to see them.

But as Sarah's mother had predicted, Patricia de Groot was perfectly willing to see Mrs. Felix Decker and the lady with her, whoever she might be. After a short wait, the maid showed them into a lavishly furnished parlor where Patricia de Groot welcomed them.

She was a tall woman whose figure was still trim and erect. Her blond hair was carefully styled, even though she hadn't been expecting company today, and her face showed the benefits of a lifetime of adequate food and rest and very little sunlight.

She did, indeed, remember Elizabeth Decker's daughter, Sarah, and had not heard she was remarried. This was not surprising since no one in society would have taken note of her marriage to an Irish Catholic ex-policeman, even if he was a multimillionaire. Mrs. de Groot ordered tea for them—Sarah would be floating after so much tea today—and they chatted about mutual friends while they waited for it to be served.

When the maid had left them alone, her mother got down to business.

"I'm sure you're wondering why we've come to see you,
Patricia."

Mrs. de Groot looked a little surprised, but she covered
it well. People in her world seldom came right to the point
about anything. "I am always happy to welcome you, Elizabeth."

"That's kind of you, but I'm afraid we have some rather
serious issues to discuss. You see, Sarah here is good friends
with Julia Longly."

Maeve would be proud of how well her mother had told
that lie, although Sarah had long since realized that all society women were skilled liars. One had to be or risk offend-
ing someone whose bad opinion could cause one all sorts of
problems.

"Julia Longly?" Mrs. de Groot echoed a bit uncertainly.

"Julia Breedlove," her mother clarified. "Ellie Breedlove's
daughter."

"Yes, I remember," Mrs. de Groot said carefully. Plainly,
she didn't want to reveal her true opinion on the subject of
Julia Breedlove Longly.

"Julia finds herself in a difficult situation," her mother
continued as if she hadn't noticed. "She desperately needs
her mother's help, but as you probably know, Ellie has left
the city."

Mrs. de Groot took a sip of her tea before replying.
"What kind of help does Julia need?"

Her mother glanced at Sarah, silently suggesting she reply to this question. Sarah gladly did so. "It seems Julia
made an unwise marriage, and she needs to find a refuge.
She would naturally go to her mother, but she doesn't know
where her mother is."

Mrs. de Groot picked an invisible piece of lint off her skirt and discarded it. When she looked up again, her expression was still strangely shuttered. "Ellie had some concerns about that marriage, as I recall."

Sarah didn't have to pretend to be surprised. "I wonder that she allowed it then."

"Julia was always a headstrong girl," Mrs. de Groot said with a small smile. "I think Ellie had long since given up trying to control her."

Sarah didn't dare look at her mother. Sarah's sister, Maggie, had been headstrong and refused all efforts to control her. Her stubbornness had led to her tragic death. Sarah knew her parents blamed themselves and mourned Maggie to this day. The Decker family knew all too well the consequences of refusing a young woman's desire to marry.

"Mrs. Breedlove might want to know her concerns were well-founded," Sarah said. "If you could tell us where we can find her, we can give her the opportunity to help her daughter."

An emotion Sarah couldn't name flickered across Mrs. de Groot's patrician face. "I couldn't possibly do that. I believe Ellie had good reasons for leaving the city and making sure no one knew where she went."

"Then she really did intend to disappear completely," her mother said with what looked like genuine surprise. "I wondered."

"Did Mrs. Breedlove leave the city because of Chet Longly?" Sarah asked, sure she was right.

Mrs. de Groot's eyes widened in surprise. "I can't speak to Ellie's reasons for doing anything she did."

"And you won't tell us where she is?" Sarah's mother asked.

"I can't." Which could mean many things.

"Then will you at least let her know that Julia needs her?" Sarah asked.

"I cannot make any promises. You are asking me to become involved in something that is none of my affair, after all."

Sarah wanted to scream. "But—"

"It's all right, Sarah," her mother said. "Patricia is correct. We had no right to ask this of her. I'm sorry to have upset you, Patricia. You must do what you feel is right. Come along, Sarah. We've done what we can."

They took their leave without even waiting for a maid to escort them. When they were inside Sarah's electric motorcar with the windows closed, giving them privacy, Sarah almost did scream. "I can't believe she refused to help."

"Don't be so sure she won't."

"What do you mean?"

Her mother smiled. "First of all, we found out something very important."

"What?" Sarah asked, honestly confused.

"Patricia knows where Ellie Breedlove is."

Sarah sat back in her seat and thought back on the conversation. "Good heavens, you're right."

"Of course I am. We gave her every opportunity to say she didn't know where Ellie was, and she never did. She was too busy refusing to get involved."

"But even if she does know, it won't help unless she tells us," Sarah said with a sigh.

"Or unless she tells Ellie that Julia is in trouble and needs her. Ellie might have gone into hiding because she was afraid of Chet Longly, but don't underestimate a mother's desire to protect her child."

Her parents had shown just such a desire when they had forbidden Maggie to marry a man they could never approve of. Sarah hoped Ellie Breedlove could help her child more effectively than her parents had done. "Do you think Mrs. de Groot really will contact Ellie?"

"I would almost guarantee it. At the very least, we are sure she knows where Ellie is and how to contact her. If all else fails, we can have Julia call on her when she is released and beg her to help."

"I would love to see that," Sarah said.

FRANK HAD GONE INTO THE OFFICE MONDAY MORNING so he would have something to do while he waited for Sarah to report back on her mother's news. Gino was also there, since they hadn't been able to think of anything for either of them to do while Sarah and Maeve were investigating.

"Maybe we should go to see this attorney Breedlove hired," Gino suggested when they'd returned from lunch after spending the morning writing up reports on what they had learned so far. Maeve could type them when she returned from her undercover tasks. "What's his name?"

"Klein," Frank said. "Why would we need to see him?"

"To find out what he's planning to do." They were in Frank's office. Gino sat in one of the client chairs and had propped his feet up on Frank's desk.

"I think we already know what he's planning to do," Frank said. "He wants to get Julia released from the asylum."

Gino gave him a mock glare. "I know that, but the question is *how*. He might know things we don't."

"Things about Julia?"

"No, things about the law. He's an attorney, after

all. They always know a trick or two to get around the rules."

"You mean they know ways to bend the law," Frank said, not bothering to hide his contempt.

"It's a skill that can come in handy," Gino pointed out with a grin.

"Seems to me that Klein should be contacting us to find out what we know. He's going to need all the help he can get to see Julia released."

"Unless he knows something we don't," Gino said.

From what Frank had heard about Klein, he probably did know at least a dozen ways to bend the law, but did he know enough facts about Julia? Frank was seriously considering contacting the attorney when they heard the main office door open.

Gino quickly removed his feet from Frank's desk and jumped up. He hurried out to greet their visitor.

"May I help you?" Gino asked.

Frank couldn't see who had come in, but he recognized the voice that replied. "Is Mr. Malloy in?"

Frank was on his feet in an instant and hurrying to his office door.

"May I tell him who's calling?" Gino asked as he had been instructed, but Frank was in the outer office now.

"Dr. Ziegler," he said by way of greeting. "How can I help you?"

The good doctor looked a bit harried. He'd pulled off his hat and not bothered to smooth down his hair. His suit was wrinkled, and his shirt collar a bit limp. But then he hadn't looked exactly neat when Frank and Sarah had visited him in his own office either. "I need to speak with you, Mr. Malloy."

He glanced at Gino, who was watching the exchange with great interest. "In private."

"Of course. Right this way." He gave Gino a glance that silently told him not to ask any questions and escorted Ziegler into his office.

The doctor took the chair Gino had vacated and Frank closed the door to give them the privacy Ziegler had requested.

"What brings you here today?" Frank asked, not certain if he should be alarmed or flattered that Ziegler had sought him out.

"I did not know where else to go, but you had given me your card, so I came here. It is about Mrs. Longly."

"I assumed as much. Is she all right?"

Ziegler curled his lip in distaste. "As far as I know, she is fine."

Frank hid his surprise at the odd reaction. "Then why are you here?"

"You were working to free Mrs. Longly, were you not?"

"I still am."

Now it was Ziegler's turn to be surprised. "You do not know then?"

"Know what?"

"She is being released."

This seemed impossible.

Or maybe not. "Then you and the other doctors agreed that she should not have been admitted to the asylum?" Which was the only way Ziegler had indicated an inmate could be released.

"Certainly not." He seemed insulted by the very suggestion.

"Then how did she get released?"

"She has not been yet, which is why I have come to you. I beg you to stop this."

"Stop what? If you and the other doctors didn't release her, then how——?"

"The judge."

"What judge?"

"How do I know? Judges can decide these things. They have a trial, and the judge says if someone can be released."

Frank thought of Klein and all the things he'd heard about him. Then he remembered what Gino had said about knowing how to bend the law. "Does this happen often?"

"Never have I heard of it, not without the doctors saying it should happen."

Well, it might be unusual, but it was certainly good for Julia Longly. "Let me get this straight. Someone brought Mrs. Longly's case before a judge who has ordered that she be released from the asylum?"

"That is what I have said to you."

Frank frowned, still confused. "That is exactly what I was working for myself, so why have you come to me?"

"As I said, you must stop this."

"Why would I even try? As you know, I never thought she should have been there in the first place."

"Then you are wrong, Mr. Malloy. I know Mrs. Longly's family hired you to help them get her released, but I do not know how to find them. But I have your card and it has your address, so I am here to beg you to help. You must stop this."

Frank had encountered a lot of liars in his time, and he could almost always tell when someone was acting in their own best interest, but Dr. Ziegler didn't appear to be doing that. He was genuinely distressed. "Why should I even try to stop it, Dr. Ziegler?"

"Because Mrs. Longly is a dangerous woman, and she will do something terrible if she is released."

IX

Victor had wanted to draw that morning, and as before, he had drawn a crude picture of Miss Winterbourne by the window and the bad lady nearby. The bad lady was still little more than a scribbled blob, but Victor was clearly disturbed by his own artwork. He refused to talk about it, though, or answer any of Maeve's questions. Maeve was determined to learn more, so this time, when Victor went down for his nap in the afternoon, she took the drawing to the kitchen.

Mrs. O'Hara looked up from kneading bread on the kitchen table and greeted her with a smile that faded when she saw Maeve's grim expression.

"What is it, girl? Has something happened to Master Victor?"

Maeve held up the drawing for her to see. "Master Victor

keeps drawing this same picture, and Mrs. Pauly won't tell me the truth about it."

"What is it?" the cook asked, squinting as if that would make Victor's crude efforts clearer.

"He says it's Miss Winterbourne, and I believe she is standing at the nursery window, and Victor tells me this"— she pointed to the scribbled blob—"is what he calls the bad lady. Mrs. Pauly insists he imagined her, but I don't think so."

The cook stared at the drawing for a long moment and tears slowly filled her eyes. "God bless him," she murmured, her voice breaking a bit. She absently wiped her flour-covered hands on her apron, pulled out one of the chairs, and sank down into it as if her legs could no longer hold her. "We didn't think he saw what happened."

"What did happen?" Maeve said, carefully laying the picture on the table, away from the bread-making mess but still where Mrs. O'Hara could see it. Then she pulled out a chair across from the woman and sat down, too.

The cook dashed a tear from her eye with a knuckle. "We don't know for sure but . . . Miss Winterbourne would never have killed herself. I know that for sure."

"You said she was your friend," Maeve said to encourage her. "What do you know about her death?"

"That's just it. We only know she fell from the nursery window. It was late evening and dark because it was winter, but the other servants hadn't gone upstairs yet, so nobody heard anything until . . ." Her voice broke again, and she wrapped her arms around herself as if for comfort. "I'll never forget her scream, as if the demons of hell were after her, and then that awful thud. I hear it in my sleep sometimes."

A tear slid unheeded down her face and a chill ran up Maeve's spine. "Did Master Victor tell anyone what he saw?"

"I only know what they told me, mind, but they said he wouldn't speak. Miss Winterbourne had put him to bed, and he may have been asleep, but her scream would've woken him. It would have woken the dead," she added grimly.

"How awful," Maeve said, thinking how *very* awful that was.

"He was hiding in his room when somebody finally thought to go upstairs. We all ran outside first because that's where she . . . she fell. The maids was screaming and I guess I was, too. Mrs. Pauly finally remembered poor Master Victor and she went up to check on him."

"Didn't Mr. Longly hear it happen?"

Mrs. O'Hara stiffened. "He . . . he was out. He didn't know anything until . . . Well, Mrs. Pauly sent Vogler for him."

So Longly wasn't even home when Miss Winterbourne died. How very interesting. And if they sent Vogler for him, they had known where he was. Had he been at his mistress's house? "Who's Vogler?" Maeve asked with creditable innocence.

"He was our driver before . . . Well, before Mr. Longly let him go."

Maeve nodded. "And I suppose Mrs. Longly was already gone, on her rest cure."

Mrs. O'Hara frowned. "Oh no, she was still here then, in her room, but she claimed she never heard a thing."

"How is that possible?" Maeve asked. "I mean, if the rest of you heard it . . ."

"Just be glad she's gone now," Mrs. O'Hara said. She

rubbed her eyes with the corner of her apron, erasing the last vestiges of her tears.

Maeve wasn't ready to let it go, though. She still had questions. "But what could have happened if Miss Winterbourne was alone in the nursery except for Master Victor? And why was the window even open? It was still winter, you said."

"Nobody knows, not for certain, and you better not let Mrs. Pauly hear you asking about it."

"But if Master Victor saw something that upset him—and he must have at least heard Miss Winterbourne's scream—then I need to know. And what if the woman he calls the bad lady was real and she was responsible for Miss Winterbourne's death?"

"That's all over now. She's gone, and you don't need to worry your head about it anymore."

"Who's gone? Do you mean Miss Winterbourne?"

Mrs. O'Hara smiled mirthlessly. "No, not Miss Winterbourne, although she's gone for sure." The shadow of grief darkened her face for a moment.

"Who then? Not Mrs. Longly, surely."

"Why not her? Because she's a fancy lady with money and jewels and expensive clothes and lives in a big house?"

Maeve could hardly believe what she was hearing. "Are you saying she had something to do with Miss Winterbourne's death?"

"I don't know," Mrs. O'Hara said with some vehemence. "Nobody knows because nobody saw it, but nobody is sorry she's gone either."

Poor Julia, even the servants held her in contempt. "Why not?"

"You're still a child, ain't you?" Mrs. O'Hara said with some sympathy. "Because with her gone there's no more screaming and fighting and sly looks and locked bedroom doors and—"

"She locked her bedroom doors?" Maeve echoed, sure she had discovered something important. "She must have been afraid of something then."

But Mrs. O'Hara only smiled that eerie grin again. "*She* didn't lock her doors. *He* did."

"What's going on here?" Mrs. Pauly asked, having appeared in the doorway.

Amazingly, Mrs. O'Hara didn't seem the least bit alarmed at being caught gossiping about the family, although Maeve couldn't help feeling a bit guilty herself. Her instinct was to snatch up Victor's drawing before Mrs. Pauly saw it, but that would only call attention to it, so she resisted the urge.

"Nothing at all," Mrs. O'Hara said. "Just having a cozy chat with Miss Smith."

Plainly, Mrs. Pauly knew she was lying but for some reason she didn't pursue it. "What's that?" she asked instead, indicating the drawing with a jerk of her chin.

"Some of Master Victor's artwork. I was just showing Mrs. O'Hara. He's very talented."

"You shouldn't encourage him to draw such ugly things," Mrs. Pauly said uneasily, looking away from the drawing. "He needs to forget Miss Winterbourne."

"I don't think children forget things easily, especially things that frighten them," Maeve said.

"What do you know about it?" Mrs. Pauly sniffed. "You're just a child yourself."

"Maybe because I still remember what it's like," Maeve

said, annoyed at being called a child twice now in just a few minutes.

Mrs. Pauly was also annoyed. "You'll keep a civil tongue in your head, Miss Smith, and you'll stop asking questions about things that are none of your concern. If Mr. Longly hears about it, he'll send you packing and no mistake."

Maeve wasn't too concerned about losing her job, but she didn't want to be banished until she had more answers about the strange goings-on at the Longly house. "I'm sorry if I offended, but it's my job to make sure Master Victor is well taken care of. How can I do that if I don't know what might be bothering him?"

"Nothing is bothering him now," Mrs. Pauly insisted. "He's safe. We're all safe, and you should be grateful. Now leave Mrs. O'Hara to her work and mind your own business."

Maeve risked a glance at Mrs. O'Hara, who looked oddly unmoved by this conversation. Then she picked up Victor's drawing and left the kitchen, climbing the flights of stairs to the nursery. Victor was still sleeping when she checked on him, so she reconciled herself to an hour or two of utter boredom, waiting for him to wake up while she was under orders from Mrs. Pauly not to gossip with the other staff.

Just when she was beginning to despair, Kate came in to clean. She glanced around. "Is Master Victor still sleeping?"

"Yes. I don't think you'll bother him if you're quiet."

She grinned at that. "Sweeping and dusting don't make much noise."

Maeve grinned back, but hers meant more. She was thinking this was the perfect opportunity to question Kate, though she would have to be careful not to alarm her.

The girl started sweeping and Maeve watched her for a

moment. She'd gotten used to having a maid to clean since the Malloys had married, and she didn't miss doing house-work, but she didn't mind it either. What better way to ingratiate herself with Kate?

"I can help. Hand me your feather duster," Maeve said.

Kate looked like she was going to protest but she must have realized how silly that would be. She handed Maeve the duster. Maeve made her way around the room while Kate finished sweeping the floor.

"How long have you worked for the Longlys?" Maeve asked after a moment.

"About three years now, I guess."

"Did Miss Winterbourne always take care of Master Victor?"

Kate paused in her sweeping, looking up so she could see Maeve's face and possibly to judge her intention. Apparently, Maeve had managed to look innocent enough to placate her. "No, she came right after I did. Before that, they had a baby nurse to look after him."

"I guess Master Victor was very fond of Miss Winter-bourne."

"We all liked her," Kate said, although her tone was stiff, as if the words hurt her to say.

"Even Mrs. Longly?"

Kate stopped again, and this time her expression had turned cold. "We don't talk about her. Mrs. Pauly must've told you."

"I'm sorry. I know I'm not supposed to ask, but everyone acts so strangely when I mention her that it scares me."

"You don't have to be scared. She's gone now, and she's not coming back. Mr. Longly promised us."

How very odd. Employers didn't make promises to their

servants. Employers often didn't consider them at all. "Were you frightened of her when she was here?"

"I told you, we don't talk about her." Kate's statement sounded almost like a plea.

Maeve knew better than to press her. Kate might report this conversation to Mrs. Pauly and get Maeve fired. She wasn't ready to leave just yet. She decided to try another tactic the Malloys had taught her. She continued to dust but did not say another word. Few people could tolerate silence, so she waited to see if Kate would try to fill it.

The silence seemed to grow bigger somehow as the seconds ticked by. Did Kate feel it, too?

Apparently she did, because after only a few minutes she said, "Mr. Longly sent her away."

"He sent Mrs. Longly away, you mean?" Maeve said, trying to look surprised.

"Yes," Kate admitted reluctantly.

"Why did he do that?"

Kate took great interest in sweeping a small pile of dirt into the dustpan. Maeve waited patiently and was rewarded when she said, "We were afraid of her."

"Why?" Maeve asked, feeling suddenly cold.

"We all thought . . . Miss Winterbourne didn't fall out of the window by accident."

"Do you really think Mrs. Longly pushed her?"

"We didn't know, but she hated Miss Winterbourne."

How strange. "Why?" Maeve repeated.

"Because Master Victor loved her."

They both looked up when the door to Victor's bedroom opened and he stuck his tousled head out. "Miss Smith?"

Maeve laid down the duster and hurried to him. "I'm right here. Did you have a good sleep?"

He rubbed one eye with a small fist. "I don't know. I was asleep."

That made her smile in spite of the lingering pall Kate's revelations had raised. "Kate was just cleaning the nursery. It's such a nice day, maybe you'd like to walk to the park so we're out of her way."

He looked up with eyes still unfocused. "I thought Miss Winterbourne was here."

Kate gave a little gasp, but Maeve quickly said, "No, darling, she's not. Let's get you ready and we'll go for that walk." She gave Kate a warning look and was glad to see the girl immediately return to her cleaning, as if nothing untoward had happened.

As she helped Victor into his jacket, she couldn't stop her sigh of frustration. Why was it that every time she found out something new, she was stopped from pursuing it? Could Julia Longly really have pushed her son's nursemaid out a window? Such a thing seemed too far-fetched even for a penny-dreadful novel. Women like Julia Longly simply did not go around killing people, not even servants. And yet, Kate seemed genuinely afraid of her, and the other servants did, too. And why would Mr. Longly lock his bedroom door? There was also the fact that he had locked Julia away in an insane asylum. Could she really be insane? But if so, why were the Malloys convinced she wasn't?

FRANK SHOULD HAVE BEEN THRILLED TO HEAR THAT JUlia Longly might be released from the asylum, but Dr. Ziegler's visit had made him question everything he knew about her. When he'd first met the good doctor, Frank had thought him merely arrogant and unwilling to admit he had made a mistake. His attitude today had been different, however. He seemed genuinely alarmed that Julia might be released. Could they have misjudged her?

"What are you going to do?" Gino asked when Ziegler was gone. Ziegler had been frustrated by Frank's inability to intervene in the legal proceedings and had left in a huff.

"I don't know what I *can* do," Frank said. They were in his office again, as they had been when Ziegler arrived, except Gino no longer had his feet up on Frank's desk. Instead, he was leaning forward on his elbows, animated by Ziegler's sense of urgency. "Ziegler didn't know the name of the judge or even what court would hear Julia's case. I can call on Breedlove, I suppose, but he's probably attending the hearing or whatever it is."

"I guess if he gets Julia out, he won't need us anymore," Gino said thoughtfully. "He's bound to let us know we're fired at least."

"I'm surprised he didn't ask us to attend the hearing, too. That's why he hired us, after all, to get evidence that would free her."

"And according to Ziegler, he didn't have support from the doctors either. So how does he think he's going to convince a judge?"

Frank had his suspicions, but there was no use in speculating. "I'll telephone Breedlove's house and see if he's home or when he's expected back. He's probably the only one who can answer our questions."

But Breedlove wasn't home and the girl who answered the phone didn't know when he would be.

"What are you going to do now?" Gino repeated with more than a trace of irony this time.

"Wait until this evening and go see Breedlove. Whatever

court proceedings are happening will be over by then and we should be able to get some answers."

I SHOULD GO WITH YOU," SARAH SAID WHEN MALLOY HAD quickly explained Ziegler's news after allowing the children to celebrate his homecoming with squeals and reports of what they had done at school that day, and then sending them back to the nursery with his mother.

"Breedlove would think that was odd. Why would my wife accompany me to a business meeting?"

He was right, of course, but Sarah couldn't help thinking her presence might be needed. "If Julia really was released, then she might appreciate some female support."

"She probably would, but Mrs. Breedlove will be there and their daughter. I forget her name." They were still standing in the front hallway, and he glanced around to make sure no one was overhearing them. No sense alarming their servants. "Let's go into the parlor."

When he had closed the door behind them, he said, "Now what news did your mother have for you today?"

"My goodness, I should have told you first thing. She located a woman who was a close friend to Julia's mother and may still be in contact with her."

"When can you see her?"

"We already did. Mother was sure she would receive us, and she was right."

He grinned at that. "Good work. Does this woman know where the mother is?"

Sarah led him over to the sofa and they sat down. "She wouldn't admit it, but she didn't deny it either. Mother believes she knows, and I agree."

"Wait, you didn't tell her Julia was in an asylum, did you?"

"Of course not. We hinted that her husband was abusing her and she needed a refuge. We said we were sure her mother would provide that for her, but we didn't know how to contact her."

"Did this friend agree to help?"

"No, but Mother believes she will if we make Julia sound desperate enough."

"I guess that depends on how soon the Breedloves want to be rid of her, assuming he's successful at getting her released."

"I'm sure if Mr. Breedlove wants your help in finding his sister-in-law, he'll tell you."

He frowned and leaned back in his seat, staring off into space.

"What is it?" she asked.

"I didn't tell you everything about Ziegler's visit. He didn't just drop by to tell me the good news. He came to ask me to stop them from releasing Julia. He claims she is too dangerous to be let out of the asylum."

"That's ridiculous," Sarah said. "How dangerous could a woman like her be?"

"I agree, but he was adamant."

"Did he explain why he thought that?"

"No. He seemed to think I should take his word for it, and when I didn't, he left."

"I don't think those doctors at the asylum know anything at all," Sarah said.

"They even admit it, but that doesn't help us. At least it looks like Julia may well be released. That's really all we could hope for."

"She'll need a place to live, though," Sarah said, thinking how bleak a future Julia might have with no income and if no one would give her shelter.

"Breedlove will take her in for now, and maybe you can find her mother."

"The mother might still be frightened of Chet Longly, though. If she left the city to hide from him, she might not want to take Julia for fear of drawing his wrath."

"Julia will probably want to hide from him, too. If no one tells him where they are, they'll both be safe from him."

Sarah smiled wanly. "You're right, or at least I hope you are. When are you going to see Breedlove?"

"I thought I'd go tonight. If they haven't had the hearing yet, at least I can warn him about Ziegler. I think he would have interfered if he had any idea where to find them."

"If you see Julia, by any chance, ask her if she knows where her mother is. If she does, then we can stop looking."

"I'll try."

THE MAID WHO ANSWERED THE DOOR AT THE BREEDLOVE house seemed surprised. Unexpected visitors didn't just drop in at this hour. The maid recognized Frank, though, and he had to wait only a few minutes until he was escorted to the front parlor where Breedlove awaited him.

The man looked jubilant. "We got Julia back," he announced without even bothering with a greeting.

"I heard you might."

Breedlove's smile faded. "Where would you have heard that?"

"Ziegler, Julia's doctor at the Manhattan State Hospital, came to my office this afternoon."

"Whatever for?" Breedlove was outraged.

"To ask me to stop you from getting her released."

"What arrogance!" Breedlove said.

"I thought so, but he obviously thought he was justified in some way."

"But why on earth did he go to you?"

"He said he didn't know how to contact you, but I had given him my card when my wife and I spoke with him about Julia. He may have thought I could convince you."

Breedlove made a sound of disgust. "I can't believe he'd be so presumptuous."

"How did you manage to get Julia released, though?" Frank asked, genuinely curious. "Ziegler had told us that for that to happen, the doctors would all have to agree and recommend it to the judge, and plainly Ziegler did not agree."

Breedlove grinned with so much self-satisfaction that Frank almost winced. "Not if you find the right judge. My attorney did that, and the judge only had to speak with Julia for a few minutes to determine that she is as sane as you and I."

So that was how Ziegler had heard about the hearing. They had taken Julia to the court. And now Frank also knew how Breedlove had gotten this accomplished. "How much did it cost you?"

"I . . . I don't know what you're talking about," Breedlove said, but the way his face turned scarlet belied his words.

"Klein found you a judge who was willing to take a bribe to declare Julia sane," Frank said patiently, as if explaining the concept to Breedlove for the first time. "I'm just curious to know how much such a thing is worth."

Breedlove's face grew even redder, but he said, "About

the same as one of those dresses my daughter is having made for her coming out, and worth every penny."

"I suppose it is, when you consider you've saved Julia from a horrible fate."

"Oh yes, that, too," Breedlove said as if he hadn't thought of it before. "I couldn't leave her in that place when I had the power to save her."

Neither man had noticed the parlor door open until Julia said, "And I must thank you for freeing me, Uncle."

The men looked up in surprise, and Breedlove smiled, although Frank didn't think he looked as happy as he might have in this, his moment of triumph.

"No thanks are necessary, my dear," Breedlove said generously.

"Mrs. Longly, it's very good to see you," Frank said, not positive that was the most appropriate greeting but he had never greeted anyone newly freed from an asylum.

Julia looked a great deal better than she had the other times he had seen her. Her hair was combed and pinned up in an attractive style. She wore a simple dress but one that had obviously been made for her. She even looked younger, with the strain of being in the asylum no longer on her face. "And I must thank you, too, Mr. Malloy. And your wife. Is she with you?"

"No, but I'll tell her you asked about her. She would be happy to call on you, if you like."

"If it suits her, although I wouldn't blame her for shunning me. Most people will, I'm sure, if not for my sojourn in the asylum then for leaving my husband, even though I had no choice in that."

"Mr. Malloy came to warn me that Ziegler tried to get his help in preventing your release," Breedlove said.

"Did he?" Julia asked but she didn't seem surprised.

"Yes," Frank said, feeling compelled to warn her. "I suppose he thought I could convince your uncle to change his mind, and he was upset when I told him I couldn't."

"The doctors in that place are used to getting their way in everything," she said with just a touch of bitterness.

"You should probably also know that he told me it would be dangerous to release you."

"Dangerous for whom?" Breedlove scoffed.

"He didn't say, but he was quite determined."

"Of course he was," Julia said. "Dr. Ziegler has personal reasons for wanting to keep me there."

"What personal reasons could he have?" Breedlove asked.

Instead of addressing him, she turned to Frank. "You recall that I told you the nurses beat me. They beat all the patients, of course, but they took greater delight in abusing someone they recognized as their better."

"I remember," Frank said, feeling the same outrage he had felt the first time.

"The nurses aren't concerned that we will report them to the doctors, as I explained, because the doctors will simply ignore the complaints. I explained that, too, but I didn't tell you the real reason why."

Frank could guess, however. "Mrs. Longly, you don't have to—"

"Oh, but I do, Mr. Malloy. My uncle needs to know so he will be prepared. You see, Uncle, the doctors didn't dare chasten the nurses for mistreating the inmates because they were doing far worse."

Plainly, Breedlove had guessed as well. "Julia, this isn't a fit topic for—"

"No, it is not, but you must hear it all the same. Dr.

Ziegler did not want to see me released because he was used to having me whenever he wanted me and using me as his concubine."

"Julia, please," Breedlove said, obviously horrified.

Frank was horrified as well, but he was also amazed at how calmly she had shared this humiliating news.

"So Ziegler has a very good reason to keep me as his prisoner in that place," she continued. "If he tries to cause any trouble, you should reveal that you know all about his debauchery, Uncle."

"I . . ." Breedlove had to clear his throat. "I certainly will," he managed.

Neither man knew what to say next. Every other topic seemed inappropriate somehow.

Fortunately, Julia saved them from having to think of something. "My uncle tells me you are trying to locate my mother so he can turn me over to her," she said to Frank.

Frank glanced at Breedlove, who was looking suitably abashed. He had obviously wasted no time in warning Julia she wasn't welcome to make her home with them. "Yes, I am. I was going to ask if you had any idea where she might be living."

"None whatsoever."

He had expected this. "We know she was afraid of your husband, so naturally, she didn't tell you where she was going, but we thought maybe you knew of a place where she had friends or had enjoyed visiting in the past."

Julia was giving him a rather odd look, as if she were just seeing him for the first time. "How clever of you to figure out that Mother was hiding from Chet."

"It was a logical assumption," Frank said, not sure if he was correct, but it seemed logical to him.

"We explained to Julia how awkward it would be for her to live with us," Breedlove said with the bravado of one who knows he is in the wrong but is determined to pretend he is not. "People would be forever asking her why she left her husband and other questions that are none of their business. This would give her all the attention when we only want the attention on Ruth."

Oh yes, Ruth was the daughter. He'd have to remember.

"Yes," Julia said with a small smile to show she understood her uncle's dilemma perfectly. "Uncle also explained that I will be much more comfortable with my mother, somewhere away from the city and the gossip I would naturally be subjected to here, even if no one ever found out my husband had sent me to an insane asylum."

"And if she remains here, someone may well find out," Breedlove added helpfully. "We simply want to protect her from that."

"Then you're willing to live with your mother if we can locate her?" Frank asked.

She smiled at that. "I would be most interested in seeing my mother again, Mr. Malloy. I hope you will continue your search." She turned to Breedlove. "You will continue to employ him to do that, won't you?"

"Of course," Breedlove said. "We want to see you comfortably settled as quickly as possible."

Settled and far away from them, Frank thought. Julia was thinking the same thing if her smirk was any indication.

"I should also very much like to see my son," Julia said to no one in particular.

Breedlove frowned. "I told you, my dear, Chet is hardly likely to agree to that."

"He doesn't have to agree. I can simply go to the house and see him."

"Perhaps you should wait until I've had an opportunity to speak with Chet," Breedlove suggested hastily. "He doesn't even know that you're free yet. Once he does, I'm sure he'll start to see reason, and a mother should be allowed to see her child."

"My thoughts exactly. Don't you agree, Mr. Malloy?"

"It doesn't matter what I think." And he was pretty sure Chet Longly would never allow Julia to see Victor if he could help it.

"Well, he'll find out soon enough that I'm free, at any rate. I've written Chet a letter asking him to send me my things, unless he's already given them to his whore. This is the dress I was wearing when those brutes came for me, and it's all I have at the moment."

Breedlove frowned. "There's no need to send him a letter. I was going to call on him tomorrow and tell him the news. I can ask him then to send your things over. He's much more likely to be amenable if I break the news to him."

"Chet is never amenable about anything," Julia said with complete assurance, "but he can have no use for my clothing. That woman he keeps is much too fat for them, so don't let him deny you, Uncle."

"I'm sure he will have no objections to returning your things, Julia," Breedlove said.

"And I am sure he will cause me as much inconvenience as he possibly can. I think you underestimate how furious he will be when he finds out you have thwarted him."

"I am fully prepared to deal with that."

Frank couldn't help wondering if he really was, but he

said, "I will continue trying to locate your mother, Mrs. Longly. My only concern is that she might still be too afraid of Chet Longly to help you."

She gave him an odd little smile. "Don't worry about that. If you bring us together, I will take care of everything."

X

Good heavens," Sarah exclaimed when Malloy had told her about Julia's confession that Dr. Ziegler had raped her repeatedly. "No wonder she was so anxious to get out of that place. It was even more horrible than we could imagine." The children were safely in bed, and they were in their private parlor upstairs where no one would disturb them.

"And that explains why Ziegler was so determined not to allow her to be released. Not only would he lose his access to her, but she might tell someone about his crimes."

"She is much more dangerous than the usual inmate, too," Sarah said. "She might tell someone with the power to do something about it, unlike most of the other women in that place, who wouldn't have the social position to even be heard."

"And most of the other women in that place will never have the opportunity since they will never be released."

"I hate to keep saying *poor Julia*, but how awful for her. I can't even imagine the humiliation of it."

"At least she managed to escape," Malloy said. "We can take a little comfort in that."

"If only there was some way to punish her husband for putting her through such a terrible ordeal."

"I'm sure my mother would say God will punish him."

Sarah smiled. "I hope she's right."

SARAH WAS ONLY TOO GLAD TO CALL ON JULIA LONGLY the next afternoon. They needed to find out if Julia would write a heartfelt message to her mother that they could deliver when they located her. This message might well convince her to help Julia escape the city, although Sarah could easily imagine Julia's resentment at having to be the one who left her privileged life in New York behind to live in seclusion somewhere in the country. She wouldn't even be able to remarry, so she was doomed to a rather lonely existence, although it would undoubtedly be preferable to spending the rest of her life in an insane asylum.

The Breedloves had no other visitors that afternoon, which wasn't surprising. No one knew Julia was there and the Breedloves had been back in the country for only a few weeks. Julia was sitting with a middle-aged woman and a girl of about eighteen when Sarah arrived. She introduced them as her aunt Amelia Breedlove and cousin Ruth. Both women were dressed in the height of fashion in gowns that were obviously brand-new. Sarah knew they were preparing to bring Ruth out in New York society, and while that didn't actually require an updated wardrobe, such a thing couldn't hurt a girl's chances of being noticed.

Sarah had also dressed with care, choosing to look like the wife of a millionaire today instead of like a private investigator's assistant. She saw Mrs. Breedlove judging her gown and registering surprise. For her part, Ruth simply looked bored and spared Sarah hardly a glance.

"I'm so glad you came," Julia said when they had offered tea and Sarah had accepted. "I wanted to thank you for coming to visit me in that place." She wore a simple day dress, probably the one she'd told Malloy was the only gown she had with her at the moment.

"We were quite moved by your story, Mrs. Longly," Sarah said. "We're very glad you were released."

"Not as glad as I am, I'm sure," she said with a smirk. "But I find it's useless to lament the past. We can only look forward. Isn't that right, Ruth?"

Ruth looked up in surprise. She was rather a plain girl, in spite of her expensive clothes and a hairstyle that some poor maid had probably spent an hour perfecting. "What?"

"Nothing," Julia said, earning a frown from her aunt. She turned back to Sarah. "My aunt is planning to bring Ruth out into society this spring."

"That was my understanding," Sarah said, turning to Mrs. Breedlove. "My husband told me you have lived in England for several years."

"Yes, but we came back for Ruth's sake. I couldn't bear the thought of her marrying an Englishman and being so far away from us for the rest of her life."

"I hope someone has warned you that society here is much different from England, and girls make their debuts in a much simpler fashion."

Mrs. Breedlove gave her a condescending smile. "America

doesn't have a queen to present the young ladies to, of course."

"We also don't have the endless parties and balls where young people encounter each other and young men have the opportunity to choose a bride from among all the eligible girls. It's become a much less formal affair in recent years."

"I wonder how you know so much about it," Mrs. Breedlove said, still condescending.

"It hasn't been so very long since I made my own debut. I thought it was all rather silly, but my parents insisted."

Mrs. Breedlove's smile had slipped a bit. "And who are your parents, Mrs. Malloy?" Sarah noticed she placed a bit of emphasis on the Irish name, which should have marked Sarah as a member of the lower classes.

"Felix and Elizabeth Decker," Sarah said, not the least bit annoyed at being quizzed in such a manner since she knew the effect those names would have on anyone familiar with New York society.

They had the same effect on Mrs. Breedlove, who stiffened in her chair. "I see," was all she managed.

Sarah glanced at Ruth to see if she had the same reaction and caught her in a yawn.

"Ruth," her mother said sharply, startling the girl into straightening her back and focusing her gaze on Sarah, although she still had nothing to say.

"I don't suppose you are involved in this year's debutante ball," Mrs. Breedlove said.

"No," Sarah said, managing not to laugh outright at the very thought. "I don't have any relations who are the right age at the moment." Or for years to come, but she didn't say that.

"Will you or your parents be giving any entertainments

during the season? I'm sure we would be honored by an invitation." Mrs. Breedlove no longer looked condescending.

"As I said, there isn't really a season here as there is in
England. I'm afraid you will be sorely disappointed if that is
what you are expecting."

"It doesn't matter anyway," Ruth said, her lower lip ex-
tended in a pout. "As long as Julia is here, I won't get invited
anywhere. That's what Father said."

"Your father doesn't know everything, dear," Mrs. Breedlove said.

"I don't know why she couldn't just stay where she was,"
Ruth said, giving Julia a black look. "Nobody knew she was
there, so how could they gossip about it?"

Sarah couldn't help turning to Julia to see how she was
reacting to Ruth's ill-considered statements. The girl could
certainly have no idea what Julia had to endure at the asylum, but her words would hurt all the same.

Julia, however, seemed merely slightly amused. "I suppose you'd like for me to return to the asylum, wouldn't
you, Ruth?"

"I don't care what you do as long as you go someplace else."

"Ruth, that is quite enough," her mother said, obviously
embarrassed by her daughter's tactlessness. "Julia, please
don't pay her any mind. She's just a child and doesn't know
what she's saying."

"I know exactly what I'm saying," Ruth insisted. "We
came all the way back here from England so I could come
out and she's ruining everything. I'll never get a husband if
she's here. That's what you said to Father."

"I said no such thing," Mrs. Breedlove claimed, although
Sarah was sure she must have. The girl wouldn't have said

so otherwise. "Go to your room, Ruth. I'll speak to you about this later."

Ruth obviously didn't mind at all being sent to her room. She flounced out with a triumphant smile.

"I'm so sorry, Mrs. Malloy. I don't know what has gotten into her. Ever since we returned to New York, she's been impossible."

"There's no need to apologize to me, Mrs. Breedlove," Sarah said, looking meaningfully at Julia, who smiled graciously.

"Or me either," Julia said, although her aunt had made no attempt to do so. "I understand Ruth's frustration. I would have been upset if someone ruined my debut."

"Nothing is ruined," Mrs. Breedlove insisted. "And I understand that Mrs. Malloy's husband is going to contact your mother, so you'll soon be able to join her and leave all this unpleasantness behind."

"Yes," Julia said with a trace of irony. "I am anxious to leave the unpleasantness behind. Has your husband made any progress?" she asked Sarah.

"He hasn't had much time since you saw him last night, but he did ask if you would write a letter to your mother for him to deliver when he finds her. It should tell her what you have been through and ask her to open her home to you. She might not be willing to take my husband's word about the situation since it seems highly unusual."

"Unusual," Julia repeated thoughtfully. "That hardly describes it, I think. But I see what you mean. Even if she still fears Chet, her motherly instincts should compel her to help me when she knows what he did to me."

"That's it exactly," Sarah said.

"I'm sure she'd never refuse you, Julia. What mother could?" her aunt said.

"So true," Julia said as if she didn't really believe it. "I know I would do anything to see my son. Do you have children, Mrs. Malloy?"

"Yes, I do, a boy and a girl." She had not given birth to them, but they were her children in every other way.

"Then you know what I'm going through. It's bad enough that Chet put me in that horrible place but being separated from Victor has been unbearable."

"I wish I could offer you some hope that you'll be able to see him, but I can't imagine your husband would ever allow it."

Julia sighed. "I fear you are right. He is a monster."

"He must be to have put you in that place," her aunt said, shaking her head in despair. "I'm so glad your uncle was able to get you released."

Julia smiled at that although it looked a little strained. "Yes, Uncle Hugh was my knight in shining armor."

Did Sarah hear a note of sarcasm? Did Julia think her uncle should have done more? Or done it faster? Or was she judging Julia too harshly? Perhaps she was simply still angry at the horrors she had endured.

"If you write the letter," Sarah said to return the subject to something less emotional, "I will be happy to come back for it so my husband has it ready."

"How quickly does he expect to locate my mother?" Julia asked with amazement.

"Soon, we hope."

"Then he knows where she is?"

"Not yet, but we believe we have found someone who does."

"Someone she trusted more than her own daughter, I guess." Now Julia sounded bitter.

"If she was trying to hide from Mr. Longly, she couldn't take the chance that he would force you to tell him," Sarah said reasonably.

Julia studied her for a long moment, as if trying to make up her mind about something. "Yes, that would explain it, I suppose."

"Are you willing to write the letter?" Sarah asked, amazed that Julia still had not agreed.

"I will be happy to write my mother a letter."

They arranged that she would telephone Sarah's home when it was ready, and someone would pick it up. Sarah had hoped for some time alone with Julia, but plainly, Mrs. Breedlove had no intention of leaving them. Sarah finally had to give up and take her own leave.

"If you need me for anything, anything at all, just let me know," Sarah said, giving Julia her calling card.

"I can't imagine what she would need," Mrs. Breedlove said. "She has us, doesn't she?"

Which was why Sarah thought Julia might need someone to talk to, but she simply smiled and allowed the maid to show her out. Sarah had thought it was cruel to force Julia to leave the city and take refuge in seclusion, but if the comfort the Breedloves were offering was any indication, Julia would be much better off bored to tears for the rest of her life.

MAEVE HAD GONE TO THE KITCHEN WHEN VICTOR went down for his nap, even though she knew she didn't dare talk to Mrs. O'Hara about Miss Winterbourne or the bad lady or anything that she really wanted to talk about. Before she could decide on a safe topic, Mrs. Pauly came in, looking a bit distressed.

"Oh good, you're here, Maeve. Mr. Longly wants to see all of us immediately."

"All of us?" Mrs. O'Hara echoed in confusion. She'd been chopping vegetables for stew and she wiped her hands on her apron.

"Yes, all the servants. I've already told Kate and Iris. Come along. He's in the family parlor."

Mrs. O'Hara took the time to remove her apron and then the two of them followed Mrs. Pauly to the small back parlor, which was the room the family would normally use every day, saving the front parlor for company.

The two maids were already there, standing in the hallway outside the door, and Maeve didn't blame them. Who wanted to be in the room with Mr. Longly, who was going to tell them something they probably didn't want to hear while they waited for everyone else to arrive? Mrs. Pauly brushed past them and entered the parlor, silently giving the rest of them the signal to follow her.

Mr. Longly was standing in the middle of the room looking like he could spit nails and no one said a word lest he take out his fury on them. Finally, Mrs. Pauly said, "We are all here."

Longly nodded once at the group of females and his valet, who stood at a respectful distance from the women. "I'm sorry to have to tell you this, but Mrs. Longly's uncle has just left. He came to tell me that my wife has been released from the asylum."

Everyone gasped, including Maeve, because this was the last thing they had expected to hear. Kate actually started crying until Mrs. Pauly hissed out her name, frightening her into getting hold of herself.

Since Maeve had been told Mrs. Longly was away on a rest cure, she felt obliged to say, "Asylum?"

"Hush," Mrs. Pauly snapped. "I'll explain it later."

"You don't have to be afraid," Longly told them all, his voice amazingly kind, considering how furious he obviously was. "She's not coming back here to live. She'll never enter this house again."

"But what if she comes to the door?" Kate asked, her voice barely a whisper.

"Then slam it in her face. You don't have to be polite to her and you must not allow her in the house. Do you understand?"

Everyone nodded except Maeve, who wasn't sure how she should feel about this. They had been hired to get Julia Longly released from the asylum and now it seemed she had been, but Maeve was no longer sure this was the best thing. At this very moment she stood in a room with six people who apparently believed Julia should not have been released and probably posed some kind of threat to them.

"Miss Smith?" Longly said.

"I . . . I'm not sure I understand what's going on," she tried. She did have questions, many questions.

"Come with me," Mrs. Pauly said, but Mr. Longly held up a hand to stop her.

"I'll explain the situation to Miss Smith," he said. "She needs to know so she can protect Victor." He turned back to the two maids. "Do you know what you have to do?"

The girls nodded. "Yes, sir," they said in unison.

He looked at Mrs. O'Hara, who said, "I understand."

"And I understand, too," Mrs. Pauly said.

"You'll need to pack up all of Mrs. Longly's things and send them over to her uncle's house," he told her. "That's where she is staying."

"Where is that?"

"He gave me the address. It's on my desk. Now try not to think about this anymore. Nothing has really changed."

No one moved for a moment, and it was plain to Maeve that the other women didn't really believe that. Knowing Julia was no longer confined in the asylum had terrified them. Even Longly was disturbed.

"Go on now," Mrs. Pauly said after a moment. "Get back to work."

The maids and Mrs. O'Hara reluctantly left the room.

"You may go, too, Mrs. Pauly. I'll tell Miss Smith what she needs to know."

Mrs. Pauly frowned, obviously loath to leave, but she couldn't disobey her employer. When she was gone, Maeve turned to Mr. Longly expectantly.

"Maybe we should sit down for this," he said with a weary sigh. He was obviously still very upset by the news Mr. Breedlove had delivered, and Maeve was glad to sit down as well. This whole situation was more than disturbing.

Maeve took a seat on the sofa and Longly took a chair facing her. He ran his hand over his face and when he looked up again, his eyes were bleak. "I don't know what gossip you have heard from the rest of the staff, but a few weeks ago my wife was committed to the Manhattan State Hospital. It is a place on Ward's Island where they keep people who are insane."

Maeve knew all this, of course, but she knew better than to say so. "Is Mrs. Longly insane?"

He seemed surprised at the question, although he may

have been surprised only that Maeve had the temerity to ask it. "Not in the way most people think of insanity, but she is dangerous."

"You mean she's violent?"

Longly winced but he said, "She can be. We think . . . She may have been violent with some of the servants."

"Miss Winterbourne?" Maeve guessed.

His expression hardened. "As you may have been told, no one knows what happened the night Miss Winterbourne fell."

"But you suspect."

"Whatever happened, I decided it was best to send Mrs. Longly to a place where she could do no further harm."

"Do you think she might harm Victor?"

An emotion that might have been fear flickered across his face. "She professes to love him, but she cannot be trusted, Miss Smith. You must never allow her near him. Do you understand?"

"Yes, sir," she said, although her mind was racing. The Malloys were convinced Julia was perfectly sane and should never have been taken from her home and locked away, but everyone in this house was genuinely terrified of her. They couldn't be pretending. Julia had certainly done things to frighten them. She may have even killed Miss Winterbourne. And now the Malloys had helped to free her.

"You're very young and you've only been here a few days, so perhaps you would prefer not to be involved in all of this. No one could blame you, so if you would like to leave, I only ask that you tell me, so we are not caught unawares."

Here was her excuse for leaving, which she had planned to do shortly in any case, but she wasn't ready to go just yet, not if Julia was a threat to Victor. "I . . . You're right, Mr.

Longly. This is all very disturbing and not at all what I was expecting when I came here. I think . . . Well, you said you would understand if I didn't want to stay, and I'm afraid I don't, but I also don't want to leave Victor until he has a new nursemaid. I'm willing to stay on for a short time, until you find a replacement for me."

He nodded wearily. "Victor will be heartbroken, but I actually expected as much. I do appreciate your willingness to stay on until we replace you, however. And I will have Mrs. Pauly write you an excellent letter of recommendation to show my gratitude."

"I appreciate that, Mr. Longly. I'm very fond of Victor, and I think it will be easier for him if he has someone new to look after him before I'm gone."

"I'm sure it will be. I only hope I can find someone he likes as well as he likes you, Miss Smith."

Maeve's conscience pricked her. When she had devised this scheme, she hadn't considered Victor's feelings in the matter. He had just been a faceless boy to her, a means to an end. Now he was a real child with feelings and whom she cared for very much. How could she not have realized this would happen? She would have to make it up to Victor somehow when this was over.

If it ever was truly over. With Julia Longly free to go wherever she wished, how could Longly and Victor and their servants ever feel safe? She needed to see the Malloys right away and tell them what she had learned. Luckily, tomorrow was the servants' half day, so she would be able to go to the house and meet with them.

"I know tomorrow is supposed to be your half day," Longly was saying, "but under the circumstances, I think it would be unwise to leave Victor. Usually, I would take him on an outing, but I don't want him to leave the house until we know how Julia is going to behave. If you would stay with him tomorrow, I'll give you an extra day's pay."

The pay meant nothing to her, but she couldn't leave Victor, not if he might be in danger. She'd just have to figure out another way to warn the Malloys.

FRANK HAD ENJOYED A VISIT FROM A POTENTIAL CLIENT that afternoon, and he was getting ready to call it a day when he heard the main door to his offices open. Since he was alone, he rose to greet whoever had entered, but before he took a step, an angry voice called, "Malloy, are you here?"

Frank hurried out to the front office, where Maeve would be sitting if she were here, and found a very angry Chet Longly. "Is something wrong, Mr. Longly?" he asked, not bothering to conceal his sarcasm.

"Yes, my wife has been released from the hospital, and you're responsible."

Frank held up his hands in mock surrender. "I'm usually pretty good at my job, but I can't take credit for getting Mrs. Longly released."

Longly didn't look convinced, but he said, "Who should then?"

"Mr. Breedlove. He was entirely responsible."

Longly curled his lip in disgust. "That's not what he said."

How strange. "What did he say?"

"He said you got the doctors to change their minds and declare her sane, so she could be released."

This was more than strange. Why wouldn't Breedlove take the credit? And more important, why lie and give it to Frank? "I don't know why he would say that, but it isn't true."

"But isn't that what he hired you to do?"

"He hired me to find a way to get her released, but before I could, he told me he had found a sympathetic judge who was willing to release Julia based on what he observed just from holding a conversation with her." Which wasn't the whole truth, but Frank didn't want to slander Breedlove by mentioning the bribe if he didn't have to.

"Oh yes, Julia can be quite charming and perfectly reasonable when it suits her purpose. I'm sure that's the side of her she showed you as well."

She had been charming and reasonable with them, of course, but Frank wasn't going to get into that. "I know you must be angry that your wife was released from the hospital but I'm not sure why you've come to me about it."

Longly ran a hand over his face, and his hopeless expression made Frank start. "I thought you'd gotten her freed, so I was going to convince you to help me get her locked up again before she does something horrible."

"Mr. Longly," Frank tried, but Longly interrupted him.

"I know, you must think I'm some heartless monster who got tired of his wife and sent her to an asylum to get rid of her, but nothing could be further from the truth."

Someone was walking down the hallway and Frank realized anyone might overhear this conversation. He quickly closed the office door and said, "Come into my office and sit down, Mr. Longly. We can speak privately there."

Longly nodded and Frank escorted him into the other room. Longly had been furious when he entered the office, but now he looked as if the anger had burned him out. He sank down wearily into one of the client chairs.

When Frank had taken his own seat behind his

desk, Longly said, "Breedlove said you were still working for him."

Frank shrugged, unwilling to confirm or deny since he always kept the identity of his clients confidential.

Longly smiled bitterly. "I see, you don't want to say. But it doesn't matter. He told me you were going to locate Julia's mother."

"Do you happen to know where she is?" Frank asked. Might as well try.

But Longly shook his head. "She isn't likely to tell *me*, is she?"

"Is that because she fears you, Mr. Longly?"

Longly seemed genuinely surprised. "Why would she fear *me*? Oh, I'll admit, I was furious with her when I realized what she had done to me, but that was years ago."

Frank frowned in confusion. "What did she do to you?"

Longly sighed. "She did what every mother of a daughter does. She worked very hard to marry her daughter off to the most eligible suitor she could find. I couldn't fault her for that, but she knew what Julia was and she never . . . She let me marry Julia in complete ignorance and then she disappeared so I couldn't even . . . Well, I did want to send her back, but taking a wife isn't like buying something, is it? One can't return her if she proves unsatisfactory."

"Did you want to return her?" Frank asked in amazement.

"You really have no idea, do you?" Longly asked, equally amazed.

"If you mean I don't know what you're talking about, then no, I don't."

"Julia is . . . I have to say it: evil. I know that sounds ridiculous. It sounds ridiculous to me, too, but I know it's true. She cares for no one but herself, and she . . . she can be violent, too."

Frank thought back to the woman he'd met at the asylum. She had been so fragile and so frightened. He couldn't reconcile his impression of her with Longly's description. "How is she violent?"

"She injured one of our servants because . . . because she imagined I favored the girl in some way." Ah yes, he must mean the maid Tamar.

Plainly, Longly was embarrassed to admit this, but Frank couldn't help remembering Julia's assertion that Longly was thoroughly debauched and seduced the servants. He could imagine emotions running high in a situation like that. Could Julia really be the one who injured her or maybe the girl had attacked Julia and gotten the worst of it?

"There's more, much more," Longly said, "but I can tell you don't believe me. That's the trouble, you see. She can be whoever she wants to be, and if she doesn't want you to see that side of her, you never will."

"You must admit that what you're telling me is hard to believe."

"I wouldn't believe it myself if I hadn't seen it, but I've lived with her for five years and she stopped pretending with me long ago."

Frank shifted in his chair, increasingly uncomfortable with this conversation. "Mr. Longly, I'm not sure why you're telling me all this."

"Because you can't keep helping her. None of us are safe now that she's free again."

"You can't think that she'll do anything untoward," Frank insisted.

"I can and I do, and Breedlove must at least suspect what

she is. That's why he wants you to find her mother, because he wants to send Julia away from his own family."

Frank didn't want to admit anything, but he couldn't let Longly believe he was right. "Breedlove is only worried about the scandal affecting his daughter's social standing. Even if no one finds out Julia was in the asylum, the fact that she is living apart from you will cause a lot of gossip. He doesn't want that to overshadow his daughter's debut."

Longly smiled again, and this time his bitterness made Frank wince. "He's wasting his time, then. Ellie knows Julia better than anyone, and she will never take her back. Why do you think she disappeared in the first place?"

Frank had thought he knew, but now he was no longer sure. Still, he couldn't take Chet Longly's word for anything concerning Julia. The man had put his wife in an asylum. Even if Julia had exaggerated his other sins, that one was unforgivable. "If you think you can persuade me to change my allegiance from Breedlove to you, I'm afraid I have to disappoint you, Mr. Longly."

"Then whatever Julia does is on your head, Mr. Malloy. Remember that."

Longly strode out without another word, not even giving Frank a chance to rise to his feet, much less show him out. His words rang in Frank's ears, though. Either Longly fully expected Julia to do something outrageous or he was trying to frighten Frank into quitting Breedlove's employ. Was he really that determined that Ellie Breedlove not be found? What could she tell them about Longly and his wife that Longly didn't want them to know?

Frank had no idea what the answers were but maybe when they next spoke with Maeve, she would be able to help. He only wished he had dared ask about the well-being of Longly's new nursemaid.

How can he say Julia is evil?" Sarah asked that evening when the children were in bed and the two of them finally had a chance to talk about their day. They were in the downstairs parlor with Malloy's mother, who took advantage of the electric lights to knit in the evenings. Frank had just told them about his visit from Longly. "They say that women tend to be dramatic, but Mr. Longly could match that, it seems."

"Can he?" Malloy asked. "I really couldn't tell if he was just putting on a show or if he was genuinely worried about what Julia might do."

"You've met her. What do you think she could do?"

Malloy shrugged. "She looked pretty harmless when we saw her at the hospital, but I've seen people do things you'd never expect."

"I suppose I have, too, but I still can't imagine Julia injuring someone. I saw her today and she still seemed perfectly normal. A little impatient with her cousin Ruth, but so was I."

"What do you mean?"

Sarah shrugged. "She's very spoiled, and she obviously resents having Julia in the house. She's heard her parents talking about how Julia's scandal might hurt her chances of finding a husband and she wasn't shy about saying she would like to see the back of Julia."

"Poor Julia. Nobody wants her," Malloy said.

"That's what happens when things go wrong for a woman," Mother Malloy remarked, not even looking up from her knitting. "She gets the blame no matter what the truth is."

"That's so true," Sarah said. "And people always believe the story the husband tells, no matter how outlandish."

"We're trying to find out the truth, though," Malloy reminded her. "And so far we don't have any reason to believe Longly, because from what we can tell, Julia Longly is not insane and never should have been sent to that place."

"Which is one thing we can certainly agree on. I wish Chet Longly had explained what he meant when he said Julia was evil," Sarah said.

"Witches," Mother Malloy muttered.

"What did you say, Ma?" Malloy asked.

"I said *witches*. That's what they always used to say when a woman displeased some man. They'd say she was a witch and hang her or burn her or something."

"And you think Chet Longly is calling Julia a witch?" Malloy asked, obviously confused.

"Not in so many words," Sarah said, "but Mother Malloy is right. When a man wanted to get rid of a difficult woman, he would accuse her of being a witch. They don't do that anymore because we're civilized now and don't believe in witches." Mother Malloy made a little huffing sound as if she disagreed, but Sarah ignored it. "Now they simply say the woman is deranged and lock her in an asylum."

"I see it now," Malloy said. "And yes, Ma, you're right. Chet Longly really wants us to believe Julia is a witch."

"Or maybe she is one," Mother Malloy said.

Malloy covered a smile with his hand. Then he said, "I thought we were too civilized to believe in witches."

"Doesn't mean they don't exist."

"She has you there, Malloy," Sarah said with a grin.

"She always has me. Now tell me, did Julia agree to write her mother a letter?"

"Yes. She'll let me know when it's ready and we'll arrange to pick it up."

"I don't suppose you've heard anything from your mother about Julia's mother?"

"Not yet. I think she wanted to give Mrs. de Groot time to contact Mrs. Breedlove and convince her Julia needs her help."

"Do you really think she'll do that?"

"I don't know if she could convince Julia's mother to help or if she'll even try, but she will most certainly convey the message that Julia needs it."

"But don't be too disappointed if Julia's mother doesn't help," Mother Malloy said.

They both looked up in surprise.

"Why not?" Sarah asked.

"Because if Julia Longly really is a witch, she'll know it."

XI

Neither Sarah nor Malloy had an answer for that, so after a moment, Sarah said, "I don't suppose Mr. Longly mentioned Maeve."

"No, and I couldn't figure out a way to bring her into the conversation since I'm not supposed to know anything about her. He did claim that Julia had injured one of the servants, though."

"He said that?" Sarah asked in surprise.

"Yes, it seems he's going to blame her for whatever happened to Tamar."

"Which is certainly why Mrs. Nailor believes it. I'd really love to ask Tamar about it, but they seem determined to prevent that. Did he mention Miss Winterbourne?"

"No, although he did say Julia had done even worse things than injuring a maid. He didn't tell me anything else because he said he could see I didn't believe him, although I was trying not to let my real opinion show."

"I'm guessing nobody would believe him or at least I hope they wouldn't."

"The doctors at the asylum must have believed him," Malloy said. "Why else would they have admitted her?"

Sarah smiled at that. "Perhaps for the same reason the judge released her."

Malloy stared at her in surprise. "You think Longly bribed them?"

"I don't know why you'd be surprised at that," his mother said. "You've taken a bribe or two in your day, I'm sure."

Malloy glared at her, but he couldn't deny it. That's how the New York City Police Department operated, and he'd been a detective sergeant there for years.

Sarah came to his rescue. "I suppose it's possible. Dr. Ziegler seemed awfully determined to keep Julia in the hospital."

"Maybe that was just because he was, uh, taking advantage of her, though," Malloy said with a meaningful glance at his mother. He obviously didn't want to mention Julia's revelation—that Ziegler had raped her—in front of his mother.

"You mean he raped the poor girl?" his mother said, outraged.

"I'm afraid so, Mother Malloy," Sarah said. "The patients at that hospital are the perfect victims. No one believes them and the only people they can complain to are the ones abusing them."

"So maybe Longly bribed Ziegler and the other doctors to admit Julia," Malloy said in resignation, "and Ziegler didn't want her released because he wanted to continue abusing her."

Sarah sighed. "I really expected the doctors in that place would be genuinely concerned about the welfare of their patients."

"You always expect the best from people," Malloy said with a smile. "I'd think you would have given that up by now."

"One can always hope," she replied with a smile of her own. "Well, Maeve will be here tomorrow afternoon. She may have more information for us."

"Are we going to let her go back there?" Malloy asked. "She's probably learned everything she can by now."

"I'm not happy about her being there either, but you know she won't leave until she's ready."

"I'll have Gino come to meet with her, too. Maybe he can convince her."

"Or they'll get into an argument, and she'll be too stubborn to come home," Sarah warned.

"What is wrong with those two?" Malloy asked of no one in particular.

"They're in love," his mother said.

Neither of them could argue with that.

GINO JOINED THEM FOR LUNCH AT HOME THE NEXT DAY so he would be there when Maeve got there. They were expecting her at any moment, but she hadn't arrived when they were finished, so they adjourned to the parlor to wait. With the children in school and Mother Malloy doing her volunteer work at Brian's school, they had all the privacy they would need.

Frank couldn't shake his restlessness and he kept walking over to the front window in hopes of seeing Maeve coming down the street.

"It would be nice to know just what has really been going on at the Longly house," Gino remarked to break the silence.

"And whose version of that is the truth," Sarah said.

"I thought we'd already decided that Longly was lying about Julia to justify locking her away in the asylum," Frank said, walking back to the sofa where Sarah sat.

"We did, but . . ."

"But what?" Gino prompted.

"It just seems strange to me that so *many* other people are also determined to blacken Julia's name."

The two men considered that for a moment.

"You're right," Frank said. "I hadn't thought of it that way, but it does seem strange."

"I can understand Mr. Longly and Mrs. Nailor blaming her for injuring Tamar and possibly even Miss Winterbourne. That would give Mr. Longly a good excuse for locking Julia up and Mrs. Nailor would swear to whatever he said."

"Because she's dependent on him," Gino said.

"Yes, and she probably hates Julia as well," Frank said.

"The neighbor, Mrs. Kindred, didn't seem to like Julia much, but she just thought Julia was a snob because she was always going out socializing with other people, presumably people richer and more important than Mrs. Kindred."

"But the groom at the Longly house told me rumor had it that Julia was having an affair with Vogler, which was why she was always having him drive her places," Gino said.

"Something Vogler denied," Frank said. "I tend to believe him because men in his situation do lie about those things, but usually they claim they really are having an affair when they aren't, instead of the other way around."

"Why would they claim they are if they aren't?" Sarah asked with a frown.

"Because they want to impress their friends with their ability to seduce an upper-class woman," Frank said with a sigh.

"But instead Vogler claimed he was taking Julia to gambling houses, which seems like an odd lie to tell about her," Gino said. "He'd even gossiped about it to other drivers in the neighborhood."

Frank turned to Sarah. "Can you imagine a woman like Julia Longly going to a place like that?"

Sarah shook her head. "I've never been to a place like that, of course, but I certainly can't imagine myself there. Men wouldn't take their wives, would they?"

"Never," Frank confirmed. "And they have women there to provide, uh, *companionship* to the customers if they want that."

Gino coughed in a rather suspicious manner, but Frank ignored him.

Sarah was too busy considering the issue to notice. "Then any female there would be considered a . . . a courtesan."

"To put it nicely, yes," Frank said. "The idea that Julia Longly would even consider going to a place like that is ridiculous."

"And even if she went once—maybe she was tricked or something—she would certainly never return," Sarah mused.

"The real question," Gino said, "is why would Vogler make up such a horrible lie about her?"

"He's not the only one making up horrible lies either," Sarah said. "Her own servants think she hurt Tamar and possibly that she killed Miss Winterbourne."

"But Maeve said they didn't know for sure what happened to either of them," Gino reminded her.

"No, but they haven't hesitated to blame Julia when Julia gave us perfectly good reasons to blame Mr. Longly."

"When you put it all together like that, it does sound like many people—some of whom don't even know each other—are purposely trying to blacken Julia's name," Frank said.

"And make her look as debauched as she claimed her husband is," Sarah said.

"What do we know about Chet Longly?" Gino asked suddenly. "Really know about him, I mean. Julia said he hurt Tamar and Miss Winterbourne, but no one else seems to think that. Has anybody else told us horrible things about him?"

Frank and Sarah considered the question for a full minute.

"We could hardly expect Mrs. Nailor to speak ill of her protector," Sarah said reasonably.

"And she might not actually know anything bad about him, since she would only know what he told her," Frank said.

"Mother said he was a bit wild as a young man," Sarah remembered.

"Which is very different from killing a servant," Gino said.

"Or sending your wife to an asylum," Sarah added.

"Which is the only thing we absolutely know he did that is appalling," Frank said.

"Except for what Julia told us," Sarah said.

"And she blamed Longly for a lot of the things other people think she did," Gino said.

They stared at one another for a long moment.

"I wish Maeve would get here," Sarah said with a sigh. "Surely she knows more now than she did on Sunday and can answer some of these questions."

But Maeve did not arrive and when it was time for Sarah to go bring Catherine home from school, Gino offered to take a note to Maeve.

"They might not let her come to the door, but I will probably be able to tell if they're at all nervous about me asking for her."

"Don't spare our feelings," Sarah said with a sad smile. "You want to see if they're nervous because something happened to her."

"I was trying not to think about that," Gino admitted sheepishly. "But yes, I should be able to tell if she's all right, at least."

"Maybe they'll even let you see her," Frank said.

"I'm not going to count on it. I did go to the door and ask about the driver job, so someone might remember me. But I'll ask."

Frank went to fetch Catherine so Sarah could write the note, and Gino set out for the Longly house.

GINO WAS STARTING TO THINK HE SHOULD GET A UNI- form of some kind. It would come in handy when he was pretending to be Mrs. Malloy's chauffeur or questioning drivers, as he had a few days ago, and now when he was delivering a message. People never looked at you twice if you were wearing a uniform. You were just doing a job. A man in a suit delivering a message was suspect, however, because men in suits didn't deliver things. He should probably find a street arab, one of the homeless children who roamed the city, and give him a nickel to knock on the Longlys' door and ask for Maeve. But then Gino wouldn't have a chance to see the reaction of whoever answered the door and judge Maeve's well-being by how alarmed that person looked.

So, Gino strolled the few blocks to the Longly house and knocked on the front door, which was already the wrong thing to do. Someone delivering a message for a servant should go to the back door. But Gino was more likely to run into someone who had already seen him inquiring about a job if he did that, so the front door was the best option.

A maid answered, and thankfully, Gino didn't recognize her. From the way she was smiling, she liked what she saw, though. "May I help you?" she asked when he didn't say anything.

"I was wondering if I could give a message to Miss Maeve Smith," he said a little uncertainly.

The girl's expression shifted subtly from pleased to knowing. "Miss Smith, is it? You should go to the back door for that."

"Should I?" he asked as if he'd never thought of such a thing. "But I'm here now. Maybe you could call her down so I could have a word with her." He gave her the smile that always got him out of trouble with his mother.

"Miss Smith don't entertain gentleman callers no matter which door they come to, mister, so I won't be going to get her for you."

Gino shrugged and kept smiling. He'd given it his best shot. "Well then, maybe you could just give her this. It's from her former employer." He held out the envelope, which was made of heavy, cream-colored paper that spoke of money. Maeve's name was neatly written on it.

The girl looked at it suspiciously. "Her former employer, you say?"

"You didn't think I'd be bringing love letters to your front door, did you?" he asked in exaggerated surprise.

She grinned at that. "How am I to know? A fellow like you could be up to anything."

"I could, but I'm a gentleman. Like you said, a gentleman caller."

She gave him a look of mock disgust and took the offered envelope. "I shouldn't be doing this. I could get in trouble if the housekeeper found out."

"She'll never find out. Miss Smith is discreet. And why don't you take this for your trouble, and buy yourself something nice?" he added, pulling a silver dollar from his pocket.

The girl glanced over her shoulder to make sure no one was watching and, seeing no one, snatched the coin from his fingers. "You get along now," she said more loudly than she'd spoken so far, in case someone was in earshot, he knew. "You've got no business here."

She'd slipped the coin and the envelope into her apron pocket.

"Thanks for your trouble, miss. I'm sorry to bother you," he replied, also more loudly. He tipped his hat and sauntered back down the porch steps. He heard the door close behind him, and he smiled. At least he could report that the maid had expressed no alarm at being asked about Maeve, which probably meant nothing untoward had happened to her. Now if she'd just deliver the message, maybe they could find out why Maeve hadn't shown up today and what was going on in the Longly house.

Gino had reached the corner before he happened to think

of another errand he could run while he was in this part of the city. The Widow Hart, Vogler's new employer, wasn't far away. The day was fine, and the sun would be shining for at least another hour. Maybe he could catch Vogler at his leisure because hadn't he promised to let Vogler know if he got any news about the maid Tamar? It also wouldn't hurt to give Vogler a chance to tell him a little more about Julia Longly's interest in gambling dens and whatever else he cared to gossip about. Men, Gino had learned, could be just as informative as women when it came to gossip.

He found Vogler in the stables behind the Widow Hart's house. He was in a stall, brushing one of the horses, which probably meant he had recently returned from an outing.

"If it isn't the investigator," Vogler said with a sly grin when Gino had greeted him. "What are you investigating today?"

"Nothing much," Gino said. "I promised I'd let you know if I found out anything about Tamar, though."

Vogler instantly stopped brushing the horse and his sly grin vanished. "You know something? Is she all right?"

"As far as I know, she is."

Vogler put down the brush and stepped out of the stall. "Where is she?"

Gino tried not to react but inwardly he was enjoying a feeling of satisfaction because obviously Vogler was more than a little interested in this Tamar. "She's working for Mrs. Nailor. She's—"

"Yeah, I know who she is. We all did. Word gets around, especially when Longly kept his fancy woman just a few blocks away. Servants talk."

And servants always knew everything, as Sarah Malloy

had often remarked. "Longly did what he said then, sent her someplace to recover."

"Is she really recovered? She was hurt pretty bad," Vogler asked with obvious concern.

"I understand she walks with a slight limp, but she seems all right otherwise. She must be if she's a maid. That's hard work."

Vogler frowned. "What do you mean, you *understand*? You mean you didn't see her yourself?"

"One of my colleagues did."

"Did your *colleague* tell her I asked about her?"

"No, my colleague wasn't permitted to speak with her. Would Tamar have been happy to know you were interested in her well-being?"

Vogler didn't like that question, probably because the answer was no, but he said, "It doesn't matter. Now that I know where she is, I can tell her myself."

"What happened to her, Vogler?"

Vogler's expression hardened. "Is this more investigating?"

"Yes, it is. If somebody hurt Tamar on purpose, shouldn't they be held accountable?"

"People like that aren't ever held accountable," Vogler said with bitter confidence.

"People like what?"

"Rich people. You should know that yourself."

How interesting that Vogler thought the person who had hurt Tamar was rich. "So, somebody did hurt Tamar on purpose. Who was it?"

Vogler glared at Gino for a long moment, but then he said, "She thinks somebody pushed her down the stairs."

"She *thinks*? Doesn't she know?"

"She . . . she doesn't remember. I told you, she was hurt

pretty bad. Broke her ankle and hit her head. Knocked her out cold."

"And no one saw it happen?"

"Whoever pushed her saw it happen," he said bitterly.

Gino nodded sagely. "Any idea who it might've been?"

Vogler hesitated only a moment. "Mrs. Longly thought her husband took too much interest in Tamar."

"Did he?"

"I don't know, but I can tell you, Tamar didn't take any interest in him."

Gino considered that. "But you didn't work in the house, did you, so how can you be sure?"

"I'm sure."

That was interesting. Maybe he and Tamar did have some kind of a relationship if she had confided in him. "Do you think Longly pushed her down the stairs to punish her for not returning his affections?"

Vogler smiled at that and looked Gino up and down contemptuously. "You're not much of an investigator, are you?"

That stung, but Gino refused to be cowed. "I'm good enough to know you lied about taking Mrs. Longly to gambling houses."

That surprised him. "Why would I lie about something like that?"

"I don't know. Maybe you could explain it to me."

"But I didn't lie."

"Don't take me for a fool, Vogler. No decent woman would be caught dead in a place like that, no matter how fancy it is."

Vogler smiled slowly with genuine mirth. "You really don't know, do you? Julia Longly isn't a decent woman."

Gino blinked in surprise. "That's an awful thing to say," he managed.

"But still true. And I did take her to those places. She'd stay for hours and come out looking a little the worse for wear, if you know what I mean."

"You can't say that about Mrs. Longly," Gino tried, horrified.

"I can and I just did. You also asked me who pushed Tamar down the stairs. You thought it was Longly, but it wasn't. It was her, Julia Longly. We all thought so. If you don't believe me, ask the other servants. Ask Tamar. And don't call me a liar again."

MAEVE HAD PUT VICTOR TO BED THAT EVENING AND was contemplating how she might get in contact with the Malloys to tell them why she hadn't been able to get away today. Her next opportunity to leave the house would be on Sunday, which seemed awfully far away, considering all the things she needed to tell the Malloys. Of course, now that Julia had been released from the asylum, they probably weren't working for the Breedloves anymore, and there was really nothing they could do anyway. Julia Longly and her problems were no longer any of the Malloys' business.

Which meant it wasn't Maeve's business either. She should have resigned on the spot when Mr. Longly told her about Julia being released. But even now, after she'd had a chance to think it through and realize the case was finished, she couldn't bring herself to leave Victor. The poor child had already lost a mother and his last nursemaid, and he was still having nightmares about Miss Winterbourne. The very least Maeve could do was wait until Longly replaced her.

How to explain that to the Malloys, though. They were already inconvenienced without her services, both at home and at the office, and now the reason for her presence here was no longer even valid. Unless they wanted to investigate Miss Winterbourne's death. Maybe that's the argument she should use.

She was still contemplating this when Kate came into the nursery. Maeve had been sitting at the table, staring out the window at the darkening street below, and she greeted Kate warmly, happy for some company.

"Your friend came by this afternoon," Kate said provocatively, sitting down at the table opposite her.

"My friend?" Who could that be?

"He didn't give his name, but he was a handsome devil. Italian, if I was to guess, and I am guessing."

Gino! She should have known the Malloys would be alarmed when she didn't come this afternoon and would do something to check up on her. "What did he want?"

"Then you do know who it was," Kate said, determined to make this some sort of romantic situation.

She shrugged as if it were of no consequence. "It was probably Gino. He worked for the same family I did. Don't tell me he wanted to see me."

Kate was plainly disappointed in Maeve's response. "He did ask me to call you down, but I had to tell him that wasn't proper. Mrs. Pauly would kill me if I did a thing like that."

"You did the right thing," Maeve said, although she was fuming to have missed a chance to speak to him. They must have been truly worried about her if Gino had actually come to the door. "I guess he wanted me to see if there was a place for him here. He was always sweet on me, although I never cared a fig for him." She was only sorry Gino hadn't seen how calmly she could deny any tender feelings for him. It would drive him crazy.

"He didn't seem too upset when I told him I couldn't fetch you, but he did leave you this."

To Maeve's relief, Kate pulled an envelope out of her pocket and slid it across the table to her. She recognized Mrs. Malloy's handwriting at once. "Oh, he brought me a message from Mrs. Brandt. She was my previous employer," Maeve said, betraying not a hint of excitement as she picked up the envelope and examined the penmanship.

"What could this Mrs. Brandt want? She was going to let you go, wasn't she?"

"She didn't need me anymore. Or rather the children didn't."

"Aren't you going to read it?" Kate asked in dismay when Maeve laid the envelope down on the table and pushed it aside.

"When I have company?" Maeve asked as if she were shocked. "That would be rude."

"But don't you want to know what it says?"

"Not particularly. I don't think she wants me back, and I'm not interested in going back, so nothing else seems that important."

"Oh," Kate said, not bothering to hide her disappointment.

"If it's anything interesting, I'll tell you tomorrow," Maeve said, giving herself time to make something up. She was certain she wouldn't want Kate to know what Mrs. Malloy's letter really said.

Kate sighed. "Mrs. Pauly said to tell you the house is locked up tight and Mr. Longly is staying home again tonight." He had forgone a visit to his mistress last night, presumably to be there to protect them if Julia Longly tried to pay them a visit. Maeve really needed to tell the Malloys how frightened everyone here was of Julia. And how Mr.

Longly had locked his bedroom door against her. And several other interesting things about Julia that had changed Maeve's opinion of her drastically.

I WISH YOU COULD HAVE SEEN HER FOR YOURSELF," Sarah said when Gino had reported back on his attempt to visit Maeve.

"I do, too, but the maid didn't seem the least bit wary of me, the way she would have been if Maeve was in some kind of distress. She acted just like she would have if a young man tried to get in to see the pretty, young nursemaid. She was intrigued and jumped to all the wrong conclusions and even teased me. I'm sure Maeve is all right."

"You didn't think to ask why she hadn't taken her day off, I guess," Malloy said.

"I did," Gino said, "but I couldn't figure out a way to ask without sounding like I had expected to meet her for some kind of assignation."

"I'm sure Maeve will appreciate your discretion," Sarah said with some amusement. "But the maid did take the letter, didn't she?"

"Yes, and she promised to give it to Maeve."

"Hopefully, we will receive a reply in a day or two."

Gino had no reply for that, but he waited expectantly, as if he thought Sarah and Malloy should do something. Finally, he said, "Aren't you going to ask me why I was gone so long?"

Sarah exchanged a look with Malloy, who shrugged. Sarah said, "Why were you gone so long?"

He told them about his visit with Vogler.

"What a horrible man," Sarah said.

"Not if he's telling the truth," Malloy said.

"And I think he is," Gino said grimly. "He doesn't really have any reason to say things like that about Mrs. Longly otherwise."

"That we know of," Sarah said, still feeling obligated to defend Julia. "I can think of several reasons why he might be angry with her and want to speak ill of her."

"I assume you're thinking of the usual reasons a man might be angry with a woman," Malloy said.

"Yes. She rebuffed his advances or she convinced her husband to fire him are the most obvious."

"Vogler did say we could ask the other servants or Tamar herself about Tamar's accident," Gino said.

"Tamar and the other servants are dependent on Chet Longly," Malloy reminded him. "They would naturally choose to blame Julia instead of him for everything."

Gino sighed. "You know, you don't have to defend Julia anymore. She's already out of the asylum, which was what Breedlove hired you to do. All he wants now is for you to locate Julia's mother so he can get her out of his house, which means we don't need to investigate any of this anymore."

"And yet you went to see Vogler today," Sarah reminded him gently.

"I know. I'm nosy, and so are you, which is why we can't seem to stop asking questions," Gino said. "But we should, shouldn't we?"

"You're right, we should. We should just concentrate on finding Julia's mother," Malloy said. "Sarah, I don't suppose you've heard anything from your mother, have you?"

"No. Perhaps I should ask her to give Mrs. de Groot a nudge to see if she has tried to contact Mrs. Breedlove."

"Is it considered good manners to nudge somebody like Mrs. de Groot?" Malloy asked with a small smile.

"Nudging is the only thing that would be considered good manners in this situation," Sarah said, returning his smile. "Asking outright would be beyond the pale."

"I'm sure Mrs. Decker is an expert at nudging, too," Gino said.

"My mother," Sarah said, "is an expert at all the social niceties."

SARAH TELEPHONED HER MOTHER THE NEXT MORNING and asked her to find out if Mrs. de Groot had made any effort to find Julia's mother. Her mother, ever mindful that operators might be listening, reminded Sarah it had been only three days since they called on Mrs. de Groot.

"Yes, but we didn't know then that Julia was back in town," Sarah said discreetly.

"*Back in town?*" her mother exclaimed. "Do you mean she . . . she left the place where she was staying?"

"She did. I realize I should have told you. She is now with her aunt and uncle."

"You certainly should have told me," her mother said, obviously irritated. "That will make all the difference. I will send over a note immediately, informing Mrs. de Groot."

"Mrs. de Groot didn't actually know that Julia had *left the city*," Sarah reminded her, still speaking in code, "and we shouldn't mention where she has been."

"Oh, that's right, I almost forgot."

"But now that she has *returned to the city*," Sarah continued determinedly, "she will need another place to stay, since her aunt and uncle aren't willing to keep her for the long term."

"Honestly, Sarah, this whole situation is so confusing."

"And tragic and sad, but all we can do is our best," Sarah said.

"That sounds like something I told you when you were a child," her mother grumbled.

"It is. Perhaps you can think of some way to impress upon Mrs. de Groot that the situation is more urgent now."

"I will do my best," she said with just a trace of irony. "Being a private investigator is much more difficult than I realized."

"Are you thinking of giving it up?" Sarah asked, managing not to laugh.

"Absolutely not. I will send Mrs. de Groot a note this very morning. I'll have a maid deliver it so there is no delay."

"What will you say?"

"Don't worry. I will be very creative."

Which made Sarah worry even more.

XII

It was almost lunchtime when the phone rang. Sarah hurried to answer it, and as she had hoped, it was her mother.

"I received an immediate reply from Mrs. de Groot," she said with a note of triumph.

"What on earth did you tell her?"

"Just that the situation had deteriorated, and Julia was in desperate need of assistance. Mrs. de Groot was obviously impressed. She invited me to visit her this very afternoon. She didn't mention you, but I was certain you would want to be included."

"You know me so well," Sarah said. "I'll drive the electric and pick you up."

They made their arrangements. As soon as she hung up, she telephoned Malloy's office. He had gone in for lack of anything else to do while Gino had gone to the neighborhood where

Julia's mother used to live to see if he could coax anyone there into giving him information about her. They knew it was probably a wasted effort, but Gino needed to feel useful.

"Good work," Malloy said when she told him about Mrs. de Groot's message.

"We don't know for sure if she is going to be helpful," Sarah warned. "But she obviously has something to tell us."

"Let's hope she's at least willing to contact Julia's mother on her behalf."

"Surely, if Mrs. Breedlove is so frightened of Chet Longly that she became a recluse, she'll be sympathetic to her daughter's plight."

To Sarah's surprise, Malloy had no answer for that.

THIS IS SUCH A LOVELY VEHICLE," SARAH'S MOTHER SAID, admiring the electric when they were on their way to Mrs. de Groot's house.

"Ladies love driving the electrics, so they make them with a feminine touch, I'm told."

"Is that a vase?" her mother asked in amazement, noticing the tube-shaped structure affixed to the inside wall of the vehicle.

"It certainly is, although I never bother to put flowers in it. I think Malloy might object."

"And it would be a bit of a mess when they started dropping petals, I suppose."

"Exactly."

Her mother looked around again. "It doesn't look very difficult at all to drive."

Sarah hazarded a quick glance in her mother's direction. "Father would never allow you to drive a motorcar."

"Never is a very long time, dear," her mother said, not the least bit discouraged.

Sarah chose not to argue. Never really was a very long time.

She parked in front of the de Groot house and they made their way to the front door. The maid seemed surprised to see them, or maybe she was just surprised to see Sarah had come along. At any rate, she escorted them to the parlor and left them there. Mrs. de Groot came in a few minutes later, looking a bit distressed.

"Oh, it really is you, Mrs. Malloy," she said when she saw them. Then she looked around as if checking for other uninvited visitors. "Are you alone?"

"It's just the two of us," her mother said with a puzzled frown. "I didn't think you'd mind if Sarah came along. She's Julia's friend, after all."

Mrs. de Groot was, Sarah noticed, not merely distressed and puzzled. She actually looked nervous.

Sarah and her mother had risen from their places on the sofa when Mrs. de Groot came in and now she asked them to sit down again and took a chair opposite them. She was dressed with her usual care, but her manner was completely different this time. Sarah had the distinct impression she wished them both in Hades.

"I'm sorry if I offended you by coming uninvited," Sarah said. "I can leave if you like."

"No, no, it's not that. I just . . ." Mrs. de Groot was wringing her hands and she made a concerted effort to still them in her lap. "When my maid told me two ladies had arrived, I was afraid you had brought Julia with you."

Plainly, Julia would not have been welcome.

"I would never assume like that," Sarah's mother assured

her. "I'm sorry if that alarmed you." Which was an odd choice of words, but Mrs. de Groot was plainly alarmed.

Their hostess drew a calming breath and managed a smile that did not quite reach her eyes. "I'm sorry if I seemed rude, but . . . Well, it's obvious to me you don't know all that happened, or you wouldn't be inquiring after Ellie Breedlove."

Sarah felt a prickle of unease. Could Ellie Breedlove have died? "You're probably right. I don't think we do know all that happened."

"Perhaps you could tell us," her mother said, using the tone that had coaxed gossip out of a thousand society matrons. "We shouldn't like to give offense out of ignorance."

Mrs. de Groot's expression could be described only as bleak. "Giving offense is the least of it, Mrs. Decker. Ellie was in fear for her life."

Sarah and her mother had expected to hear something like that, but the words still stunned them.

"Perhaps I should explain," a woman's voice said, startling all of them.

The pocket doors separating the parlor from the room next door slid open and a woman appeared. She was middle-aged and careworn, her face lined the way need and hard living marked the faces of women who lived in the city's tenements, but she was dressed as fashionably as the other three women in the room.

All three of them rose as the woman made her way into the parlor.

"Ellie," Sarah's mother said in surprise.

Sarah knew a moment of relief. At least the woman wasn't dead.

"Elizabeth, I'm sure I never expected you to be looking for me," Ellie replied.

Before her mother could reply, Sarah said, "I'm afraid I'm the one who is looking for you. My mother was just helping me."

Ellie Breedlove nodded. "Please, sit down. I'm curious about why you're so concerned about Julia."

The women sat down, and Ellie took a chair beside Mrs. de Groot.

Before Sarah could begin to explain, Ellie said, "Patricia here told me you claimed that Julia was being abused and needed a refuge. Let me just say, I don't believe that for a moment, so why don't you tell me the real reason you are here."

Sarah blinked in surprise, and a glance at her mother told her she was equally bemused. "I suppose I should start at the beginning."

"That usually results in less confusion," Ellie agreed.

Sarah drew a steadying breath. She'd been trying to decide how much of the story to tell, but now that she had met Ellie Breedlove, she knew she would have to tell it all if she hoped to get any sympathy from this woman. "Chet Longly put Julia into the insane asylum on Ward's Island a few weeks ago."

Mrs. de Groot was suitably horrified, but Ellie Breedlove gave an anguished cry, clapped a hand over her mouth, and began to weep uncontrollably. Mrs. de Groot jumped up to comfort her friend, taking her hand and offering a handkerchief and patting her shoulder and whispering comforting words as Ellie's body shook with sobs.

While Sarah was surprised, she shouldn't have been. She would probably have reacted the same way if she learned

someone had locked away her beloved daughter. Mrs. de
Groot looked up at Sarah and her mother beseechingly, and
Sarah realized they couldn't allow Ellie to keep weeping like
this. She would exhaust herself.

"Do you have any brandy?" Sarah asked.

Mrs. de Groot pointed to a cabinet on the far side of the
room, and Sarah located a variety of liquors and glasses. She
poured some brandy into one and delivered it to Mrs. de
Groot, who urged Ellie to take some. She choked a bit, but
after a few minutes she was calm again.

"You must forgive my display," she said, mopping up the
last of her tears with her own handkerchief.

"I'm sure we all understand completely," Sarah's mother
said. "That was shocking news indeed."

"Indeed," Ellie said. "I'm so very glad you went to the
trouble of finding me and telling me, though."

"Yes, we thought you would want to know, but there's
much more to the story that you also need to know," Sarah
said.

"I don't imagine I'll want to hear it, but there's no choice,
is there? You've told me the most important thing, so nothing else really matters now, does it?"

Sarah didn't know if it did or not, but she said, "Your
brother-in-law, Hugh Breedlove, and his wife and daughter
recently returned home from London."

"How surprising," Ellie said. "I never thought Hugh
would leave England."

"They wanted to bring their daughter out into society in
New York, I believe."

To Sarah's surprise, she smiled at that. "I guess they were
afraid Ruth wouldn't catch on over there and attract the
right sort of husband."

"I suspected that, too, but at any rate, they came back to the city. They were hoping Julia would use her social connections to help them meet the right people, and they were shocked to learn that Mr. Longly had committed her to the hospital."

"Poor Hugh, I'm sure he was stunned."

Sarah blinked again, but she continued. "Mr. and Mrs. Breedlove were concerned about the scandal if people found out where Julia was. They thought it would affect people's opinion of their daughter."

Ellie nodded her understanding. "Of course. No one wants to marry into a family where there is insanity."

"They had also visited Julia and found her to be completely rational, so they felt a grave injustice had been done to her."

Ellie's expression hardened. "How could they possibly judge such a thing?"

Which was not the response Sarah had expected, but plainly, Ellie didn't fully understand what had happened. "They hired a private investigator to help them prove Julia was sane and get her released from the asylum."

"Those meddling fools!" Ellie cried, turning to her friend. "We have to stop them."

"You want to stop them from getting Julia released?" Sarah's mother asked in confusion.

"Of course I do."

This wasn't making any sense. Sarah's mother didn't understand either, so it wasn't just her. "It's too late to stop them," Sarah said. "Mr. Breedlove found a friendly judge and Julia was released a few days ago."

"Released?" Ellie echoed in despair. "That can't be. How could they release her? Chet would never allow it!"

"He didn't know about it," Sarah said.

"No!" Ellie cried. "She can't be free. She just can't!"

Sarah couldn't believe this was happening. None of it made sense.

"This was why we have been looking for you, Mrs. Breedlove," Sarah said as calmly as she could in hopes of calming Ellie, too.

Ellie turned her furious gaze to Sarah. "To torture me?"

"Ellie," Sarah's mother tried, "you must see the problem. Obviously, Julia cannot go back to Chet after what he did, and your brother-in-law is concerned about people finding out Julia was in the asylum and ruining his daughter's chances, so he doesn't want to keep her either. Under the circumstances, the logical place for her to go is to her mother."

"And that is why you have been looking for me? Because you think I will take Julia and protect her from a cruel world?"

Sarah's mother gave her a desperate glance. Someone was obviously confused, but Sarah wasn't sure who it was.

"Mrs. Breedlove," Sarah said gently, "we know why you have been in hiding these past years, but you don't need to be afraid that anyone will find you. We still don't know where you are living, and Julia will also need to disappear from the city. The two of you will have each other."

Ellie Breedlove stared at Sarah as if she had grown a second head. Finally, she said, "You claim to know why I have been in hiding and then you prove that you have no idea by threatening to bring Julia back into my life."

"Threatening?" Sarah echoed in surprise. "I didn't intend to threaten you."

"And yet you did. You obviously don't know anything at all about Julia or why Chet would have sent her away."

"We don't know for sure, of course, but it's easy to guess," Sarah said.

"Is it? Perhaps you will tell me what you think it is."

"We think he . . . Well, at least two of the women who worked in the Longly home were . . . injured."

"And you think Chet injured them?" Ellie said.

Sarah couldn't miss the skepticism in her voice. "We did think so," she said carefully.

"What if I told you that you were wrong? What if I told you Chet Longly would never hurt a woman?"

"Then who . . . ?" Sarah began, but she didn't need to finish the question because suddenly she knew, even though she had excused every single bit of evidence that proved it. "Not Julia?" she said, her voice hardly more than a whisper because she didn't want to say it at all.

"Why not Julia?" Ellie asked, angry now that Sarah had refused to see it. "Because she's a woman? Do you think all women are good and pure and kind?"

"No, of course not," Sarah insisted. She'd known too many female murderers to claim that.

"Then why couldn't you believe Julia was the one?"

"I . . ." Sarah caught herself. Why hadn't she? "Because," she said after a long moment, "Mr. Longly had sent his wife, who was apparently completely sane, to an insane asylum where she was doomed to spend the rest of her life. What kind of a man does a thing like that?"

"A desperate one, I would imagine," Ellie said. "Did that never occur to you?"

"No, it did not. When my husband spoke with him, he didn't offer any explanation as to why he had done it, so we had to assume the worst."

Ellie frowned. "Why did your husband speak to him

about this? In fact, why are you involved at all? None of this is any of your business."

"I told you, Ellie. Mrs. Malloy is a friend of Julia's," Mrs. de Groot said.

"Actually, that isn't completely true," Sarah said, knowing she couldn't mislead this woman any longer. "I explained that Mr. Breedlove hired a private investigator to help get Julia released. That private investigator is my husband."

Mrs. de Groot was appalled, and Ellie Breedlove was furious. "How dare you trick me into coming here?" Ellie demanded.

"She believed Julia was an innocent victim of a cruel man," Sarah's mother said, no longer able to hold her tongue when someone was maligning her daughter. "She thought she was saving Julia from a horrible fate."

"And Julia was quite convincing," Sarah said. "But how can you be so sure she was the one who injured the two servants?"

Ellie stared back at Sarah as the color drained from her face.

"Ellie, dear," Mrs. de Groot said urgently. "It's too much for you. I can tell them."

"No," Ellie said, her voice hoarse with some emotion Sarah didn't even want to name. "I'll tell them. I want them to know exactly what they've done."

Sarah wanted to at least defend her mother, who had done nothing at all, but Ellie gave her no chance.

"Julia had always been . . . difficult. We blamed it on her being spoiled because she was an only child. She liked to get her way and she could be charming when she did, but she wasn't pleasant when she didn't get it. Her father adored her, and he always made excuses for her, so naturally, he was her favorite parent. When she said she wanted to go to a finishing school in Switzerland, he resisted at first, but she had made up her mind, so she kept at him until he finally agreed. I have to admit, the house was very peaceful with her gone, and at first her letters were cheerful. She loved the school, she loved her teachers, everything was wonderful. But slowly, that changed. She didn't like one particular girl, and the other girls always took her side, it seemed. Then she started asking to come home. She hated it there and couldn't believe we had forced her to go there."

"Which wasn't what happened at all," Mrs. de Groot said, in case they had missed the point.

"Girls that age can be unreasonable," Sarah said.

"Yes," Ellie said a little bitterly. "They can also be selfish and self-centered, which Julia always was. That is why her father refused to allow her to come home. She needed to learn how to get along in the world, he told her, so she wouldn't be coming home until the end of the school year."

That sounded like the right decision to Sarah, but judging from Ellie's expression, it had not been. "Did she run away?" she asked, remembering her own sister, Maggie, who had done just that when their parents had refused to allow her to marry the man she loved.

"Oh no," Ellie said, her eyes bleak. "I only wish she had. The girl, the one Julia didn't like, she died."

"Oh," Sarah's mother said, her face ashen as she was plainly remembering how Maggie had died.

"It was a terrible accident," Ellie continued, although her tone indicated it was not an accident at all. "The girl fell out of a window on the top floor of the school."

This time it was Sarah who cried out, but it couldn't be true, could it?

Ellie's sharp gaze speared Sarah, holding her fast. "You know something, don't you? What is it?"

But Sarah only shook her head in silent denial.

"You can't mean Julia had something to do with that girl falling," Sarah's mother said. "That's too . . . too terrible to even contemplate."

"Isn't it?" Ellie said almost cheerfully. "I only wish I had never had to contemplate it. They couldn't prove anything, of course. Julia is much too clever for that. She chose a time when the girl was alone, so no one saw anything, except no one saw Julia anyplace else either. All the girls knew how much Julia hated this girl, and the window . . . Well, it wasn't easy to fall out of, and someone thought they'd heard her screaming *No, no*, before she fell. At any rate, they were all sure Julia had pushed her. They were going to send Julia home because none of the other girls would stay if she did."

Sarah had never fainted in her life, but now she knew how it must feel before it happened. Her head felt disconnected from her body and all the heat had drained out of her, leaving her chilled to the bone.

"Mrs. Malloy, are you all right?" Mrs. de Groot asked.

"Sarah?" her mother said, her voice sounding faint and far away.

But Sarah shook off the tempting oblivion of unconsciousness. "One of the servants . . . I told you some servants were injured," she said, sounding faint and strangled even to her own ears. "One of them fell."

"Out of a window?" Ellie demanded.

"Yes. She . . . she died."

Sarah's mother and Mrs. de Groot gasped, but Ellie simply closed her eyes and shivered.

"But that isn't all," Mrs. de Groot said. "Tell them the

rest, Ellie." She turned to Sarah and her mother. "So you'll know this is real and not something she made up."

"Who could make up a story like this?" Ellie asked. "And yes, there is more. They wanted to send Julia home, but they couldn't put a young girl like her on a ship alone and no one was willing to travel with her, so my husband had to go to Switzerland himself to bring her back. He was furious, of course. He blamed the school. He never believed Julia had done anything wrong."

"And they had no proof," Sarah said.

Ellie smiled mirthlessly. "Even if they did, they couldn't put one of their students on trial for killing another. No one would ever attend that school again."

"And no one would ever convince your husband in any case," Sarah's mother guessed.

"No," Ellie said. "He went to fetch her. She told me they had locked her up for the two weeks it took him to get there, but who could blame them? At any rate, she'd gotten her way again. She was going home."

"She must have been grateful that he came for her," Sarah's mother tried.

"I think that's what he expected, but . . ."

"But she wasn't?" Sarah guessed uncertainly.

"She must not have been. I don't know for sure because my husband didn't tell me."

"Why not?" Sarah's mother asked.

"Because he never came home."

Sarah's head seemed to be floating again. This couldn't be true.

"Never came home?" her mother echoed uncertainly.

"He disappeared from the ship. They decided he had fallen overboard."

"And no one saw a thing," Sarah said, her voice echoing in her ears and the pain holding her heart in a viselike grip.

"I was devastated," Ellie said. "I could hardly think, so I didn't figure it out until later, when Julia was complaining, blaming her father for forcing her to go to that school and then insisting she stay there when she told him how unhappy she was. Her father was gone and all she could talk about was the ways in which he had somehow wronged her."

"But you can't believe she had anything to do with her father's disappearance," Sarah's mother said.

"What else could I believe?" Ellie said. "A girl she doesn't like gets pushed out of a window and then her father, whom she blames for her troubles, somehow falls overboard on an ocean liner, all within a few weeks."

"And now one of her servants falls out of a window," Sarah reminded them. She could hardly breathe.

"You said two servants were injured," Ellie remembered. "What happened to the other one?"

"She . . . she fell down the stairs. No one saw it and she can't remember what happened."

"But she survived?" Mrs. de Groot said.

"Yes, although she was badly hurt."

"Thank heaven she lived, at least," Ellie said.

"Is that why you left the city, Ellie?" Sarah's mother asked.

Ellie sighed. "You'll think me a coward, and I am. I know that, but I couldn't take the chance that Julia would start to blame me for sending her to that school or for something else entirely. When I realized what must have happened, I tried to keep her happy by giving her everything she wanted, and when she decided she wanted to come out, even though she was too young, I let her do it. Then she met Chet Longly and decided she'd like to get married."

"But how could you let them marry if you thought she'd killed two people?" Sarah asked, newly horrified.

"How could I have dared try to stop her?" Ellie asked, her voice like ice. "I did try to warn him, though. I told him what she'd done, even though I knew what a risk I was taking, but she convinced him I was unhinged by my husband's disappearance. Did I mention that she can be charming when she wants to? She can also appear perfectly reasonable and explain away everything with a string of beautiful lies."

"I know that all too well," Sarah said. "Remember, she fooled me, too."

Ellie studied her for a long moment with what might have been sympathy. "Yes, well, by the time she was finished with him, Chet thought I was a bitter old woman who resented her beautiful young daughter and was out of my mind with grief. I'd done all I could, so when they were married, I left the city and told no one where I was going so Julia could never find me."

"She did tell me," Mrs. de Groot added, "because she knew she could trust me."

"And you proved she could," Sarah said.

"Now you see why I did what I did, but Patricia was upset by your initial visit," Ellie said. "She knew Chet wasn't abusing Julia. Julia would never stand for it, but I had to know what was going on and why someone was trying so hard to find me."

"You took a risk," Sarah said. "It might have been Julia trying to lure you out of hiding."

"I see now why you were worried that Julia was with us,"

Sarah's mother said. "How awful it must be to fear your own child."

"Now you know the truth about Julia," Mrs. de Groot said, still holding Ellie's hand for comfort. "I hope that means you will stop trying to help her."

"I can't tell you how sorry I am that we got involved in all of this," Sarah said. "Mr. Breedlove was outraged at the way Mr. Longly had treated Julia, and you must understand, we had only his and Julia's word for what had happened."

"Sarah has rather made a career out of helping women who have been treated unfairly," her mother said. "And you must admit, being sent to an insane asylum when you aren't insane would be a horrible fate."

"And you were quite right, Mrs. Breedlove, when you said Julia could be charming," Sarah said. "She seems perfectly rational, and she had a logical explanation for everything anyone had accused her of."

"I'm furious at you, of course," Ellie said wearily, "but you aren't the first people she's taken in, and you probably won't be the last."

"Ellie, why did you weep when you heard Julia was in the asylum if you believed that was where she should be?" Sarah's mother asked. Sarah had wondered that, too.

Ellie smiled sadly. "Out of relief. For that one moment, I thought it was over, that Julia was in a place where she could no longer hurt anyone, and I didn't have to be afraid anymore."

"I only wish we had found you sooner," Sarah said. "Maybe we could have stopped her from being released."

"Perhaps," Ellie said, "but Julia would never have given up trying to be free, and she's capable of fooling most everyone when she sets her mind to it."

"At least she won't fool us anymore," Sarah said. "I will immediately tell my husband what you've told me, and your brother and sister-in-law, too."

"We can only hope they believe you," Ellie said, "because Julia will have used all her powers to convince them she is the innocent in all of this."

"They are already determined to find Julia another home, although they had pinned their hopes on you, Mrs. Breedlove."

"I can't imagine Julia will want to stay with them for long, but I'm sure it suits her purposes at the moment," Ellie said. "You could warn them and advise them to be kind and even offer to help her find a place of her own. That might get her out of their house at least."

"I certainly will. Can you possibly forgive me for . . . for believing the wrong things?"

"I think you believed the wrong person," Ellie said sadly. "I am still furious, of course, but I can't blame you. I know how convincing Julia can be, and she is the one I'm angry with. Poor Chet must be beside himself. I wish I could offer him some comfort or at least some support, but I'm afraid he must hate me for leaving him with Julia."

"And you'd best not let anyone else know you are in town," Mrs. de Groot said.

"Will you stay here or return to your home?" Sarah asked.

"I don't know. I'd like to know what happens with Julia, and I suppose I'm safe here with Patricia for a little while if no one tells Julia where I am."

"Neither of us will breathe a word," Sarah promised, and her mother solemnly agreed.

"If Ellie decides to go home, I can always reach her," Mrs. de Groot said.

"If we hear anything, we will let you know," Sarah said. "Is there anything else we need to know about Julia? Is her son in any danger, for example?"

Her mother muttered, "Oh dear," and Mrs. de Groot winced at the very thought of harm coming to the little boy.

"I honestly don't know," Ellie said. "Julia may love her child, in her own way, but she loved her father, too, and she still killed him when he displeased her. She must hate Chet after he sent her away, so she may use Victor to hurt him."

"Mr. Longly knows she is free, so I'm sure he's taking precautions," Sarah said. "He obviously understands what she's capable of."

"Poor little Victor," Ellie said, brushing away a tear. "I would dearly love to see him."

"Perhaps when this is over, you will," Sarah's mother said.

But they all knew this would never really be over as long as Julia was free.

MAEVE HAD GONE DOWN TO THE KITCHEN TO SIT WITH Mrs. O'Hara while Victor napped that afternoon. Sarah's note had only confirmed Maeve's worst fears about Julia Longly. All of this was disturbing enough, but it took on a new sense of urgency now that Julia was free. Maeve had sat up last night composing a reply listing all the things she had learned from the staff here and addressed the envelope, but hadn't figured out how to mail it without drawing unwanted attention.

Would Julia really try to harm anyone in this house? Maeve could easily imagine her wanting revenge on her husband, who had sent her away. She must hate him with a passion, and if she had pushed a maid down the steps and a nursemaid out a window, what might she do to the husband who had betrayed her? Maeve didn't even want to guess.

Of course, attacking another female and attacking a man were two very different things. Then Maeve remembered little Victor. Attacking a child was easy. Would Julia try to get revenge on her husband by harming her son or would she hesitate to harm her own child? Maeve instinctively reached down and touched her skirt, just where the knife was strapped to her leg underneath. Although it was unlikely Julia would be able to get into the house, Maeve would be ready for her if she did.

Maeve had been half listening while Mrs. O'Hara complained about the butcher when they heard someone pounding on the front door. Maeve was on her feet in an instant, and Mrs. O'Hara quickly wiped her hands from her bread making.

"What on earth?" Maeve muttered, hurrying out to see.

Mr. Longly was out, so they were there with just the other servants and Victor. If Julia tried to force her way in, they would have to stop her.

Mrs. Pauly was already there. She had stepped into the parlor and was looking out the front window to see who was on the porch. "Good heavens," she muttered, and went straight for the front door.

"Don't let her in," Mrs. O'Hara cried.

"It's not her," Mrs. Pauly snapped. "Go back to the kitchen."

But neither Maeve nor Mrs. O'Hara moved, and Maeve caught a glimpse of the maids, who had gathered at the top of the staircase to see as well.

Mrs. Pauly opened the door, and Mr. Breedlove came bursting through the door without waiting for an invitation.

"Where is Longly?" he demanded.

"Mr. Longly is out," Mrs. Pauly said, frowning her disapproval. "I don't know when he'll be back but if you'd like to wait—"

"I need to see him right now. Where is he?"

Mrs. Pauly's mouth, already frowning, tightened even further because they all knew Mr. Longly was visiting Mrs. Nailor, but she certainly had no intention of saying so. He had taken to seeing her during the day so he could be home after dark in case Julia tried to sneak in. "I really couldn't say," she tried.

"He's with his fancy woman, then. Is that it?" His gaze swept over the foyer, finding Maeve and Mrs. O'Hara. He frowned when he saw Maeve. She instantly lowered her head. Would he remember she worked for Mr. Malloy? He'd seen her only the one time and people rarely remembered secretaries. But he must not have recognized her because his gaze skittered away, back to Mrs. Pauly. "I need to see him. Something terrible . . ." On that, his voice broke, and he looked as if he might weep.

"You're not yourself, Mr. Breedlove," Mrs. Pauly said, easily sizing up the situation. "Mrs. O'Hara, would you make some coffee? Maeve, help me here."

Maeve couldn't refuse, so she hurried to be of assistance. Hopefully, Breedlove was too upset to remember who she really was. Mrs. Pauly took one of Mr. Breedlove's arms and Maeve took the other, still keeping her head lowered so hopefully he wouldn't look her full in the face and jog his memory. They escorted him into the front parlor and helped him sit down in one of the overstuffed chairs.

"Can I get you something while we wait for the coffee?" Mrs. Pauly asked. "Some brandy perhaps?"

"Whiskey if you've got it," he said, rubbing his face with both hands.

Mrs. Pauly signaled Maeve to fetch the drink, which she did, but she let Mrs. Pauly present it to him. He took a large gulp and wiped his mouth with the back of his hand. When he looked up, his eyes were so full of pain, Maeve had to look away.

"When will Longly be back? I need to see him."

"Perhaps you could tell us why you need to see him," Mrs. Pauly said, ever protective of her master and also painfully aware that Mr. Breedlove was currently sheltering their violent mistress.

"Yes, it . . . it's my daughter. My Ruth. She's dead."

XIII

Sᴀʀᴀʜ ᴀɴᴅ ʜᴇʀ ᴍᴏᴛʜᴇʀ ᴄʟɪᴍʙᴇᴅ ɪɴᴛᴏ ᴛʜᴇ ᴇʟᴇᴄᴛʀɪᴄ motorcar, but Sarah made no attempt to drive away. She simply sat and stared out through the front window, stunned by her own shame and guilt.

"You couldn't have known," her mother said.

"Couldn't I?" Sarah asked. "I could have at least doubted Julia a little bit. Instead, I championed her, finding a reason to believe everything she said and to doubt everyone who spoke against her."

"But even her own mother acknowledged how good a liar she is. She must have been fooling people all her life, and she must be excellent to have fooled you. You also had good reason to believe her. What I said about you in there is true, you've dedicated your life to helping other women. Heaven knows, this world isn't kind to us, and Julia Longly appeared to need even more help than most."

"That doesn't excuse me from being so wrong about her and now—"

"It's not your fault she's free, Sarah. Yes, you and Frank were investigating, but in the end, it was Mr. Breed-love's money that freed her. You can take neither credit nor blame."

"Even if that's true, Mother, we need to do something now. After what Ellie Breedlove just told us, I can't believe Julia won't want revenge on her husband and possibly others as well."

"You may be right, but what can you do to protect them?"

Sarah shook her head, which was now so muddled, she could hardly think. "We can warn them if nothing else. And get Maeve out of the Longly house so she's safe, at least. I'll take you home and—"

"You will not take me home. I have to know what's happening. Take me to your house and we can call Frank and tell him to go there as well. Then we can fetch Maeve or whatever you decide to do."

"Father will be furious if I involve you in this," Sarah protested.

"Not as furious as I'll be if you don't. Start this vehicle up and get going. I'm sure Julia isn't wasting any time thinking about reasons why she can't do something."

Sarah had to admit she was probably right. She pulled away from the curb and headed back to her home on Bank Street.

RUTH IS DEAD?" MAEVE ECHOED. SHE COULDN'T HAVE heard him correctly.

Breedlove looked up at her and frowned, obviously still trying to place her.

"What happened, Mr. Breedlove?" Mrs. Pauly asked, shooting Maeve a disapproving glare. Plainly she didn't appreciate Maeve's bluntness.

"She . . . she fell out of the window," he said with so much wonder that Maeve knew he could hardly believe it himself. If she hadn't known Miss Winterbourne's fate, she would have doubted it, too.

"The window?" Mrs. Pauly echoed, exchanging a horrified glance with Maeve, whose blood had turned cold.

"We can't figure out how it happened," he was saying. "It was a nice day, so the windows were open, but Ruth isn't a child. She knows better than to lean out an open window."

Maeve's stomach knotted like a fist, but she couldn't let her own shock keep her from learning as much as she could. "Mr. Breedlove," she said, knowing she was earning Mrs. Pauly's ire again but willing to risk it, "why do you need to see Mr. Longly about this?"

"He . . . he needs to know," Breedlove said a bit uncertainly.

Mrs. Pauly frowned. "Yes, but—"

"And Julia said he could help," Breedlove added with a bit more confidence. "Yes, she said Longly would know what to do."

Maeve glanced at Mrs. Pauly again, but this time the woman refused to meet her eye. She must understand, as Maeve did, that Julia had sent Breedlove here to make sure Mr. Longly heard just how Ruth had died so he would feel the proper amount of fear and horror.

"Where was Julia when Ruth fell?" Maeve asked.

Mrs. Pauly gasped at her audacity, but Breedlove was

trying to think. "I don't . . . In her room, I suppose. She's still recovering from her ordeal at the . . . the hospital."

"Of course she was," Mrs. Pauly said, silently warning Maeve not to speak again. "I'll see if I can locate Mr. Longly for you, if you'd care to wait."

"Yes, I . . . I suppose I can wait a little while. Julia is with my wife."

Maeve winced, but she followed Mrs. Pauly into the foyer.

"Leave that poor man alone," Mrs. Pauly warned.

Maeve could only nod. She had learned all she needed from him already. "I should check on Master Victor," she said, and hurried up the stairs.

The maids were still there on the landing, although they had moved back away from the railing so Mrs. Pauly wouldn't see them. "What happened?" Kate asked.

"Mr. Breedlove's daughter fell out the window," Maeve said, knowing they didn't need any more details to understand.

"Mrs. Longly is living with them, isn't she?" Iris asked.

"You know she is, you ninny," Kate snapped. Both girls had gone pale.

"I need to run an errand," Maeve said. "Can you listen for Master Victor, and if he wakes up, keep him busy until I get back?"

"You can't leave," Kate insisted.

"I have to. It's very important. I need to tell someone that Miss Breedlove is dead."

"Why? Whose business is it?" Kate asked.

"I won't be gone long," Maeve said, ignoring the question because she couldn't tell the truth. "Master Victor might still be asleep when I get back."

With that she headed for the back stairs. She could probably slip out without anyone noticing.

SARAH PULLED THE ELECTRIC INTO THE BUILDING THAT had once served as a stable for their house and now had been converted into a garage. She took a moment to plug the charging cord into the device they had had installed, then she and her mother made their way into the house. Her maid, Hattie, came to greet them and offered to bring them refreshment, which they gratefully accepted. Sarah went to telephone Malloy at the office, hoping he would be there.

Fortunately, he was. Sarah couldn't tell him much on the telephone, but he easily understood that Sarah had spoken with Ellie Breedlove and that Sarah's opinions on everything had changed. They decided he would wait a few minutes and fetch Catherine from school on his way home. Then Sarah could tell him everything and they could decide what to do next.

Sarah and her mother had just settled themselves in the parlor to wait for the two of them to get home when someone rang the doorbell rather insistently. Hattie was frowning at the rudeness when she passed the parlor doorway on her way to answer it, but then they heard her say, "Miss Maeve," in surprise and they both jumped up and hurried out to the entrance hall.

Maeve was panting and holding her side, having plainly run from somewhere. "Thank heaven you're here," she said when she saw Sarah.

"What is it? What's happened?" Sarah demanded.

"My goodness," her mother said. "Let the poor girl catch

her breath. Come inside and sit down, Maeve, while Hattie gets you something to drink."

Hattie took the hint and hurried away while Sarah and her mother escorted Maeve into the parlor. When she was seated, she looked up at them with tragic eyes. "Julia killed Ruth Breedlove."

Sarah and her mother gasped.

"How do you know?" Sarah asked when she could speak again.

"Mr. Breedlove came to the Longly house to tell Mr. Longly. Julia sent him," she added ominously.

"Good heavens," her mother exclaimed.

"Wait a minute," Sarah said, her head swimming. She had trusted Julia. How would she ever be able to look at herself in the mirror again? "How did Mr. Breedlove know Julia had killed Ruth?"

"He didn't," Maeve said. Her breath was back now, and she stared up at them both intently. "All he knew was that Ruth fell out of a window, but *we* knew about Miss Winterbourne, so the housekeeper and I knew what message Julia was sending her husband."

"What on earth did Mr. Longly have to say?" Sarah's mother asked.

"He wasn't home. He was . . . Well, I'm not supposed to know, but he was visiting his lady friend."

"Mrs. Nailor?" Sarah asked.

Maeve nodded.

"How many is that now?" Sarah's mother asked.

"How many of what?" Maeve asked when Sarah didn't answer.

Hattie arrived, carrying a tray with three glasses of lemonade on it. She stopped short, obviously feeling the tension in the room, but Sarah said, "Thank you so much, Hattie. Just set it down and we'll serve ourselves."

Hattie proceeded warily and left as soon as she had deposited the tray on a table.

"How many what?" Maeve repeated, a little desperate now.

Sarah handed Maeve one of the glasses. "Mother and I just visited Mrs. de Groot again. We met Ellie Breedlove there."

"She came out of hiding?" Maeve asked in wonder. "Did she believe your story about Julia being abused?"

"Not for a moment. She knew . . ." Sarah's voice stuck in her throat as she remembered the horrors that poor woman had endured.

"What did she know?" Maeve asked, obviously recognizing Sarah's distress. "What did she tell you?"

"Julia isn't what we thought," Sarah's mother said when Sarah couldn't speak. "She . . . she apparently killed a girl she didn't like at her boarding school."

Maeve shook her head in silent denial, but Sarah said, "I'm so sorry. We were as shocked as you."

"Did she . . . ? Please don't tell me she pushed the girl out a window," Maeve said.

Neither Sarah nor her mother could bring themselves to answer her.

Maeve groaned and covered her face with her hands.

"But why would Julia kill her cousin?" Sarah's mother asked of no one in particular.

"Ruth was rather rude to her when I was there," Sarah said. "She made it clear she didn't want Julia living with them because she was afraid it would hurt her chances of finding a suitable husband."

"But to kill the girl." Her mother shook her head in silent wonder. "Wouldn't she be afraid someone would guess?"

"No one ever held her accountable for the girl she killed at school," Sarah said.

"That's right. They just sent her home," Sarah's mother said.

"She . . . she apparently killed her father, too. He disappeared from an ocean liner," Sarah said.

Maeve groaned. "And no one saw her. No one saw her push Miss Winterbourne either," Maeve said.

"But surely she didn't expect to get away with it again," Sarah said. "She must know Mr. Longly suspects her, and when Ruth died the same way . . ."

"And Mr. Breedlove said Julia sent him to tell Mr. Longly," Maeve said. "She wanted him to know. She wanted to frighten him."

"What is she going to do now?" Sarah wondered aloud. "She must have something in mind."

"I don't know, but I'm sure she's not feeling very charitable toward Mr. Longly after what he did to her, so I suspect she's going to want to get back at him," Maeve said.

"Thank heaven we have you home, at least," Sarah's mother said. "Getting you away from there was the first thing Sarah thought of when we found out the truth about Julia."

Maeve looked up at them in despair. "But I can't come home now. I can't leave little Victor alone."

"He won't be alone, dear," Sarah's mother argued. "I'm sure Mr. Longly has servants."

"You don't understand. I have to protect him."

"Maeve, you can't think Julia will be able to break into the Longly house and harm him," Sarah said. "Besides, he's her child, too."

"I don't know what she might do when she's already killed four people," Maeve wailed. "I have to get back to Victor." She rose, setting her untouched lemonade back on the table. "I had already gathered some information that made me believe Julia wasn't the innocent victim she pretended to be. It's all in here." She pulled the unmailed envelope out of her pocket. "I was going to send this today, but I never got a chance. I guess it doesn't matter, though, since you know the truth now, too."

"At least wait until Malloy gets here," Sarah said. "He'll certainly have some ideas about what would be the best thing to do."

"And I'm sure he wouldn't want you going back to that house," her mother added.

"Nothing is going to happen to me there. They don't even know who I am. But someone has to protect Victor, someone who really understands the danger he's in."

"If Mr. Longly thinks he needs protection, we can send Gino over there," Sarah argued.

"Then send him, but I'm going back there until you come up with a better plan. That little boy needs me." With that Maeve left, ignoring Sarah's pleas to at least take a minute to discuss it.

Sarah stood in the front doorway watching Maeve hurry back down Bank Street and wished she could go after the girl and drag her back.

"You can always get her later," her mother said when Maeve was out of sight and Sarah finally closed the front door. "If Mr. Longly finds out who she is, he'll insist that she leave anyway."

She was right, of course. Chet Longly wouldn't appreciate knowing they had put a spy in his own house. "I just hope getting thrown out of that house is the worst thing that happens to her."

Maeve went to the back door, hoping she wouldn't attract attention. With any luck, Victor would still be asleep, and Mrs. Pauly might not even know she had been gone. She was halfway up the stairs when Mrs. Pauly said, "Miss Smith."

From her tone, she knew Maeve had been gone. She turned slowly to find the housekeeper standing at the bottom of the stairs. "I just need to check on Master Victor."

"Kate is with him. Come down here."

Having no choice, Maeve descended the stairs. Mrs. Pauly glared at her the whole time.

"Where have you been?" she asked when Maeve reached the bottom.

"I . . . I needed to run an errand."

Mrs. Pauly snorted at such a lame excuse. Servants ran errands only when their employer ordered them to. "I should fire you right now, but . . . I'll need to discuss it with Mr. Longly. In the meantime, go up and see to Master Victor. Kate is needed elsewhere."

Maeve gladly made her escape. She found Kate and Victor in the nursery. He was building something with his blocks while Kate sulked. When Maeve apologized she gave her a dirty look and left without a word.

"Kate said you left," Victor informed her when they were alone.

"I just had to go out for a few minutes."

"I don't want you to leave me anymore."

Maeve thought her heart would break. "I don't want to

leave you either." She sat down beside him and started to help him with his building project.

Maeve was beginning to think she might get away with her little errand when Kate came back into the nursery a few minutes later. "Mr. Longly wants to see you." Which meant he had returned home, and Mrs. Pauly had probably told him about her "errand." Kate looked a little smug, which told Maeve she was in trouble. Well, what had she expected?

"I don't want her to go," Victor said.

"Your papa wants to see me," Maeve said as cheerfully as she could manage. "I won't be gone long, though."

After getting Kate's promise to stay with Victor, she made her way downstairs. She wasn't too worried. She was a good liar and could make up a story on the spot if necessary. She would just have to wait to see what Longly's complaint was before deciding on her excuse.

Mrs. Pauly was waiting in the hallway outside the formal parlor. That seemed strange. Mr. Longly had seen Maeve in the family parlor before. She didn't dare ask Mrs. Pauly anything, though, judging from her expression. Mrs. Pauly opened the parlor door and said, "Miss Smith is here." She stood aside for Maeve to enter and closed the door firmly behind her.

Maeve hesitated, surprised to see Mr. Breedlove was still there. Both men were standing and turned when she entered the room. She should have bowed her head so Breedlove wouldn't get a good look at her, but it was too late now.

"Yes, that's her," Breedlove said. "I thought she looked familiar."

Maeve winced. So much for hoping he didn't recognize her. Longly was obviously furious and holding his temper with only the greatest effort. "Breedlove tells me you work for that private investigator he hired."

Maeve wasn't sure whether denying it would help or hurt so she said nothing.

Longly wasn't deterred. "So this Malloy character sent you here to spy on me. What were you supposed to find out?"

She could answer that one easily. "Mr. Breedlove wanted us to find out why you sent Julia to the asylum and if she really deserved that. We didn't think she did, at first, but now I know the truth, Mr. Longly, and I've already told my boss how dangerous Julia is."

Longly stared at her in astonishment. "You know that Julia is dangerous?"

"That's ridiculous," Breedlove said, glancing anxiously at Longly. "Julia isn't insane. We even found a judge to agree with us about that."

Maeve gave him a disgusted look. "You found a judge who was willing to free Julia for the right price."

Longly turned on Breedlove. "You bribed the judge?"

"It wasn't like that, Chet," Breedlove insisted, backing away from him. "I was simply able to convince the judge to speak with Julia and decide for himself."

"By bribing him," Longly said. "No wonder the judge didn't notify me that my wife was having a sanity hearing and no wonder he didn't even ask her doctors for their opinions."

"We couldn't leave Julia in that place," Breedlove said a little desperately. "Have you seen it?"

"Of course I saw it. My choices were to have her arrested for murder or put her in that place. I couldn't make a public spectacle of her. Victor's life would be ruined, so I chose to have her quietly locked away where she couldn't hurt anyone else."

"What do you mean?" Breedlove asked. "Julia never hurt anyone."

"You just told me Ruth is dead," Longly reminded him baldly.

Breedlove blanched. Had he forgotten his daughter was dead in the discussion of Julia? And could he really not suspect the truth? "But Ruth just . . . just fell out a window."

"But people don't just fall out of windows, do they?" Maeve asked. "A child maybe, but not grown-up people who know better."

Breedlove's eyes were full of pain. "It was an accident," he insisted.

"Was it?" Maeve asked. "Then how do you explain the fact that Victor's nursemaid fell out of a window just a few weeks ago after Julia decided Victor loved her more than he loved his mother?"

"That's . . . ridiculous," Breedlove repeated, but with far less confidence this time. He turned back to Longly. "Tell her."

"No one saw it, but we knew Julia pushed her," Longly said. "She hated Miss Winterbourne."

Breedlove was shaking his head. "But if no one saw it, how can you—?"

"And then there's the girl at Julia's boarding school," Maeve continued relentlessly. "Julia hated her for some reason and the girl died when she fell out a window."

Breedlove was speechless, but Longly was seeing her with new eyes. "How did you know that?"

"Julia's mother told us."

The two men stared at her in wonder.

"You found Mrs. Breedlove?" Longly asked.

"Where is she?" Breedlove asked. "Where has she been?"

"I don't know where she's been, and I wasn't the one who found her, but one of our operatives questioned her. She told us everything." Maeve turned to Longly. "She told us what happened to Julia's father, too."

"I didn't believe Ellie when she told me," Longly said. "Julia said her mother had always been jealous of the special relationship she and her father had. She told me her mother was using the tragedy of her father's death to turn me against her."

"She can be very convincing."

"What are you talking about?" Breedlove cried in dismay.

Longly stared at Breedlove for a long moment, probably choosing what words he would use to tell this awful tale. "Julia pushed your brother off that ship."

"No!" Breedlove nearly shouted. "It was an accident."

Neither Maeve nor Longly responded. After a moment Maeve said, "I understand that Ruth didn't like Julia living with you."

Breedlove frowned as if unsure whether Maeve was trying to trick him in some way. "Ruth was worried about being accepted into New York society. Having a close relative in an asylum would be difficult to explain."

"So, she wanted Julia to leave your house and go far away, someplace where her scandal wouldn't touch your family," Maeve guessed.

Breedlove pulled himself up to his full height as if fending off an insult. "We only wanted the best for Julia. People can be very cruel, and we wanted to protect her."

"Mr. Breedlove," Maeve said patiently, "Julia has pushed

three people to their deaths, that we know of. Now your daughter, who had a difficult relationship with Julia, has also fallen to her death. Do you think you should continue to defend her?"

Breedlove opened his mouth to respond but no words came out. He glanced at Longly, whose icy glare forbade any argument. "My wife is alone with Julia," he said, his voice a hoarse whisper. Without another word, he pushed past Maeve, threw open the parlor door, and practically ran out of the house.

For a long moment, both Maeve and Mr. Longly stared after Breedlove. Maeve decided she should be the first to break the silence if she had any hope of salvaging her relationship with Longly. "I'm so sorry I had to lie to you, Mr. Longly, but you must understand how outraged we were when it seemed that you had put a perfectly sane woman in an asylum."

"I think I can understand your outrage, Miss Smith, but I can never forgive your lying," Longly said coldly.

"I never lied," Maeve said. "I really am a nursemaid and I do care about Victor. I want him to be safe."

"So do I, Miss Smith, which is why I can never trust someone who came into my home with the express purpose of freeing my murderous wife and who has placed everyone in this house in danger."

"But I know what she is now, and I would never—"

"Don't tell me what you would never do, Miss Smith, because we know you will do or say whatever you must to accomplish your purpose."

"But I didn't—"

"Enough," he nearly shouted. "I've heard all I need to hear. Pack your things and leave this house at once."

"But Victor will be so upset," she argued, ignoring Longly's command to stop. "He's lost so many people in his life already."

"He's only known you a few days, Miss Smith. He'll hardly remember you a week from now, and even if he does, he doesn't need a woman hired to free his murderous mother taking care of him."

"But—"

"How do I know you aren't in league with her even now?" Longly went on. "Is that it? Are you planning to let her into the house some night so she can murder us all?"

"No!" Maeve cried in anguish. "I'd never want any of you to come to harm."

Longly's lips stretched into the rictus of a smile. "I made the mistake of believing another woman once when she said the same thing, and now I have to pray she doesn't come for my son."

"Mr. Longly, please—"

"Get out of here, Miss Smith. Don't make me send for the police to have you arrested for trespassing."

"What shall I say to Victor?" Maeve asked in despair.

"Whatever you like. You're a good liar. I'm sure you'll think of something."

With that she surrendered to the inevitable. How would she explain her failure to the Malloys? To Gino? She had been so certain she could accomplish something here, and now all she had to show for her efforts was a brokenhearted little boy.

Victor jumped up when she came back into the nursery and ran to her, throwing his arms around her. "You came back!"

Maeve glanced at Kate, who was glaring at her knowingly. She must have guessed Maeve was going to get fired. Servants didn't get summoned to the parlor to be commended. But Maeve had to focus on Victor. She loosened his grip on her and stooped down so she could look him in the eye. "Yes, I did, but I have to go again. I'm so sorry, Master Victor," she said quickly when he started to wail. "Your father told me that my mother is very sick, and I have to go home to take care of her."

"But you're supposed to take care of *me*," Victor argued.

He was right, of course. "Yes, but you have other people here who can look after you, and my mother is all alone."

"I don't want you to leave," Victor said, crying now. "Can I go with you? I could help."

Now Maeve was crying, too. "Your papa would miss you too much if you left him. He loves you very much, and he couldn't stand to be parted from you." That much, at least, was true. "You can help me pack my things."

"No need for that," Kate said with more than a trace of bitterness. "I put your things in your suitcase while you were downstairs."

So, she had known. Everyone had probably known. Servants always knew everything.

Kate went into Maeve's bedroom and brought out the suitcase. "I can't believe you took Mrs. Longly's side after the things she did," Kate said.

"I didn't know," Maeve said, defending herself.

"Mr. Longly didn't deserve this. He's a good man. After Miss Winterbourne died, he sent us all away for a few weeks, until he could send Mrs. Longly away and we'd be safe from her. Then you do this to him."

Maeve had no answer for her.

Victor was sobbing in earnest now, and Maeve had no idea how to comfort him. Anything she might say—that she would visit him, that she would write to him—would be a lie and he would simply be disappointed. Chet Longly would never allow her to contact his son again.

Kate had to hold Victor so he wouldn't follow Maeve down the long stairs. She slipped out the back door without a word to anyone. She supposed they were all secluded behind closed doors, so they didn't have to speak to her. They must hate her now, and she supposed she couldn't fault them for that. She'd been working to free a woman who had hurt and killed two of them and terrified all of them. When she thought about that, she even hated herself.

SARAH HARDLY KNEW HOW TO COMFORT MAEVE WHEN she came in the front door dragging her suitcase and looking as if she'd lost her best friend.

"Where is Mr. Malloy?" Maeve asked when she'd had a good cry on Sarah's shoulder.

"He came home with Catherine not long after you went back to the Longly house. When I told him what happened, he went to the Breedloves' house to see what he could find out. If we can find any proof at all, maybe this time they can arrest Julia and put her in prison, where she belongs."

"And what about your mother?"

"She decided she should go right back to Mrs. de Groot's house and tell Ellie Breedlove what happened. She needs to be on her guard even more now, don't you think?"

"Yes, but thankfully, Julia doesn't know we found her unless . . ."

"What is it?" Sarah asked in alarm, seeing the color drain from Maeve's face.

"I . . . I happened to mention that we'd found Mrs. Breedlove."

"Who did you tell?"

"Mr. Longly and Mr. Breedlove."

"Did you tell them where she was?"

"I don't know where she was and I don't even know where she is now, so I couldn't have told them that."

"Then she's not in any danger."

"Unless Breedlove tells Julia that we found her," Maeve said. "I wonder what lengths Julia would go to for that information."

"Don't think about that. I'm sure Mr. Breedlove isn't going to mention it to her."

But they both knew that was something Breedlove would most certainly mention to her.

"I think Mr. Breedlove believed me when I told him Julia killed the girl at school and Miss Winterbourne and even her father. At least I frightened him. He ran home so his wife wouldn't be alone with Julia."

"Julia won't be happy with them if they throw her out," Sarah said, "although they can't possibly allow her to stay if they believe she killed Ruth."

"I know why she sent Mr. Breedlove to tell Mr. Longly about Ruth's death," Maeve mused. "But didn't she realize they would throw her out and she'd be all alone in the world?"

Sarah rubbed her arms, warding off a sudden chill. "She wanted them to know. She wanted all of them to know. She obviously no longer cares if anyone knows what she is. She must hate her husband with a passion beyond all reason to cut herself off from everyone who might have supported her. He had the courage to lock her away, and he would have left her there for the rest of her life, ignoring any disapproval her family or friends or society as a whole might offer. Julia wouldn't have ever been able to hurt anyone again. His plan would have succeeded, too, if the Breedloves hadn't returned from London when they did."

"And if we hadn't helped them," Maeve said bitterly.

"At least nothing we did actually helped free her, although I'll never forgive myself for failing to see through her."

"What do we do now?"

"I don't know, at least not yet, but I'm sure Julia has a plan to exact her revenge. She isn't one to forget what her husband did to her. He's the one in danger now, I'm afraid."

XIV

WHEN FRANK AND GINO ARRIVED AT THE HOUSE THE
Breedloves were renting, they found the whole street eerily
quiet.

"I thought this place would be swarming with rubber-
neckers," Gino said.

"It would be if something like this happened on the
Lower East Side," Frank said. "I guess people here are a little
more civilized." He glanced around at the houses next to the
Breedloves' and directly across the street and saw a few cur-
tains twitch but no other signs of life.

"Or they're scared," Gino said, eyeing the large brownish
stain on the sidewalk in front of the Breedloves' house.

"They couldn't possibly suspect that the girl was mur-
dered," Frank said with more certainty than he actually felt.

"But seeing Ruth after she fell must have been horrible,
which would explain why all the neighbors are hiding,"

Gino said. "What would they have done with the body, do you think?"

"I'm guessing they just called an undertaker."

"But not the police?"

"Not if they thought it was an accident, and from what Maeve said, they did until Breedlove talked to her and Longly."

"Let's see what they think now."

Frank knocked on the door and they waited a little longer than usual for someone to answer. He was just about to knock again when a red-eyed maid opened the door.

"We're not receiving visitors," she said.

Frank handed her his card. "Tell Mr. Breedlove I need to see him immediately."

"But—"

"Just tell him."

She frowned at his rudeness and closed the door in their faces, leaving them standing on the porch.

"Do you really think Breedlove would send us away?" Gino asked.

"I hope not, but who knows? People do crazy things when they're frightened, and Breedlove must be terrified if he believed Maeve and Longly."

After another long wait, the door opened and the maid escorted them in, although her expression told them how reluctantly she did so. "Mr. Breedlove will see you in the parlor."

She led them in and didn't even bother to announce them.

Breedlove had been pacing but he stopped when Frank and Gino came in.

"Did you hear? About Ruth?" He looked like a man on

the edge. His hair was mussed from running his fingers through it, and he had stripped to his shirtsleeves.

"Yes. What happened?"

"We don't know what happened or at least how it happened. It was early this morning. My wife and I were still asleep, and Ruth is usually still asleep at that hour as well." Frank noticed he still referred to his daughter as if she were alive. "We were awakened by a scream. It was . . . chilling."

Breedlove's face had gone white, and Frank grabbed his arm and steered him to a chair. When he was seated, Frank motioned for Gino to fetch him something from the sideboard where a few liquor bottles were lined up.

When Breedlove had been fortified, Frank asked, "Who was in the house at the time?"

Breedlove frowned at the question, obviously thinking it of no importance. "The family, of course. The servants and . . . and Julia." His voice caught on her name. "No one else."

"When you heard the scream, what did you do?" Frank asked.

"We . . . Well, it took us a few minutes to figure out what we had heard. By then the servants were running to see. They'd been up for hours, doing their work."

Of course they had.

"Where were they going?" Gino asked. "The servants, I mean."

"Outside. That's where the scream was from and then they heard . . ." His voice caught again, and he looked up at them in helpless horror. "They heard Ruth hit the street shortly after."

Frank winced but he had to find out everything. "Where was Julia during all this?"

"I have no idea!" Breedlove cried, stricken. "I would have thought she was in bed like the rest of us."

"When did you see her?"

"I don't know. I guess she was with us when we reached the front door and ran outside to find . . ." His words choked off in a sob and then he was weeping like a man who had lost his only child.

Frank laid a hand on Breedlove's shoulder and squeezed, offering what little comfort he could. "Where is Julia now?"

Breedlove needed a minute to clear his throat. "Gone," he managed to choke out.

"Gone? You mean she left the house?"

"Took her luggage and vanished, thank heaven."

"How is your wife?" Frank asked.

"She was hysterical, as you can imagine. The doctor was here and gave her a sedative."

"I hope he left one for you, too."

Breedlove smiled mirthlessly. "I can't go to sleep. What if Julia comes back?"

Which was a good question, although Frank was pretty sure her work here was done. "How did Julia get away?"

Breedlove frowned in confusion. "What do you mean?"

"If she took her luggage, she had some kind of conveyance. Did she take a cab or . . . ?"

"No, the maid told me a private carriage came for her."

A private carriage? "Any idea who it belonged to?"

"None. It didn't exactly have a coat of arms on it," Breedlove said bitterly, obviously remembering his years in London. "Who cares anyway, as long as she's gone?"

But Frank cared and when Breedlove's grief wore down

to a reasonable level, he would want revenge and then he would care as well.

"Can Gino and I take a look at the room Ruth fell from?" Frank asked.

"What on earth for?"

"To see if we can figure out what happened and—"

"We know what happened. Longly and that girl of yours told me. Julia pushed her out the window."

"I'd like to see if there's any way I could prove it so we can get Julia locked away once and for all."

The pain on Breedlove's face was almost too much to bear but after a few moments, he rose stiffly and pulled the bell cord to summon the maid. At Breedlove's instruction, she took them upstairs and showed them which room was Ruth's, although she wouldn't go inside.

"Where was Julia Longly staying?" Frank asked her.

The girl blinked her red-rimmed eyes and pointed to the room across the hall.

"Did you see the carriage that took Mrs. Longly away?"

The girl nodded.

"Can you tell me what it looked like?"

"It was black with red trim."

"Did it have any decorations on it? A picture on the door or anything?"

The girl frowned. "It's funny. I didn't look at it too close, but now that you ask, it had a little picture on the corner of the door."

"What was it? Could you see?"

"I think . . . It doesn't make sense, but I think it was a picture of two coins."

"Coins?" Gino echoed. "You mean like money?"

"Yes, except who puts a picture of money on their carriage?" the maid asked.

"That does sound strange," Gino said, although the look he gave Frank said he didn't find it strange at all.

Frank thanked the girl and sent her off to grieve in private. The two men stepped into Julia's room and Gino closed the door behind them.

"Do you have an idea about the coach?" Frank asked Gino.

He nodded. "Remember Vogler said he used to take Julia to gambling dens?"

"Ah yes, then the coins make sense. And she's known there. Would they take her in, though?"

"A beautiful woman with good manners and class?" Gino said. "They'd make her the hostess."

"You're probably right, and they'd protect her, too. I doubt even the police would want to go into a place like that to get her."

"Before we worry about arresting her, we need to see if we can find any evidence to charge her with a crime," Gino reminded him.

They took a minute to scan the room. It was plainly designed for the daughter of the house, with pink drapes and bedclothes. The wallpaper was flowery and the furniture delicate and feminine. What must have been Ruth's clothes from yesterday were draped over a chair and her dressing table was a jumble of brushes and combs and hairpins.

The window still stood open, the slight breeze stirring the drapes. Frank walked over and peered out, not surprised to see the brown bloodstain on the street directly below. "How did it happen, do you think?"

Gino took his turn looking out, then stepped back. "She must have somehow convinced Ruth to come to the window."

"But even if she was leaning out to see someone or something in the street, she wouldn't have fallen. Not easily, at least."

Gino stuck his head out the window and verified Frank's theory. "It would make it easier to push her, though," Gino said.

"She wouldn't have gone without a fight, I'd guess," Frank said.

"Do you think they'll do an autopsy?"

Frank shook his head. "Why would they even think of it if they thought it was an accident?"

"Maybe we can convince Breedlove to do one?"

Frank wasn't so sure, but if it could prove Ruth was pushed, perhaps Breedlove would consider it.

WERE THEY MEAN TO YOU?" BRIAN SIGNED TO MAEVE, his darling face screwed up into a concerned frown.

As soon as Brian and Catherine had learned Maeve was back, they had stormed downstairs to reclaim her as their own. Both of them had noticed Maeve's red eyes.

"A little," Maeve said, "although the boy I was taking care of was very sweet."

"Not as sweet as we are," Catherine insisted, signing and speaking so everyone could know what she thought.

Maeve wrapped her arms around both children and hugged them to her. Sarah smiled at them, wishing they didn't ever have to face the kind of ugliness she knew was out in the world.

"Let the girl rest now," Mother Malloy said from where she'd been watching in the doorway. "She's had an ordeal."

"Thank you, Mrs. Malloy," Maeve said, standing up and

signing for Brian's sake. "But I think I'd like to spend some time in the nursery with the children to remind myself why I never want to leave here again. I'm sure you could use a little rest yourself after having their care while I was gone."

Mother Malloy grinned, her fingers moving with her words. "You're right there, girl. Go on now, go have a tea party or something."

"Not a tea party," Brian begged, trailing behind and trying to get Catherine to see his signing. But she was ignoring him, as sisters will, so Sarah knew he was doomed to endure a tea party with the girls. Her heart was so full, she thought she might cry, but she didn't want the children to see her with red eyes, too. She didn't want the sadness of this case to invade their home any more than it already had.

Malloy and Gino finally returned, but not until after they'd had supper and put the children to bed. Maeve had gone to bed as well.

"Julia is gone," Malloy reported to her.

"What do you mean, gone?"

"She packed up all her things and left in a private carriage."

"Good heavens," Sarah said. "She must have planned that."

"We thought as much," Gino said.

"But where would she go?" Sarah asked, trying to imagine how a woman would manage completely on her own.

"We think she may have gone to one of the gambling dens she frequented," Malloy said. "I'm waiting to hear from an expert on the subject."

Sarah could guess who that might be. "Did you find out what happened to poor Ruth?"

"Just that she fell out the window, but we convinced

Breedlove to let my friend Titus Wesley go to the funeral home and look at Ruth's body," Malloy said. Wesley was an undertaker more skilled than most of his kind and he had often aided Malloy in investigations. "Breedlove wasn't too happy about it, but I promised him Wesley wouldn't actually do an autopsy."

"What was he looking for then?" Sarah asked. The three of them were in the parlor where they could speak privately and not upset the servants.

"Bruises," Gino said. "Anything to indicate someone forced her out the window."

"Did he find them?"

Malloy and Gino exchanged a look. "Slight bruising on her wrists and a scratch on her arm."

"That proves something, doesn't it?" Sarah asked.

"Not enough to interest the police," Malloy said. "And we did try. They pointed out the body was in pretty bad shape and how could anyone know if the injuries were caused by the fall or something else?"

Sarah sighed. "I was afraid of that. So, what do we do now?"

"I'm not sure there's anything we *can* do," Malloy said. "Breedlove certainly doesn't need us to help him free Julia anymore." Sarah winced. "Longly would probably have us arrested if we tried to interfere—he doesn't trust us at all—and I can't think of any way to help them without their cooperation."

"Especially when the only way to help them is to lock Julia Longly up again," Gino said bitterly.

They sat in silence for a long moment, brooding over the stalemate. Then Gino said, "How is Maeve? Longly told us he fired her."

"She's very sad to have left Victor but happy to be home," Sarah said. "She's gone to bed. I don't think she got much rest at the Longly house."

"I should go see her," Gino said.

He was halfway out of his chair when Sarah said, "Wait until tomorrow. Her emotions are a little ragged right now, and she might . . . Well, I don't think she'd like for you to see her cry."

"You think she'd cry if she saw me?" Gino asked, outraged.

"I think she might feel safe enough to cry with you," Sarah said gently.

He sank back into his seat, a little stunned. "You think so?"

"I know so," she said briskly. "But she would hate showing weakness. She'll be stronger tomorrow. Now, we have to reconcile ourselves to the fact that there is nothing we can do until Julia makes the next move."

"What do you think she might do?" Malloy asked.

"I only wish I knew, but if I were she, I'd be plotting ways to get back at my husband for what he did to her."

"We did stop by Longly's house and advise him not to sleep there," Malloy said. "Or in his mistress's house either. He's going to a hotel tonight, or at least he said he would, someplace Julia won't find him."

"That makes sense," Sarah said. "I can't imagine she would try to push Chet Longly out a window, but there are many other ways to kill someone."

"Especially if he's sleeping," Gino said.

"But he can't stay in a hotel forever," Sarah pointed out.

"Which is why we need to wait to see what Julia will do next."

* * *

MOTHER MALLOY AND MAEVE HAD ALREADY TAKEN the children to school and Frank and Sarah were lingering over breakfast when someone started pounding on their front door.

"What on earth . . . ?" Sarah said.

Frank jumped up, guessing this wasn't a visitor his maid should be confronting. "I'll get it, Hattie," he called, hurrying down the hall.

He opened the door to find Chet Longly on his doorstep. "Where is she?" he demanded.

"Maeve?" Frank asked, confused. "She took my daughter to school. You did fire her, after all—"

"Not Maeve," Longly nearly shouted. "*Julia.* And what has she done with Victor?"

Frank muttered a curse. "Get in here, Longly, and tell me what happened."

"I thought you'd know what happened," Longly said, allowing Frank to pull him inside. His face was nearly purple with rage. "You were the one who advised me to leave my house unprotected last night."

"For your own safety, and I told you, we aren't working for Julia or even Breedlove. We know what she is now, and we'll help you all we can, but you have to tell me what she's done."

"Mr. Longly?" Sarah said, using her rich-lady voice, the one she used to influence servants and calm hysterical people and anyone else who needed calming.

Longly turned his suspicious and still-angry gaze to her.

"This is my wife, Longly. She's going to help you, too,"

Frank said, trying to sound reasonable when he really wanted to shout out some curses.

"Please come in and sit down and tell us what happened," Sarah said, taking his arm.

As if her touch were magic, his anger instantly melted into despair.

"She took him. Julia took my son," Longly told her with all the pain a loving parent could feel.

"She won't hurt him," Sarah told him. "It's you she wants revenge on."

"Hurting Victor would be the worst sort of revenge," he replied, and Frank knew he was right.

Sarah would know it, too, but she wasn't going to destroy Longly's hope. She led him to a chair, and he sat down, slumping like a man bearing the burdens of the world.

"Now tell us," Frank said, taking a seat beside Sarah on the sofa and across from Longly.

"I went to a hotel last night, as you suggested. I don't know why I bothered. I hardly slept a wink. The house was locked up tight, though. I checked every door and window before I left. I was awake before dawn this morning, so I went home. I wanted to have breakfast with Victor. He's been upset since . . . since Miss Smith left." He glanced up guiltily but did not admit his error there. "Everything was still locked when I got there. I went up to check on Victor and he was gone."

"Did you search the house?"

"Of course I did," he snapped, angry again. "I woke up all the servants first thing. One of the maids was sleeping in the nursery, but she didn't hear a thing. We searched every corner of the house, and all the doors were still locked. Victor couldn't have gotten out by himself."

"How do you think she got in?" Frank asked, his mind running through the possibilities. "Did one of the servants help her?"

"They're all terrified of her, so no, I don't think so. I think she must have a key."

"A key?"

"She used to go out at night, after the household was in bed and when I was . . . out." He meant at his mistress's house, they assumed.

"Your former driver told us she went to gambling dens," Sarah said as gently as one could say something like that.

"I didn't want to know. I hoped . . ." Longly sighed with infinite weariness. "I hoped that one night she simply wouldn't come home. I even considered killing her myself, but I couldn't do that to my son. The scandal . . . That was why I tolerated her as long as I did. I wanted to protect him, but when she killed Miss Winterbourne . . ."

"Of course, of course," Sarah said, leaning forward and nodding to confirm he had made the right decision. "Placing her in the asylum was really your only option."

Longly gave Sarah a look so full of gratitude it made Frank blink. "Do you know where she is? You said Vogler admitted he took her to gambling dens. Could she have gone to one of them?"

"It's possible," Sarah said. "There aren't many places a woman in her position could go with relative safety."

"Or take a kidnapped boy," Frank added, "if that's what happened."

"That's most certainly what happened. Who else would want to kidnap Victor?" Longly asked bitterly.

"One of the servants noticed the carriage that took Julia

away from the Breedloves' house. I've been trying to identify the markings on it," Frank said.

Just then the telephone startled them all with its shrill ring.

"That could be my answer now." Frank got up and hurried out into the hallway where the candlestick telephone sat on a table.

As he had suspected, his good friend Jack Robinson was calling. "It took me half the night," Jack complained good-naturedly. "Jocelyn says you owe us a dinner to make up for my being out so late."

"Sarah will be only too glad to repay you," Frank assured him. Sarah had recently delivered Jack and Jocelyn's baby and Jack had been more than helpful in several of Frank's cases. "What did you find out?"

"The Wishing Well is the name of it. It's one of Lou Lawson's places," Jack added, naming one of the most powerful gangsters in the city who was, oddly, also a friend to Frank's family, "but he wasn't pleased when I told him what might be going on there."

"How can a man who owns half the illegal businesses in New York be offended by anything?" Frank asked.

"We all have standards," Jack said with a laugh. Until recent months, Jack Robinson had also owned a lot of illegal businesses, a career he'd given up for his bride. "Is there anything else you need?"

"An address if you have it."

Jack provided it and then warned Frank to schedule their celebratory dinner before his baby girl started walking. Frank smiled to hear Jack refer to her as *his* baby girl.

"We have a possible location for Julia," Frank told Longly

and Sarah when he had hung up with Jack. "Are you familiar with the Wishing Well?"

"No. What is it?"

"A gambling den, I understand. The carriage that took
Julia and her luggage away from the Breedloves' house had
a design painted on the door. One of my contacts managed
to trace it there."

Longly jumped to his feet. "Let's go, then. I don't want
Victor to be in danger another second."

Frank held up both hands to stop him. "Wait, Mr.
Longly. You can't just go barging into a place like that. First
of all, they'll be closed now and locked up tight. They also
have armed guards who won't hesitate to kill you, and if
Julia has found refuge there, she must be under their protection."

"Do you think . . . ? What do they want with a woman
like Julia?"

"Whatever you are thinking and more, I would imagine.
If she's been frequenting the place for a period of time, she
has at least one protector there."

"Lover, you mean. Yes, I can see that. Julia always did
know how to use her charms. That's why I first started locking my bedroom door." Longly glanced at Sarah and instantly realized he had said more than he'd intended. "I'm
sorry, Mrs. Malloy. I didn't mean . . ."

"That's all right, Mr. Longly. You can't shock me. But I
imagine it took a lot of willpower to resist your wife."

Anguish flickered across his face. "By the time Victor
was born, I had realized how evil Julia was. I knew I couldn't
have any more children with her, no matter how much she
pleaded with me. She must have realized the power she

would have over me through my children, but so did I. That was when I locked her out and . . . made other arrangements."

"You found Mrs. Nailor," Sarah said, making Longly flush with embarrassment. "She seems like a lovely woman."

Longly had nothing to say to that.

Frank cleared his throat to change the awkward subject. "If we hope to find Victor and rescue him without incident, we need a plan."

"Do you have one?" Longly asked in surprise.

"Not yet, but my partner and Miss Smith will be arriving soon, and we will make one."

"Then I'm staying right here," Longly said. "Whatever you do, I want to be there."

"That might not be the safest thing for Victor," Sarah said, her voice gentle again. "You must trust Malloy. He has done this sort of thing before."

"And Victor is my son, Mrs. Malloy. You can't expect me to sit by and let others rescue him."

"Yes, I can," Sarah informed him, "if that is what will get the job done."

THAT EVENING, WELL AFTER DARK, GINO PULLED THE electric motorcar up to the curb in the shadowed area between the streetlights. They were close enough for the doorman to see they had arrived in a fancy vehicle but far enough that he couldn't see much else.

"Are you ready?" he asked Maeve.

"I will be," she said. "Give me your flask."

"Dutch courage," Gino joked, pulling it out of his coat pocket.

"It would be if we were really going to drink it," she said with an impish grin that made him want to kiss her. He handed her the flask. She uncorked the top and tipped a little in her mouth. While she swished it around, she handed the flask back to him so he could do the same. They both opened their doors a crack and spit the whiskey into the street.

"Splash a little on you so you reek of it," Maeve suggested.

Gino did as she suggested, although he'd have to listen to a lecture from his mother later on the evils of strong drink. She'd never believe the truth of why his suitcoat smelled like a distillery. "Are you sure you can act drunk?"

"I can act anything. Let's go."

Gino jumped out of the electric and hurried around to formally open her door for her. To his surprise, she let out a boisterous laugh, as if he'd done something hilarious, and leaned into him when she took his arm.

"Is the sidewalk moving?" she asked him happily and hissed under her breath, "Laugh!"

He managed a chuckle. "I think it might be. Hold on to me. I won't let you fall."

She laughed again and almost lost her footing. He was so engrossed in her performance, he almost forgot his own part until she pinched his arm through his coat. "Where is this place, anyway?" Gino asked too loudly, looking around with the uncertainty of one too drunk to be sure. "They said it was right here, but I don't see it."

"What might you be looking for, sir?" a voice asked.

Gino did a creditable job of looking puzzled while he searched the shadows for the person who had asked the question.

"Up here, sir," the voice said, so they both looked up, owl-eyed.

"There he is," Maeve informed Gino, pointing to the stoop of one of the brownstone houses on the block.

"Is this the Wishing Well?" Gino asked with exaggerated pronunciation.

"It certainly is. Come right in."

Gino tipped his hat to the doorman, then tipped his hat to Maeve, and then they both made their way carefully up the stoop to where the liveried doorman awaited. Since Gino wasn't really drunk, he noticed the man looking them over for signs of wealth. "I promised the little lady I'd win her enough for a diamond ring," Gino bragged, pulling out a wad of cash that made the doorman blink. He couldn't know it was mostly single dollar bills rolled up with a few larger denominations on the outside.

"Better put that away, sir. They'll take care of you inside," he said.

"You hear that, honey?" Gino marveled. "They'll take care of us inside."

"Sure they will," Maeve said. "If this fellow ever opens the door."

The fellow jumped to the task, ushering them in and closing the door firmly behind them.

The place was noisier than Gino had expected. They had a piano player, and although he was playing what might be considered soothing tunes, it just added to the noise from the tables, forming a cacophony of sound. If Victor called for help, no one would hear him.

"Oh, look," Maeve said, pretending to be taken with the beauty of the roulette table. She watched the wheel spin with comic fascination. "How do you play this?" she asked one of the gamblers, who took the question as an opportunity to try to look down Maeve's low neckline.

Gino drunkenly elbowed him out of the way. "I'll explain it to you," he told her. He began to do so, giving an explanation that had no basis in fact and even less in logic, but it gave them both a chance to look around the room and see if they could identify anyone.

Sarah Malloy had given them such an excellent description of Julia Longly that Gino felt sure they would have no trouble identifying her, but no woman in the room even came close to what he imagined she looked like. All the females were obviously harlots whose clothes and gaudy face paint served to advertise their profession. Even Maeve looked classy by comparison, although she had taken pains to paint her face and alter the gown she'd borrowed from Mrs. Malloy to make herself look cheap.

At the urging of the croupier, Gino bought some chips and proceeded to lose a few turns of the wheel.

"Come on," he told Maeve grumpily. "Let's try something else."

"You said I could keep your winnings, but you don't have any winnings," Maeve complained.

Grabbing her hand, he dragged her over to watch some men throwing dice. Gino was pleased to note the two of them were a cause for amusement to the other gamblers. That was according to plan, but they weren't going to find Julia Longly if she wasn't here.

Maeve was pretending to be fascinated by the tumbling dice and the shouts of victory or dismay from the gamblers. From the corner of his eye, Gino saw one of the bawds leading a gambler out into the hall and up the stairs. If Julia was really here and she had Victor with her, she'd most likely be hiding him in a bedroom out of sight.

With a little grin of anticipation, Gino bent down and

kissed the back of Maeve's lovely neck, just as he had fanta-
sized about doing for a very long time now. He felt her
flinch of surprise, but true to her character, she turned and
offered him her throat, which he immediately began to
cover with kisses.

"Get a room, you two," one of the gamblers grumbled.

"You got one?" Gino asked with just the right amount of
innocence.

One of the bouncers stepped up and whispered something to Gino, who took the hint and slipped him some
bills. They were quickly escorted to the stairway.

"Any room," the bouncer said. "Just make sure nobody
else is using it," he added with a grin.

Maeve shot Gino a look that made his breath catch, then
raced him up the stairs. At the top, she paused to let him
catch her and for one blissful moment, she let him kiss her.
But only for a moment. "Nobody's watching us now. You
check those rooms. I'll take these," she said against his lips.

He reluctantly released her and moved down the dimly
lit hallway to check those rooms.

Maeve gave him an adoring smile once his back was
turned and he couldn't see it. Then she turned to her own
end of the hall. The sounds coming from behind the first
closed door indicated the couple that had gone up before
them were quite busy. Maeve moved on. The next room was
empty. Curiously, the third door had a key sticking out of
the lock, but the door was open when she tried it. After
listening for a few seconds and hearing nothing, she opened
it wider, letting the light from the hallway spill across
the bed.

The light revealed two small, very dirty feet.

XV

THE CHILDREN HAD BEEN DIFFICULT TO SETTLE THAT evening. Oddly, they had protested Sarah's involvement. They had wanted Maeve, but she had explained that she and Gino had to do some investigating that night. The children weren't happy, so they resisted all attempts to placate them until fatigue finally claimed them.

As she paced the parlor, Sarah almost wished the children had taken even longer to fall asleep. At least she would have something to do. There had been no role for her in Malloy's plan to rescue Victor Longly, so she had to content herself with waiting. They would most likely bring the boy back here, a place Julia wouldn't know about, unless they were certain Julia was no longer in a position to find him again. So, Sarah was to keep the home fires burning, as it were.

"You'll wear yourself out," Mother Malloy told her from where she sat knitting by the light of the electric lamp.

"I just can't seem to sit still, though. I keep thinking about that poor little boy."

"She's not going to hurt him," Mother Malloy said with confidence. "At least not while there's a chance she can use him to bring her husband to her."

"You seem very sure," Sarah said.

"I've known women like her before. They don't care for nothing or no one except themselves."

"Julia seems more than just selfish, though," Sarah said.

"She is. Selfish women are a dime a dozen, but even they have a care for their own. No, Julia Longly is a breed apart. She'll get what she wants and the devil take it. She doesn't even care if she puts herself in danger."

Sarah was mulling the truth of that when someone started pounding on their front door and ringing the bell at the same time. It was far too soon for them to have rescued Victor, but Sarah couldn't stop the spark of hope that bloomed in her heart as she hurried to answer it.

But it wasn't whom she had expected. "Mrs. Ellsworth," Sarah exclaimed in surprise. Her neighbor looked as if she'd run across the street and forgotten to catch her breath.

"It's Theda," Mrs. Ellsworth gasped. "It's early but the baby is coming."

Sarah smiled and gently guided her neighbor into the house. Mrs. Ellsworth's daughter-in-law had extracted a promise from Sarah that she would deliver her baby when the time came, even though she only occasionally practiced as a midwife since her marriage to Malloy. She served as a backup to the midwives at the maternity clinic she had started on the Lower East Side, and occasionally delivered babies for her friends. Theda was one of her friends. "Tell me what's going on," Sarah said. It was indeed a bit early, but only a couple weeks. Babies kept their own schedules.

Mother Malloy had come out to see what the excitement was about. "Is it Theda?"

"Yes!" Mrs. Ellsworth reported excitedly. "She's been having contractions all day. I knew but she didn't want to tell me. She was afraid I'd get too excited, so I pretended not to notice."

Sarah smiled. Mrs. Ellsworth got excited over everything, so the birth of her first grandchild would certainly be such an occasion. "How far apart are the contractions?"

"Theda won't tell me," she wailed, forcing Sarah to somehow keep a straight face. "She just told me it was time to get you. Please, hurry!"

"First babies are hardly ever in a hurry. Just give me a few moments to get my bag." She knew the Ellsworth house would be well supplied with clean sheets and towels and blankets, so she didn't need to bring her own. All she would need was her medical bag with its various implements and supplies. She hoped only that Theda's delivery would be an easy one because dealing with Mrs. Ellsworth would be difficult enough.

MAEVE PUSHED THE DOOR OPEN A BIT WIDER SO THE hallway light illuminated the small figure huddled on the bed. The boy was curled up, his little body shuddering the way a child does when he has cried himself to sleep uncomforted.

Maeve hurried to him. "Victor, darling, wake up." She shook him gently.

He opened his eyes and stared at her warily. "Miss Smith?" he asked, fisting one eye.

"Yes, it's me. Don't be frightened. I'm going to take you to your papa. Would you like that?"

His little face pinched up as he scanned the room. "Is she here?"

"Your mother? No. Only me. We'll go in just a minute. I have to do something first."

Maeve considered calling for Gino, but she didn't want to raise an alarm and besides, he'd soon notice she wasn't in the hallway anymore and come looking for her.

They had discussed several ways to send an alarm, but basically, the plan was just to cause some sort of disturbance. Fortunately, this room faced the front of the house, so she quickly pulled a pillowcase off one of the pillows. The window wasn't locked, and she had no trouble pushing it open. She waved the pillowcase frantically for as long as she dared, hoping not to attract the attention of the doorman below.

But what if no one had seen it? She draped the pillowcase over the windowsill so it would be still visible to those on the street. She couldn't see anyone at all out there, but wasn't that the point?

"No, Mama!" Victor cried.

In an instant Maeve realized her position. She stood in front of an open window and Julia Longly had seen her.

SARAH FOUND THEDA ELLSWORTH ENSCONCED IN HER bed with her husband, Nelson, holding her hand and looking quietly frantic. Theda herself seemed relatively calm and more than a little excited.

"I did just what you said," Theda reported before Sarah

could even greet her. "I walked around and waited until the contractions were ten minutes apart to call for you."

"Is everything all right?" Nelson asked. He had removed his suit jacket, which was unusual for the normally dapper banker, and rolled his shirtsleeves up, as if he were preparing to deliver the baby himself. "She seems to be very uncomfortable."

"That's perfectly normal," Sarah said with a reassuring smile. "That's why they call it labor. Delivering a baby is hard work. Now if you'd give us some privacy, Nelson, I need to examine Theda to see how far along we are."

Nelson gave Theda a questioning look.

"Yes, go," she told him with a grin. "We don't need you for this part."

He made his escape with comic alacrity.

Sarah helped Theda into position so she could see the baby's progress. "You're almost completely dilated," she exclaimed in surprise. "I can already see the baby's head."

"I'm not surprised," Mrs. Ellsworth said. "I untied every single knot in this entire house."

"You did what?" Sarah echoed in surprise.

"To loosen the way for the baby," Mrs. Ellsworth said as if Sarah were simpleminded.

Sarah had heard that old superstition before, so she should have expected it from her notoriously superstitious neighbor.

"She even untied the knots in my nightdress," Theda complained. "It's practically falling off of me."

"Oh my, maybe we could find one of Nelson's nightshirts for her. Surely, it wouldn't have any ribbons on it."

Mrs. Ellsworth did as instructed, and in a moment, Theda was decently covered again.

"I also put a knife under the bed," Mrs. Ellsworth reported, "and unlocked all the locks in the house."

Sarah waited a moment to see if she was finished. "Is that all?"

Mrs. Ellsworth frowned. "Did I forget something?"

"No," Sarah assured her. "Are you boiling water?"

"I put it on before I went to get you. I'll go check."

When she was gone, Sarah said, "She means well. She only wants the best for you."

"I know. I do love her, but all the superstitions can be a bit overwhelming. Oh!"

Sarah placed her hand over Theda's stomach as the contraction did its work.

"How long was it since the last one?" Sarah asked.

"I had one just before you came in, but I didn't look at the clock that time."

"Are you feeling the urge to push?" Sarah asked.

"I think so. What should I do?"

Sarah took some wrist straps from her bag and attached them to the headboard. Then she helped Theda sit up, arranging pillows behind her for support. "When the next contraction starts, slip your hands into these straps like this." Sarah demonstrated. "That will give you some leverage. Then bear down. Your body will tell you what to do."

No sooner did she say the words than the next contraction came upon her. Theda's eyes widened but she quickly took hold of the straps and when the time came, she pushed as if she'd been doing it all her life.

"Good job! If your mother-in-law doesn't hurry back, she might miss the birth!"

"Is it that close?" Theda asked. "It's been so easy."

"The hard part is coming," Sarah said.

They had put a rubber sheet beneath the regular sheet, so Sarah wasn't worried about the mattress, but she grabbed several towels from the stack Mrs. Ellsworth had prepared and spread them out to catch the fluids that would come with the baby. It was only a couple of more minutes before Theda said, "Another one!" and grabbed for the straps.

Sarah put her hand on Theda's stomach and watched as the baby's head emerged a little more.

"Only one or two more pushes and I think we'll have a baby," Sarah said. She grabbed for her stethoscope and checked for a heartbeat, something she hadn't had time to do yet. There it was, strong and loud, so loud it seemed to have an echo.

Mrs. Ellsworth came back just then, carrying a pail of hot water. "Is something wrong?" she asked in alarm, seeing Sarah holding the instrument to Theda's stomach.

"No, everything is fine. I was just checking the baby's heartbeat. Can you drop those instruments into the water for me?"

"Another one," Theda cried as Mrs. Ellsworth did so.

Mrs. Ellsworth gave out a squeak of surprise, but Sarah focused completely on Theda. As she had expected, the baby's head emerged.

"He's so beautiful," Mrs. Ellsworth exclaimed.

Only a grandmother could call a newborn covered with blood and slime and with its tiny face scrunched up from the effort of being born beautiful, but Sarah had to agree.

"Is it a boy?"

"Don't know yet," Sarah informed her cheerfully. "One more push should tell us."

Theda had sagged back against her pillows. "I don't think I can do it."

"Yes, you can. Only one more push. Don't you want to see your baby?" Sarah taunted her cheerfully.

"Ohhh," Theda moaned as the next contraction began. "I can't!" she insisted even as she did, bearing down with everything she had.

The baby slipped free in a tangle of umbilical cord.

"It's a boy!" Mrs. Ellsworth exclaimed happily.

And he was screaming in outrage even before Sarah could clear his mouth. He was a bit small, Sarah noted, especially considering how big Theda had been the last few months, but his lungs seemed to be operating just fine. She wrapped the towel around him and used a pair of tongs to fish her scissors out of the pail of hot water. She cut the umbilical cord and then handed the baby off to Mrs. Ellsworth, whose eyes seemed to have doubled in size as she stared at the new arrival.

"Can I see him? Let me see him," Theda cried, and her mother-in-law hurried around the bed to show him to his doting mother.

But Sarah now realized that there was too much umbilical cord here. She sorted through it, finding the end she'd cut and where it went back into Theda, attached to the afterbirth that would emerge soon. But there was another cord, and both ends of it were still inside, and when she looked, she saw just the tip of a set of five tiny toes.

Theda's baby had a twin, and its umbilical cord was now pinched in the birth canal, and the baby would die if it wasn't born quickly.

MAEVE DROPPED TO HER KNEES JUST AS JULIA'S BODY would have slammed into hers. Julia went sprawling, grabbing the windowsill as her feet tangled with Maeve's skirts.

Maeve gave a moment's thought to lunging up and pushing Julia out the window, but she couldn't do that. She'd be no better than Julia and besides, Victor was watching. She couldn't do that to the child. Instead she heaved Julia up and slammed her onto the floor, and in another instant, Maeve was straddling her, knees pressed against Julia's arms. Julia was fighting with all her might, and she had started to yell, but she froze when Maeve pressed the knife to her throat.

Thank heaven she had strapped it to her leg this evening as she had every day she'd lived in the Longly house.

For a long moment the two women stared at each other in the shadowy light from the hallway.

"You won't kill me," Julia said.

She was right, of course, but Maeve bared her teeth in what she knew was a terrifying grin. "Try me."

The room went dark for a moment as someone large appeared in the doorway.

Maeve held her breath until Gino whispered, "Maeve?"

"I've got Julia," she said.

He moved out of the way so the light could come in and he saw them.

"Victor is on the bed. Get him and we'll go."

"You won't get far," Julia said. "Everyone in this house will try to stop you."

"Miss Smith?" Victor said. The poor mite must be terrified and horribly confused. "Is she the bad lady?"

"Yes, she is, but she won't hurt you. This is my friend Gino and he's going to take you to your papa."

"How are you going to make sure she doesn't raise the alarm?" Gino asked.

Maeve gave that a moment's thought. "Put your foot on her throat," she said.

He hesitated only a moment, and she moved the knife just far enough for him to accomplish it.

"If you so much as breathe hard, Gino will stomp down and you'll die," Maeve said, jumping up.

Julia plainly didn't believe her and she lifted her now-freed hands to push Gino's foot away, but bless him, he pressed his foot down harder, making her gasp, and she went still.

Maeve grabbed the other pillow and quickly used her knife to cut the pillowcase into strips. These she used to tie Julia's hands. She stuffed one into her mouth and tied it into place with the last strip.

"That should hold her for a few minutes," Maeve said.

"Someday you have to tell me how you learned to do all this," Gino said. "Come on, Master Victor," he said in the voice he probably used on his younger brothers when urging them to join the fun. "How about a piggyback ride?"

Still the boy hesitated, looking first to his mother, lying bound on the floor, and then to Maeve.

"It's all right. You're safe with us," Maeve said.

"It's awfully quiet downstairs," Gino said.

Maeve glanced back at the window where the pillowcase still hung halfway out. She'd done what she could. "Let's go."

They slipped out into the hall and Maeve closed the door behind them and turned the key. That should hold her for another few minutes. She pulled the key out and threw it down the hallway, where it would eventually be found but not anytime soon.

"The back stairs must be here somewhere," Maeve said, hurrying off into the darkness.

They had just found them when they heard Julia calling for help. She'd wasted no time removing her gag. She would easily attract the attention of the doorman, and someone would come up to release her, but that would still give them plenty of time to get away.

Maeve went down the stairs first, moving carefully in the dark. They reached the bottom without incident, and as they had figured, a door led to the alley that ran beside the house. Maeve held the door for Gino and his companion, and then took the lead in case she ran into any obstacles. She didn't want Gino falling down with Victor.

They were almost to the end of the alley when three very large and threatening men appeared and blocked their way.

THERE'S ANOTHER BABY," SARAH SAID, TRYING TO KEEP the panic from her voice but knowing she hadn't succeeded.

"Another baby?" Theda and Mrs. Ellsworth said in unison.

"A twin. Two, there are two, and the other one is breech."

"What does that mean?" Theda asked, Sarah's panic affecting her as well.

We couldn't have that. Sarah took a deep breath and managed what she hoped was a reassuring smile. "It means it's coming feetfirst, but that's just fine, because I'll have something to hold on to when I give this little one some help being born."

"What can I do?" Mrs. Ellsworth asked, her own voice less than steady.

"Just hold that one tight."

"A contraction is coming," Theda said.

"Push," Sarah told her, and both tiny feet appeared. She wanted to grab her stethoscope and try to find a heartbeat, but what if she didn't? She wouldn't be able to hide that from Theda and Mrs. Ellsworth. Besides, she knew new-borns could survive a little while without breathing and still be just fine. The question was, how long had the cord been pinched? There was no way to know.

Sarah grabbed more towels from the stack and positioned them. Were the little feet too pale? She couldn't tell. Didn't want to know. When the next contraction came, Sarah held the feet tightly in her left hand and pulled while she quickly wrapped the emerging body in one of the fresh towels to keep the baby from getting chilled. If he gasped in shock, he could inhale fluid and choke to death when he tried to breathe on his own.

If he ever did.

Or she. She saw now it was a girl, but that couldn't pos-sibly matter. Keeping her alive was all that did.

"What's happening?" Theda asked, her voice thick with tears.

"The body is born. We're going to get the head out with this next contraction, but you're going to have to push like you never pushed before. For your baby, Theda," Sarah re-minded her.

And when it came, she did push, crying out in anguish with all the pain and dismay and hope that every mother has felt.

Is that a signal?" Chet Longly asked, squinting into the darkness.

"It's certainly unusual," Jack Robinson observed, watch-ing the white cloth being waved out the window. "Not something you usually see in one of these places."

Frank shook his head. "Of course it's a signal."

"Then they've found my boy," Longly said with obvious relief.

"But they still have to get him out," Jack said. "Shall we go?"

Frank didn't bother to answer. He just climbed out of his motorcar and left it to the others to follow. They were half a block away and anything could happen while they were closing that distance. He trusted Gino and Maeve, but he didn't trust anyone else in that house, and he knew they would do what Julia Longly wanted if pressed.

The three of them had just reached the porch of the Wishing Well when a woman started yelling.

"Help me! Get somebody up here. I'm locked in!"

"That's Julia," Longly said, peering up at the woman ironically leaning out an upstairs window as she called for help. "Why doesn't somebody push her?"

No one had an answer for that.

"Miz Julia, is that you?" the doorman called, staring up at her with a puzzled frown.

"Of course it's me, you moron. Get somebody up here. I'm locked in."

"How'd you get locked in?" the doorman asked.

"Just get someone," she screeched. She ducked back inside, and the doorman disappeared into the house.

"That must mean Gino and Maeve have the boy," Frank said. "Now we need to do our part."

The three of them hurried up the stairs and into the gambling den. No one inside seemed too alarmed at the moment. Either they hadn't heard Julia's cries for help over the noise they were making themselves or a woman calling for help was no cause for concern here.

"What should we do?" Longly asked.

"Just wait," Frank advised.

They stood in the doorway to the main room for only a moment before one of the bouncers noticed them. "Welcome to the Wishing Well. Can I help you gents?"

"We're looking for a friend," Frank said. "We were to meet him here."

The bouncer looked them over and he stopped when he reached Jack. "Mr. Robinson, we don't see you much anymore."

"I'm an honest man now, Roger. That's what marriage will do for you."

"Remind me never to get married," Roger replied. Then he glanced at Chet Longly, who was plainly agitated and not looking at all like a man out for a pleasant evening with friends. "Something the matter with him?" he asked Jack, jerking his thumb at Longly.

Although no one else seemed to notice, Frank could hear the muffled sound of a woman's screeching voice, but then everyone looked up at the jarring sound of splintering wood. Julia must indeed have been locked in and without a key, too.

Everything stopped, even the piano player, and for a moment the only sound was the click click click of the little ball making its way around the roulette wheel. Everyone was looking up expectantly. The breaking down of a door was always the prelude to good entertainment for this crowd.

"Hurry," a female voice cried, and then she appeared at the top of the stairs. "O'Connell, where are you?" she shouted.

One of the well-dressed men at the roulette table looked surprised and made his way with dignified purpose but not too quickly, in case anyone thought him at the beck and call of a female, to the hallway where he could see her.

"They've taken the boy. They've . . ." She had seen her husband, and how could she not since he had stepped forward to stand beside O'Connell? "You!" she screamed with all the venom and hatred a woman could feel.

Oddly, Frank noticed she had something that looked like a bandage trailing from one wrist, but he had barely registered this when she fell on Longly. She would have raked her nails across his face, but he caught her wrists and held them.

"Kill him!" she shrieked. "O'Connell, kill him!"

GINO AND MAEVE STOPPED DEAD AT THE SIGHT OF THE three men.

"Is that the boy?" one of them asked.

Maeve didn't know whether to answer or not, and apparently, neither did Gino. They stood no chance of overpowering these three men if they wanted to take Victor, though.

After an awkward silence, the man said, "Miss Smith, I guess you don't recognize me in the dark."

Maeve blinked. "Mr., uh, Lawson?"

"That's right. And this must be Mr. Donatelli. You have the boy?"

"Yes, sir," Gino said, knowing Lou Lawson was on their side.

"Good, my colleagues here will escort you to your motorcar. Do you know where to take him?"

"Yes, we do," Maeve said. "We just didn't know you'd be here."

"I decided I should take an interest in this situation," Lawson said.

A loud crash made them all start.

"It sounds like the time has come for me to step in. These gentlemen will protect you until you can get away."

With that he was gone, heading toward the entrance of the Wishing Well with no apparent sense of urgency.

"Come along, miss," one of the men said. "Do you need help with the boy?"

"No, thanks. It's not far to my motor," Gino said. Maeve smiled because she knew he would never ask for help in front of her.

"Let's get out of here," she said.

THEN THE BABY WAS FREE, AND FOR ONE INSTANT SARAH froze, staring down at this tiny scrap of life who, she realized, was staring back at her with the most perplexed expression Sarah had ever seen, as if wondering why on earth Sarah had put her through all that.

"Is it . . . all right?" Mrs. Ellsworth asked tremulously.

Which galvanized Sarah. She quickly cleared the baby's mouth, then picked her up by her feet and held her upside down and slapped her little bottom, making her howl like a banshee and putting her brother to shame. Within seconds the pale little body pinkened and the little hands tightened into fists and Sarah wrapped her in a towel and held her close to comfort her.

"It's a girl," she informed them over the baby's wails.

Theda stared at her in shock, and Mrs. Ellsworth said, "I knew it. This is why we could never get a good reading with your wedding ring, Theda."

Sarah carried the baby girl around the bed so Theda could see her, too.

"I want to hold them. I want to hold them both," Theda said, tears of happiness and relief running down her face.

Sarah and Mrs. Ellsworth quickly rearranged the pillows so Theda could hold both of her children. Sarah showed her how to position them to nurse, and soon they were happily suckling away, which helped deliver the afterbirth.

"I suppose someone should tell Nelson," Mrs. Ellsworth said while Sarah was helping Theda change into a clean nightdress with the knots all tied up.

"My goodness, he must be going crazy," Sarah said.

"I want to tell him myself," Theda said, glowing like a new mother should. "Mother Ellsworth, go fetch him but promise you won't say a word."

When she was gone, Sarah checked to make sure she had some smelling salts in her bag.

KILL HIM!" JULIA ONCE AGAIN COMMANDED THE MAN who was obviously her protector in this place. From the way the bouncers held back, Frank understood he was also the manager or even part owner.

O'Connell grabbed Julia's arm and shoved her behind him, as if to protect her from Longly. "Who are you?"

"That's my husband," Julia said for him. "You said you'd kill him for me. You promised."

Plainly, O'Connell found this revelation a bit embarrassing, but he wasn't going to let that stop him. He drew back his fist, but Longly sucker punched him in the stomach. He doubled over and Longly landed another punch right on his nose, sending a geyser of blood spouting across the floor. Julia screamed and lunged for Longly again.

Frank grabbed her but caught only one arm and she swung on him, catching his cheekbone with one small fist and startling him into letting her go.

By then the bouncers had jumped in to grab Longly and Frank and probably Jack, too, although Jack had yet to even move to help his companions. But Frank had witnessed his share of bar fights in his years with the New York City Police, so he shoved the bouncer who came for him back into the crowd at the roulette table, which jarred the table and scrambled all the bets and gave the patrons the excuse to join the melee.

O'Connell had finally caught his breath and was coming up to help his lady, so Frank planted his foot on O'Connell's lower back and shoved him into the gambling room as well. One of the bouncers had grabbed Longly from behind and pinned his arms, and Julia was pummeling him with her fists, so Frank grabbed Julia from behind.

Jack, he noticed, had made short work of the bouncer who had tried to tackle him and now moved to free Longly. He had just succeeded in doing so when someone emitted an ear-piercing whistle that froze everyone.

The man who stood in the doorway wasn't particularly large or imposing, but all the Wishing Well employees raised their hands as if displaying that they held no weapons and retreated at least one step at the sight of him.

The only person who seemed unmoved was Julia, who continued to struggle against Frank's hold and mutter the kind of curses one would expect to hear on the docks.

"Mrs. Longly," the man in the door said, startling her into stillness. "You forget yourself. Anyone might think you were insane."

The words obviously stung, and Frank marveled that he

had spoken them, but they had the desired effect of silencing Julia, at least for the moment.

From somewhere in the other room, O'Connell had collected himself and he emerged tentatively but with as much dignity as he could manage while holding a handkerchief to his nose to stanch the blood. "Mr. Lawson, it's good to see you."

Which was an odd thing to say, but Frank imagined O'Connell was under a lot of strain. Lawson was, after all, his employer.

"Since when do you allow people to hold kidnapped children in my establishment?" Lawson asked mildly.

O'Connell's face turned scarlet, but it was Julia who replied.

"He wasn't kidnapped. I'm his mother. I have as much right to him as anyone."

Frank knew Sarah would have argued that, too, under normal circumstances. It hurt him to know that these were not normal circumstances, though, and even Sarah would agree to that.

Frank realized that he was still holding her, and when she shrugged against his restraint, he let her go. She straightened her dress, which he noticed was quite a bit less modest than the ones she would have worn as Longly's wife. Then she smiled at Lawson in a way no lady ever smiled at a strange man.

"I don't know who you are, but you should know what this man has done to me." She glanced at Longly just to make sure Lawson knew whom she was talking about. "He sent me to an asylum. He would have locked me away for the rest of my life just so he could enjoy his mistress in peace."

A murmur of shock went through the crowd or perhaps it was just a murmur of interest. This crowd probably didn't shock easily.

"You have indeed been done a great injustice, Mrs. Longly. I'm not sure how to make it up to you, however."

Julia glanced at Longly again. "You can let me . . ." she began, and then launched herself at Longly. This time she did rake his face with her nails, and she clamped her hands around his throat before anyone could even think to stop her. The force of her attack sent both of them to the floor, and Julia scrambled over him and put her knee on his throat.

Frank and Jack each grabbed one of her arms and lifted her free of him even as she kicked and screamed in protest. Longly came up gasping, and Julia was now shouting her curses and fighting both of them with all her strength. At that moment three men came in the front door.

"We'll take her from here," one of them said.

"Ziegler," Julia cried. "I won't go with you. Tell them, O'Connell! I won't go with them."

She fought like a tiger, but the two orderlies had handled much worse cases than Julia Longly, and after only a few moments, she was gone, bundled into the ambulance and on her way back to the Manhattan State Hospital.

O'Connell must have given some sort of signal because the piano player began to play again. He was a little hesitant at first, but when no one objected, he began to play with more enthusiasm.

"Thank you for your timely appearance, Mr. Lawson," Frank said with a small smirk.

Lawson smirked back, but he wasn't smiling when he turned to O'Connell. "I'll want to know what's been going on here. Come to my office tomorrow."

O'Connell could only nod.

"I think our work here is done, gentlemen," Lawson said with a nod to Frank and his two cohorts.

They made their way out to the dark street. Frank glanced up to see that Maeve's signal still dangled from the window. "We need to make sure Maeve and Gino got away with the boy."

"They did," Lawson said. "My men made sure of that. Where were they going to take the boy?"

"Your house, wasn't it?" Longly said to Malloy.

"Yes, since Julia was still loose when they found him. We'll take you there and then you can take your boy home, Longly."

"I don't know how to thank you, Malloy."

"Just knowing your boy is safe is thanks enough," Frank said.

XVI

FRANK WAS GLAD TO SEE THE LIGHTS WERE ON IN HIS house. That probably meant Gino and Maeve had made it home with Victor and were awaiting news of how the rest of the plan had gone.

His mother answered the door and she put her finger to her lips to indicate they should keep their voices down. "The boy is asleep, but he wouldn't be separated from Maeve. They're in the parlor."

Longly didn't wait for an invitation. He could see his boy lying on the sofa, his head in Maeve's lap, and he went straight to them, falling to his knees when he reached them so he could see the boy for himself.

Frank noticed that Gino stood behind Maeve and when Longly approached, Gino put a hand protectively on her shoulder.

"He's fine," Maeve assured him. "He's just exhausted."

Longly laid a hand on the boy's head and lowered his own to hide his tears of relief. He'd blinked them away when he raised his head again. "I was wrong about you, Miss Smith. I owe you an apology."

"I can't blame you for misjudging me, but we were always trying to do what was right. We just had to figure out what that was. What happened to Julia?"

"Dr. Ziegler took her back to the hospital," Frank said.

"I hope they're ready for her there," Jack Robinson said with feeling.

"I spoke with him at length today," Longly said, rising to his feet again. "They're going to put her in the ward with the dangerous patients so she can't escape and won't attract the attention of any sympathetic judges."

"And sadly, the Breedloves won't ever try to get her released again either," Maeve said.

"So we may finally be free of Julia," Longly said.

"We can let her mother know, too," Maeve said. "I'm sure she wants to meet her grandson."

Longly looked at Frank. "If you'll tell me how to get in touch with her, I'll arrange a visit as soon as possible."

"And Gino and Maeve will have to tell us how they found Victor and made their escape," Frank said.

"Maybe later," Gino said. "I think we need to get Victor and his father home."

Something had been niggling at Frank and he suddenly realized what it was. "Where's Sarah?"

NELSON HADN'T REQUIRED THE SMELLING SALTS, BUT IT was a near thing. Fortunately, Sarah had thought to have a chair ready for him. Now he was taking turns with Theda holding the babies and counting fingers and toes the way new parents did.

"What did Mrs. Ellsworth mean about your wedding ring not telling you something?" Sarah asked.

Theda grinned. "If you tie a woman's wedding ring to a string and hold it over her belly, the way it moves—back and forth or up and down—will tell you if the baby is a boy or girl."

"Oh, I see," Sarah said. "And you kept getting both results."

"Yes, and now it looks like there was a reason." Theda winked, and Sarah covered her mouth to hide a grin.

"Something is going on at your house," Mrs. Ellsworth said. She was peering out the window, which wasn't unusual. Nothing much happened on Bank Street that Mrs. Ellsworth didn't notice.

"Oh my, I forgot in all the excitement. They were rescuing a little boy tonight. This must mean they brought him home, safe and sound," Sarah said after checking the street herself. Both of their motorcars were parked at the curb in front of the house instead of being put away in the garage, and another one Sarah didn't recognize had just pulled up. She hoped this meant the mission had been successful and everyone had gathered here before going home.

"You should go see what's happening," Mrs. Ellsworth said.

"I can't leave Theda," she protested.

"Nonsense. We're here and you'll just be across the street."

"Yes, I'll be fine," Theda said. "Besides, now we also want to know if they rescued the little boy."

After some more urging, Sarah decided to duck across

the street just long enough to hear the news. The front door was still slightly ajar when she arrived, so no one noticed her slip in. Two large men she did not know were standing in the hallway, obviously waiting for someone. They nodded politely. She stepped past them and saw the sweet tableau of Maeve and Victor on the sofa with Longly hovering protectively over them.

"Sarah," Malloy said. "How did everything go?"

"Just fine," Sarah said. "And I see you have Victor back."

"Yes, and Julia is safely locked away again."

Sarah sighed with relief and looked around at the remainder of her guests. She was a bit surprised to see the man known as Lou Lawson. He also nodded a greeting when their eyes met, and Sarah smiled broadly.

"Mr., uh, Lawson, do you know where I've been?"

"I don't think I do, Mrs. Malloy," he admitted. "I've just arrived."

"I was across the street, making a delivery."

"Across the . . . *Theda?*" he asked, his eyes growing wide with surprise when he realized she was talking about his stepdaughter.

"Yes, indeed. I'm sure they would be happy to see you. Nelson could use the support."

Instantly, the tough gangster vanished, and Lou Lawson was a man beguiled by the prospect of a new life in his family. "My wife's nose will be out of joint when she finds out I saw the baby first," he said. "But I'm willing to risk it."

In a moment he and his two henchmen were gone.

"Is it a boy or a girl?" Maeve asked.

Sarah smiled and made them wait for a very long moment. "One of each," she told them. "One of each."

Author's Note

MANY THANKS TO DR. MICHELLE SKEEN, WHOSE WORK triggered my interest in psychopaths and who provided her expertise in checking the book for accuracy. Mental illness was, of course, poorly understood in 1901, when this book is set, and many treatments were cruel and barbaric by today's standards. The Manhattan State Hospital was indeed a massive structure, built in the Kirkbride style as I described. Certainly fresh air and sunshine would have benefitted the patients there, even if it didn't cure them.

Ward's Island was long a dumping ground for New York City, beginning in the 1840s, when over one hundred thousand paupers' graves were moved from Manhattan to the island. The island was also the site of a hospital for sick and destitute immigrants, known as the State Emigrant Refuge. Other tenants included an immigration station, a homeopathic hospital, a rest home for Civil War veterans, the Inebriate Asylum, and the New York City Asylum for the Insane, which became the world's largest mental institution and is now the Manhattan Psychiatric Center, still located on the island.

Please let me know if you enjoyed this book, and if you send me an email through my website, www.VictoriaThomp son.com, I will put you on my mailing list and send you a reminder when my next book comes out.

Keep reading for a preview of the
27th Gaslight Mystery

MURDER IN ROSE HILL

by *USA Today*
bestselling author Victoria Thompson.

IT'S A GIRL!"

Sarah Brandt Malloy held up the squalling infant she had just delivered so the mother could see it.

"Poor mite," the woman said wearily, raising her head from the pillows to see better. "I was hoping for a boy. They have an easier time of it in this world."

Sarah couldn't argue with that. Males had a lot of advantages, and when you started your life as the illegitimate child of a penniless mother, as this baby was, those advantages helped.

"I know you'll do your best for her, Mary," Sarah said.

Mary sank back on the pillows and sighed. "I already been doing my best, and if it wasn't for this clinic, I'd have birthed her in an alley."

Which was why Sarah had founded the clinic in the first

place, to give women like Mary a safe place to have their babies. "Don't lose heart," she said, handing the baby to Miss Kirkwood, one of the other midwives employed at the clinic. "You can stay here until you recover and then we'll help you find a job."

Mary didn't reply, but Sarah didn't notice because she was busy massaging Mary's stomach to encourage the delivery of the afterbirth. Miss Kirkwood had cleaned up the baby and wrapped her in a fresh blanket, but when she tried to hand the child to the mother, Mary turned her head away.

"Don't. I'm not going to keep her. I can't."

"You don't have to decide right now," Sarah said as gently as she could. "As I said, you can stay here until you have your strength back. Then you can decide."

But Mary shook her head. "I already decided. It's best for her. I don't want her growing up in the streets like I did."

Growing up in an orphanage wouldn't be much better for the child, but Sarah knew better than to argue with a woman whose hormones were still running wild from childbirth. "At least nurse her a little," Sarah urged. "It's for your own good. You'll recover faster if you do."

Miss Kirkwood offered the baby again and this time Mary took the tiny bundle, even though she was obviously reluctant.

"I don't know what to do," Mary complained. Miss Kirkwood showed her how to put the baby to her breast, and soon the child was suckling happily.

"She don't have much hair," Mary observed after a few moments.

"It will grow," Miss Kirkwood said, brushing her fingertips over the baby's downy head. "It looks like it will be blond, like yours."

Mary didn't exactly smile but her frown relaxed a bit. Sarah said a little prayer that Mary would fall in love with her baby, as most mothers did no matter what their circumstances. But if she didn't, Sarah would do everything she could to give both Mary and her baby a chance in life.

When Mary and the baby were both cleaned up and comfortable, Sarah bundled up the soiled towels and sheets and was getting ready to leave the new mother and her child to rest when someone knocked on the bedroom door.

It was one of the other women who were currently staying at the clinic. This woman had given birth a few weeks ago and would soon leave. "Mrs. Malloy, there's a lady here, and she asked to see you in particular."

That was odd. Prospective patients didn't usually ask for Sarah since she came to the clinic only occasionally. She had been lucky today to find one of the residents was in labor, so she got to help with a delivery. She had once made her living as a midwife, but rarely had a chance to make a delivery anymore now that she was a rich matron able to sponsor charities.

"She asked for me by name?" Sarah said to clarify.

"Not by name, but she wanted to speak to the lady in charge, and I thought she must mean you."

Sarah smiled and thanked her.

"I'll take care of those," Miss Kirkwood said, taking the bundle of dirty linens from her.

Sarah made her way downstairs and found a young woman waiting in the parlor of the large house she had purchased and remodeled into the clinic. The parlor was now a waiting room of sorts with comfortable chairs for the neighborhood women who had a home in which to deliver but who still came to the clinic for prenatal care. "May I help you?"

The woman rose. She was probably in her late twenties with ash brown hair and chocolate-colored eyes. She wore a dark skirt and jacket with a white shirtwaist, what had come to be a sort of uniform for women who held paying jobs, and a rather sensible hat. She didn't look like the type of woman who needed the services of a charity clinic. "Are you Mrs. Malloy?"

"Yes."

"The lady who answered the door said you founded this clinic," the woman said.

"I started it, yes. I was a midwife myself, so I knew there was a need for it. Are you looking for a place for yourself?" The young woman was slender as a reed, but she might still be expecting.

She smiled at that. "Oh no, not at all. I didn't even want to talk to you about that. It's something else, something to do with women's health, though, so I thought perhaps you might be able to help me."

Sarah had to admit this was intriguing, so she invited the young woman to sit down and asked one of the expectant mothers who had gathered in the hallway to eavesdrop on their visitor if she would fetch them something cool to drink.

While they waited, the young woman said, "I am Louisa Rodgers. I'm a reporter for the New Century magazine."

"I see," Sarah said. This was quite impressive since not many reporters were female. "Are you writing an article about women's health? That's what you said, isn't it?"

"Yes, well, I'm writing about something that affects women's health: patent medicines."

Sarah couldn't help wincing. "If you're looking for some sort of endorsement, I'm afraid you've come to the wrong place." Advertisements for these medicines often featured recommendations from various medical professionals even though the preparations seldom contained anything that actually cured or even treated diseases.

"Oh no, Mrs. Malloy. I'm . . . well, just the opposite, in fact. I want to write an article about how dangerous these potions can be."

Sarah needed a moment to absorb this. "And your magazine has assigned you to do this?"

"Well, yes," Miss Rodgers said almost defensively. "I hope you don't think that just because I'm a female that—"

"No, no, nothing like that," Sarah hastily assured her. "I would be the last person to think that. I'm just surprised that a magazine would want to publish something unflattering about these nostrums. Don't magazines usually avoid controversial subjects?"

Miss Rodgers lifted her chin in a show of defiance. She wasn't a beautiful girl, but her confidence and determination made her quite striking. She actually looked as if she relished taking on this monumental task. "The *New Century* wants to make a name for itself as a progressive publication. We want our readers to know they can trust us to tell them the truth and will always be concerned with their well-being."

That was a noble cause, but Sarah had rarely seen any commercial enterprise succeed at it. "I must say, I'm glad they have given this assignment to a woman."

Miss Rodgers shifted uncomfortably in her chair. "Yes, it is an honor, but I must do an excellent job at it or . . ."

She didn't need to explain. If a woman was entrusted with an important job and failed at it, that would make it all the harder for the next woman to be trusted. "Why have you come to me and how can I help?"

Miss Rodgers smiled. "I was in the neighborhood talking to women and trying to find some who regularly use patent medicines. I wanted to know if any of them had been cured or even helped in any way."

"And did you find any?"

"No one who had actually been cured, although most of them swear by whatever concoction they are taking," she said with a sigh.

"People never want to admit they made a mistake, and as you probably know, these medicines often contain alcohol or drugs that actually do ease pain and make one feel a little better, if only temporarily."

"Exactly. Then I thought perhaps a doctor might be willing to tell me the truth. I know some people become . . . well, ill from taking these medicines and end up in a doctor's care as a result."

"Did you think you'd find a doctor at this clinic?" Sarah asked.

"No, but I thought a woman—a nurse or midwife— might be more willing to tell me the truth, and since you deal with only women at this clinic, I hoped some of them might speak freely as well."

Sarah had to admit her logic was sound. Unfortunately, in Sarah's experience, just because *she* thought people should do something didn't mean they actually would. "I'm perfectly willing to ask our ladies if they have ever tried a patent medicine, and it's highly likely that they have."

"So many people use them," Miss Rodgers agreed.

"Yes, well, you have to admit the advertisements are quite impressive, although it's difficult for me to believe that one tonic can cure things as varied as cancer and a toothache."

Miss Rodgers smiled. "And it seems they all cure *catarrh*, whatever that is."

"It simply means *congestion*, although they are never quite clear about what type of congestion they intend to cure."

"Are you aware of anyone here who uses any of these so-called medicines?"

Sarah had no intention of violating anyone's privacy, especially knowing the ladies in the hallway could hear every word, so she was careful with her reply. "I know many women use Lydia Pinkham's Vegetable Compound for female complaints, although the ladies here aren't having their monthly periods, so that isn't a problem for them."

"Indeed it isn't," the woman Sarah had asked to bring them drinks said, carrying in two glasses of lemonade. "Here you are, nice and fresh."

"Thank you so much, Annie," Sarah said.

"I've taken that Lydia Pinkham's myself," Annie said, handing each of them a glass. "My monthlies were that painful, but Pinkham's helped a lot."

Several women in the hallway murmured their agreement.

"Lydia Pinkham's is twenty percent alcohol," Miss Rodgers said knowledgeably.

"Is it now?" Annie asked. "Is twenty percent a lot?"

Miss Rodgers looked a little startled by the question, but Sarah said, "Enough to get you drunk if you take too much."

"Peruna's is almost fifty percent alcohol," Miss Rodgers added, naming another popular brand.

"I knew a woman took Peruna's, three bottles a day," Annie recalled. "Couldn't hardly walk straight. I guess that explains it. Glad I stuck to Pinkham's."

"Thank you, Annie," Sarah repeated more forcefully.

Annie finally took the hint and rejoined her compatriots out in the hallway.

"Isn't Pinkham's also used for change-of-life symptoms?" Miss Rodgers asked.

"Which is also not a problem for our ladies," Sarah replied with a smile to soften her words.

Miss Rodgers seemed a little chagrined. "No, of course not. But . . . older women do use it, don't they?"

"Women of all ages do, I'm sure." Sarah sighed. "Don't misunderstand me, Miss Rodgers. My first husband was a physician, and no one worked harder to cure his patients than he did but . . . Well, we really know very little about how the human body works and how diseases are contracted and how to treat them. Doctors are often guessing when they treat a patient, and a treatment that cured one person might kill another."

"Which is why many people don't trust doctors and refuse to see one even when they are very ill," Miss Rodgers said. "And many others can't afford to visit a doctor even if they would like to."

"Exactly. I'm a nurse and a midwife, and I deal with the same issues. The birthing process should be the same for every woman since all women have the same organs, and yet every birth is unique, and sometimes even years of experience don't help me with a particularly difficult birth. And of course not everyone can afford to hire a midwife and some must give birth alone, which can be dangerous and even fatal for both mother and child. That is why I started this clinic."

To Sarah's surprise, Miss Rodgers was nodding as if she understood completely. If she had been researching this subject, she probably did.

"So naturally, people who are poor or who just don't trust doctors will look for an easier way to cure themselves, and if that comes in a bottle they can buy cheaply, they will do that," Miss Rodgers said, "even if the bottle contains only alcohol and water."

"Or opium or morphine or Heroin," Sarah added. "All those things will ease pain, which allows people to feel better or at least think they do for a little while."

"But they will also create a dependence," Miss Rodgers said with a frown that told Sarah she must have seen this herself.

"Yes, an addiction that forces the patient to continue purchasing the so-called medicine, making the manufacturer rich but doing nothing to cure the patient. People who would never dream of going to an opium den or taking drugs of any kind and even people who are morally opposed to liquor in all its forms can become enslaved to these nostrums, believing them to be actual medicines. Miss Rodgers, if you can educate the public about this, you can eliminate a lot of needless suffering."

"That is just what I intend to do," Miss Rodgers said. "I wonder if . . . if you'd allow me to interview the ladies you have staying here and anyone else who would like to speak with me."

"It isn't my place to allow anyone to do anything here. These ladies are free to speak with you or not, as they choose, but I will certainly invite them to do just that." Sarah glanced over her shoulder at the women gathered in the hallway. "I imagine you will have at least a few willing volunteers."

"I'm very grateful, Mrs. Malloy. This is so important." Miss Rodgers's eyes were shining with the fervor Sarah had often seen in would-be reformers.

"Yes, it is. I'm afraid I am going to have to leave soon. I must get home, but you are welcome to stay as long as you like and return if you need to. In the meantime, here is my card." Sarah handed her a calling card with her home address. "Feel free to contact me if I can be of any help."

Miss Rodgers thanked her profusely, and Sarah had to jump out of the way of the women surging into the room to speak with Miss Rodgers. Plainly, they were willing to help her or at least were bored enough to consider speaking with her a novelty.

Sarah hadn't heard of the *New Century* magazine. It might be truly new or perhaps she just hadn't noticed it before. A lot of magazines were being published now that advances in printing had enabled them to have so many pictures, some even in color. The articles were interesting, and the stories entertaining. She remembered reading a wonderful biography of Abraham Lincoln serialized in one of the magazines. If she remembered correctly, it had been written by a woman, too.

Sarah checked on Mary and her baby again, finding them both sleeping. Miss Kirkwood reported that Mary had successfully fed the child and seemed to be softening toward her.

"But if she decides to take her, we must make sure she's really going to keep her," Miss Kirkwood said.

"I know. Selling babies is still much too easy in this city. We'll keep a close eye on her to make sure she really wants to keep the child." Desperate women could sell their babies to unscrupulous people who used them as child prostitutes or even worse. An orphanage would be far better than that, at least.

When she'd gathered her things, Sarah walked past the

parlor on her way out. She saw Miss Rodgers in deep conversation with several of the residents. Sarah waved and Miss Rodgers waved back. "Contact me if you need me," Sarah called. Miss Rodgers nodded and went back to her conversation.

Outside, Sarah found her electric motorcar sitting just where she'd left it. Two street urchins had agreed to guard it for a nickel apiece. They had allowed a group of children to examine it closely, but it was still there and unharmed, so Sarah's nickels were well spent. She rewarded the boys and thanked them.

She loved her electric. It was so quiet and easy to drive compared with the gasoline-powered motor her husband drove. Malloy would probably prefer an electric of his own, but they were getting the reputation of being a vehicle for females, so he had resisted. Who could understand men?

Sarah checked the watch pinned to her bodice and realized she was probably going to be late for supper. Mary's labor had taken much longer than anticipated, but she couldn't leave in the middle of a delivery, even though she would have been leaving Mary in very capable hands. Sarah so rarely got a chance to deliver a baby, she wasn't going to miss one.

She was still thinking about Mary and her baby and what would become of them when she noticed a crowd gathered around a newsboy, jostling for a chance to buy a paper.

"Extra! Extra!" the boy was shouting. "President McKinley shot!"

Good heavens. Sarah pulled to a stop, earning the ire of all the vehicles behind her, but she ignored the shouts. "Here, give me a paper!" she cried, leaning out the window and holding up her penny for the single-sheet publication the boy was selling.

"Here, I've read it," a man said, handing her his copy. He wasn't quite as generous as Sarah had thought, though. He took her penny.

She didn't care. She quickly skimmed the short article. The facts were few, since it had apparently just happened this afternoon at the Pan-American Exposition in Buffalo, New York. The president had been greeting people in a receiving line in the Temple of Music and some man had concealed a pistol in a handkerchief and shot him with it. They thought the man was an anarchist. According to the article, the president had survived the shooting, but they had no further information about his condition. The would-be assassin was in custody.

Sarah could no longer ignore the shouts from the wagoners or the horn blasts from the other motorists who were blocked by her vehicle, so she started out again, although her mind was spinning. As awful as it was to hear that the president had been shot, the news had even more significance when she realized what it might mean for her old friend Theodore Roosevelt.

She had known Theodore all her life, and he had been a police commissioner when she had first met Detective Sergeant Frank Malloy. Theodore had learned to respect Malloy's abilities and sought his services more than once in solving crimes that required a special touch.

So much had happened since then. She and Malloy were married now, and they were rich, through no fault of their own. Malloy had left the police force and opened a private investigation office. Theodore had campaigned vigorously for McKinley when he first ran for president and was appointed assistant secretary of the navy for his trouble. Then he had fought in the Spanish-American War and returned a hero, which resulted in his getting elected governor of New York. When McKinley's vice president died in office, he chose Theodore to be his running mate for his second term.

Now McKinley had been shot, and Theodore Roosevelt was next in line to the presidency.

Photo by Monica Zibutis/Monica Z. Photography

Victoria Thompson is the Edgar® and Agatha award-nominated author of the Gaslight Mysteries, the Counterfeit Lady series, and numerous historical novels. She lives in the Chicago area with her family.